BY KELMAN OUT OF PESSOA

First edition published in 2011 by Les Figues Press, Los Angeles, as Book 4/5 of the TRENCHART Recon Series.

Second edition published in 2023 by Les Figues, an imprint of punctum books, Earth, Milky Way.
https://punctumbooks.com

ISBN-13: 978-1-68571-134-4 (print)
ISBN-13: 978-1-68571-135-1 (ePDF)

DOI: 10.53288/0500.1.00

LCCN: 2023934873
Library of Congress Cataloging Data is available from the Library of Congress

Les Figues is an imprint established under the punctum books Special Collections initiative.

Doug Nufer

By Kelman Out of Pessoa

LES FIGUES

Contents

Introduction

Louis Bury

> Here we come across another, very positive feature of play: it creates order, is order. Into an imperfect world and into the confusion of life it brings a temporary, a limited perfection... The profound affinity between play and order is perhaps the reason why play, as we noted in passing, seems to lie to such a large extent in the field of aesthetics.
>
> —Johan Huizinga, *Homo Ludens*

Games: Works of literature are often described as ludic, or game-like, but few, if any, have ever been the product, in form and substance, of an actual game.

By Kelman: Doug Nufer wrote *By Kelman Out of Pessoa* by going to the track once a week for an entire horseracing season, placing bets on behalf of three fictional characters,[1] the results of which, in turn, dictated the structure and plot of the novel.

Games: Nufer did not just play any type of game, but a gambling one in which he wagered his own money in the name of art. As a species of game, gambles attract those drawn to risk, to the commingling of fantasy (the world of the game) with reality (actual money).

---

1 Following the Portuguese poet Fernando Pessoa, Nufer calls his narrator-characters "heteronyms." Distinct from its dictionary definition, which refers to a word spelled the same as another but possessing different sound and meaning (like "lead" [to conduct] and "lead" [a metal]), Pessoa's usage of the term "heteronym" refers to a fabricated authorial persona with a fleshed out biography and an identifiable literary style. Pessoan heteronyms differ from pseudonyms and noms de plume in that they have a biographical back story and defining stylistic traits and are not just false names.

Games: I am playing a game in this introduction based on tosses of a die: a wager, one Nufer also makes in *By Kelman*, that an arbitrary, invented literary structure can be as apt a receptacle (and generator) of content as any of the more common, traditional forms.

Predecessors (literary): James Kelman. Fernando Pessoa. Harry Mathews. Gilbert Sorrentino. The OuLiPo.

By Kelman: "Aspects of the hysteria within [Nufer]," the mob of gambling heteronyms that take turns as the novel's narrators—Cal Nipper, Kelly Lane, and Henderson Will—obsess over sums ($200 losses) at which professional gamblers, by training, barely flinch.

Predecessors (theoretical): Johan Huizinga, *Homo Ludens*. Roger Caillois, *Man, Play and Games*. John von Neumann and Oskar Morgenstern, *Theory of Games and Economic Behavior*. And, further afield, Ludwig Wittgenstein's *The Philosophical Investigations*, Blaise Pascal's *Pensées*.

By Kelman: In other novels in Nufer's oeuvre, such as *Negativeland* (Autonomedia, 2004), loss is the dominant motif, even a term of value. Here, however, the characters, less confident, seek "the comfort to be gained by gain alone, gain in and of itself, gain, however minuscule, gain." The constraint determines the attitude: constraints of restriction, like the rule in Nufer's *Never Again* that no word can be used twice, create a fictional world permeated by loss and absence; constraints of permutation, on the other hand, like the one used in *By Kelman*, create a world in which the inhabitants crave correspondences and connections.

By Kelman: The Course, "a weekend seminar" for aspiring horseplayers and the system according to which the heteronyms structure their wagers, smacks of the self-help claptrap Nufer assiduously sniffs out and derides in his fictions. And yet, treacly as its cant may be—"YOU ARE A WINNER! A WINNER!"—The Course provides the perplexed protagonists with much-needed purpose and direction. Like constraint, its appeal is that of system.

Games: The literary accounting of critics and lay readers alike is shot through with the language of wins and losses, successes and failures, pleasures and disappointments—with the rhetoric of games and game playing.

Games: Consider art a complex betting game in which participants—artists, critics, audiences, institutions—wager both money and reputations but must pretend, for the sake of decorum, that no bets are being placed. By Kelman suggests that our (false) modesty cannot conceal the speculative nature of the enterprise—suggests, too, that the size of the stakes matters less than their import to the participants' lives.

Games: The difference between the type of order play produces and the type of order art produces is that the former tends towards reductive simplicity, the latter towards complexity, even entropy.

Games: The odds of my throwing the category "Games" four consecutives times are 1/81. Unlikely as these odds seem, every gambler knows that they're an eventuality to hit and that, when they do, it's rarely a happy occasion.

Games: The odds of five consecutive throws: 1/243. My frustration at having to write, improbably, in this category for so many consecutive throws inadvertently illustrates the way in which plot and narrative are built in to the very form of *By Kelman,* irrespective of its content, illustrates the way in which games inherently possess a dramatic structure.

By Kelman: Henderson Will, the queer node in Nufer's psychic triad, thinks, alternately, in Spoonerisms and in chiasmus: "His mind would work as his work would mind: backwards." Contrarian to the core, Will is considered "the key" to the heteronyms' gambling enterprise: "If we could come to terms with him," muses Kelly Lane, "maybe we would solve a major puzzle of the scheme."

Predecessors: Each of the novel's principle literary influences can be seen as the embodiment of a novelistic desire. Kelman: the desire to write about horse betting and have it be something other than mere genre fiction. Pessoa: the desire to make an elaborate show of masking and unmasking aspects of oneself. Mathews: the desire, destined to remain unsatisfied, to impose order upon experience through the use of permutational procedures. Sorrentino, via Flann O'Brien: the desire to let one's characters run amok, ceding, to the extent possible, authorial control.

By Kelman: The rough, grainy argot of the track—"boxed in," "bobble," "chalk," "punter," "spit the bit," "mudder," "early speed," "late speed," "tactical speed," "post position," "getaway play"—resembles the rarefied realm of literary patois in that both at once blunt and exacerbate the force of lived experience.

By Kelman: The racing season, like the novel form an arbitrary unit of length and organization, appears, by book's end, sculpted and purposive: "[Kelly Lane] wonder[ed] why she, too, now thought of the season in the shape of a whole process, an arc or plot or sequence that leant itself to some meaning or theme rather than as an artificial construct of actual opportunities to win money, wherein the opportunities themselves constituted all that should have mattered to her or to any of us."

By Kelman: The novel ends with Nufer's heteronymic mob in the black (+$362) and with Kelly Lane as the big winner of the group (+$756). Speculating that her win "was what it was, no more and no less than a game," the novel ends with this curious sentence, set off as its own paragraph: "Only the results were official." The novel's closing tension comes from the disjunct between the dry, quantitative record of the wagers and the narrative spun out of it: from the gulf between the raw data of our lives and the qualitative meanings we craft of them.

By Kelman: The concern, expressed best by Kelly Lane, is that the analogy between life and games is too accurate, too thoroughgoing an analogy: "Maybe the only dread any of us should have is that at the end we'll be back where we started, with no more insight than what you would expect to be manifested by the tokens of a board game."

By Kelman: Perhaps Henderson Will, the heteronym who "only could long so go nothing for playing," is seen by Kelly and Nipper as "the key" to the puzzle that is the novel because of his intensified linguistic and cognitive capacities: playing for nothing, or, rather, "nothing for playing"—living his life as though it were merely a game and nothing more—would be akin to thinking in run-of-the-mill linguistic ruts, something he, as well as Nufer himself, seems constitutionally incapable of doing.

Games: Literary games always sport at control, only to see the effort collapse under the weight of their—of life's—irreducible complexity.

By Kelman: Case in point: though I'm looking for a way to conclude this introduction, the rules of the game I'm playing, designed to make the task of writing more manageable, now compel me to write on a category, "By Kelman," about which I have no appropriately summative thoughts. The best I can do is to stage even this unwanted disruption as a necessary part of the whole.

Predecessors: Blaise Pascal's famous wager—that it's a good bet to believe in God because if you win you gain everything and if you lose you lose nothing—was a bet, ultimately, not about God's existence but about the nature of life itself: that we humans possess more purpose and meaning to our movements than mere board game tokens. The irony of this plea, framed cannily as a wager, is that in order to make it, in order to assert his hope that we aren't just wooden tokens adrift in the cosmos, Pascal resorts to the reductive language of gaming (as if the possible outcomes of the bet could be so simple as either "gaining everything" or "losing nothing"). Nufer's novel—and ludic literature more generally—plays, gleefully, in the fraught space of this irony.

Preface

Doug Nufer

The study of literature isn't generally thought of as a course to make you rich, so when a wagering system sprang from the pages of "A Wide Runner" by James Kelman in *Not Not While the Giro and Other Stories,* I was skeptical. Readers familiar with Kelman's workhorse characters might question whether sensible investment advice could ever come from men who live in pubs and die in vats of acid. A work of art, moreover, does not exist in order to provide tips for how to beat the races; and, particularly in Kelman's work, the delusions the archetypical loser exploits so as to pursue his shabby dreams must, in all artistic and intellectual honesty, result in failure. Be that as it may, the stop-at-a-winner money management system and the speed handicapping selection method used by John and Jock in "A Wide Runner" not only illustrate sound principles of racetrack strategy, but also offer a blatant opportunity for exponentially charged financial gain, in light of the heteronymic possibilities touted by the work of Fernando Pessoa.

Unlike some of the stories from that maiden collection, "A Wide Runner" has not been reprinted in other anthologies. Its use of slang that may seem vaguely obscure or frankly obscene to readers outside of the Scottish punter community, and its focus on a subculture that international publishing concerns evidently deem unmarketable, may well have rendered the story that has the potential to revolutionize the betting markets of the world obsolete, but what do acquisitions editors and publishing house accountants know of high finance? Whatever choices these publishers and Kelman made with respect to this 5,000-word story, we are more interested in the choices the player may make, in light of what Kelman and, by extension, Pessoa here reveal.

"A Wide Runner" begins as the young narrator, Jock, is discovered sleeping in a London college garden shed by a man who subsequently offers him a job as a porter at the college. Jock meets John, a porter near retirement age who is prone to bet and mostly lose huge sums on the horses. Whatever social standing the elder John might have had has been eroded by his need to borrow money from nearly everyone he knows, and so John may take Jock for a new, untapped friend (not to mention, a surrogate son) and a fellow seasoned punter who can appreciate the finer points of the game. Work, trips to the betting shop, and hours at the pub keep Jock and John occupied until John wins a hefty multiple bet payoff. This enables him to embark on a well-capitalized foray into a system that someone he knew used successfully before going broke for other reasons.

"The system is quite well known, nothing startling; it's called stop-at-a-winner and in principle consists of a minimum 1 bet and a maximum of 4," the narrator conveys John's explanation, unveiling a progression that increases according to the proportions 2–4–6–8. Win or lose, the betting stops after the fourth bet, but once you win, you go home. "In theory, to choose one winner from four is not too difficult," and yet, "When somebody's on a losing streak, everything can go crazy."

Once they decide to place bets according to the stop-at-a-winner progression, they determine a method to pick the winners. To assist his characters in their quest to chart previously uncharted territory (or to demonstrate how thoroughly dedicated they are), Kelman poses an equine virus that puts a halt to all horse racing, so in order to ply their scheme, the punters go to the dogs. That is, they study the results of greyhound races in the stacks of newspapers John just happens to have at hand to see which methods have proven to be most successful. The records they study aren't nearly as sophisticated as the *Daily Racing Form* past performances available to handicappers in the US, but they think this approach is more sophisticated than what most punters do at the track just because it is a plan. This approach also demands fidelity to the method chosen, so that once they see that the "time dog" (the dog posting the fastest time in its recent races) is most often the winner, Jock and John become speed handicappers. Committed to this method of picking winners and to the stop-at-a-winner betting system, our men "don't need no fucking luck," John says, because they "eliminate the fucking middle man," i.e., the bettor himself.

Fair enough. Most people assume that racetrack success is purely a matter of luck and many know that you often beat yourself by second-guessing bad decisions made worse as you identify yourself as a loser, not just for a day at the races but for a lifetime of missed opportunities, simply because you don't have what it takes to be able to look into the mirror and say, "You are a winner." What's harder for readers who don't habitually play the races to grasp is the need John has to share his bankroll with a partner whose bets are to be identical to his own. And yet, this sort of symbiotic co-dependence is not uncommon at the track. Punters will share information and match each other's bets. Even a by-the-numbers method such as speed handicapping can prod debate over which figure best represents what the runner will do next. More than strategy, though, and more to the point of the alliance between Kelman's characters, punters who join forces get moral support. Could it be, then, that this is a lame ploy to thwart your weaknesses by creating another entity that can stand in for you, an entity that can function as a third person or even as, some might say, the "fucking middleman" the process is designed to eliminate?

Yes and no. Driven by a notion that stop-at-a-winner is so powerful that no off-site bookie will take their bets, they spend hours commuting to and from the track, although it seems extravagant to go to such lengths to attend just one or a few races. But they keep to their system and their bankroll grows, even surviving the occasional three-day losing streak. John and Jock are comfortable playing the favorites their method often picks, and so their system seems like a key to the mint rather than a variation on the classic sucker gambit of chasing your losses. But another losing streak eventually sets up a decisive finish: Jock follows the method and system, betting a "time dog" longshot while John backs the favorite because circumstances make the "time dog" look like a bad play. The "time dog" wins, the younger man hauls in a bundle, the friendship sours, Jock leaves; John stays and resumes losing.

Now, a general reader might think Jock was right to quit a winner, that the system, however successful it may have been in the short run, was ruinous, and that the brunt of the story is meant to focus not on the young and feckless Jock, but on the old and pathetic John. A reader versed in the arts of handicapping and wagering might think that, as crude as the selection method and betting scheme were, such a system might well generate profits, particularly if it applied more advanced selection techniques and multiplied wagers according to a more aggressive progression.

Readers of Portuguese poet Fernando Pessoa, meanwhile, have another idea: rather than pair up into a single betting entity, Kelman's characters should have split up into heteronyms. What better way to "eliminate the fucking middle man" than to create separate bettors, each following a peculiar scheme? Like the heteronyms Pessoa created to write poetry, comment on each other's work, and intrude into his own life, the heteronym horseplayers would each follow their own approach to picking winners.

These beings may seem similar to characters in fiction or drama, but to apply the principles of Pessoan heteronymy to the track, you must appreciate how they differ from literary characters: one difference is, these characters act in the real world. Whether they act strictly in character or in a way which embodies the quirks of their creator, they publish work in their own names. By setting them loose in the world as autonomous individuals, Pessoa (or you, the boss of your own private gambling mob) could only claim to have a kind of remote control over them. Another difference is, as Pessoa explains, "The origin of my heteronyms is basically an aspect of hysteria that exists within me." As a measure to control the potential for hysteria, then, each of the heteronym punters would use the stop-at-a-winner wagering system outlined by Kelman.

Unlike James Kelman (1946–), Fernando Pessoa (1888–1935) is not someone whose books could be expected to contain practical references to the track. Nevertheless, any entrepreneur who would breed racing heteronyms inspired by Kelman out of Pessoa should consider the poetic bloodlines. Pessoa wrote poetry under three principal heteronyms as well as under what he called an "orthonym" of his own name, in addition to employing some sub-heteronyms, as he created separate bodies of work that variously echo pastoral and classical traditions and the verse of Walt Whitman. Pessoa's line on his entries was: "[Alberto] Caiero has one discipline: Things must be felt as they are. Ricardo Reis has another kind of discipline: Things must be felt, not only as they are, but also so as to fall in with a certain ideal of classic measure and rule. In Álvaro de Campos, things must simply be felt."

Because none of these heteronyms, not even Campos, displayed much aptitude for the sporting life, I do not recommend reviving them for the purpose of teaching the basics of pari-mutuel wagering and then sending each off with a bankroll in order to win your fortune(s). Besides, Caiero and company were Pessoa's problems; or, the solutions inspired by his own hysteria. You have problems of your own, serious personal problems that may only be resolved by a workout at the track. To attempt to deal with these problems without first familiarizing yourself with the most efficient selection methodologies and ways of integrating these into a coherent heteronymic deployment strategy would be a terrible mistake. But not as much of a mistake as ignoring them.

No matter what you do, these heteronyms of yours are there, festering inside of the fucking middleman that is you, infecting you with the hysteria of insurmountable desire. Without them, you are nothing. With them, you can be a winner. But only with my help.

From Doug Nufer, *Divide and Conquer: Lose Yourself and Beat the Races* (Reno: Off-track Books).

Sources

Kelman, James. *Not Not While the Giro and Other Stories*. London: Minerva, 1989.

Pessoa, Fernando. *Always Astonished: Selected Prose by Fernando Pessoa*. Translated and edited by Edwin Honig. San Francisco: City Lights, 1988.

———. *Fernando Pessoa & Co.: Selected Poems*. Edited and translated by Richard Zenith. London: Grove Press, 1998.

"From time to time, every confirmed horseplayer is racked by doubts about what he is doing with his life."

—Andrew Beyer,
Picking Winners

"These people aren't real. I'm making them up as they go along..."

—Gilbert Sorrentino,
Imaginative Qualities of Actual Things

Doug Nufer

By Kelman Out of Pessoa

To those who conceive of me to think of them as they might be.

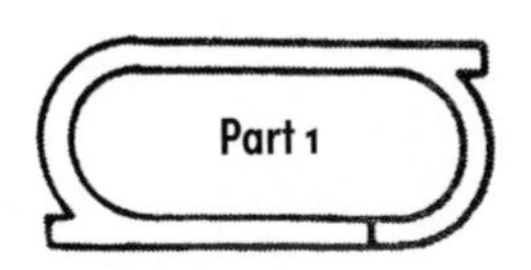

Live Workout: Emerald Downs, Auburn, Washington

2003 Season

Cal Nipper by Kelly Lane

He would be expecting a ride while wondering if he shouldn't go, as if he had a choice. He would be a guy who, spending $4 on a *Daily Racing Form,* could never let it go to waste by not putting it to use. Thrifty, careful, by-the-numbers: the kind of guy who retired in his mid-forties and managed to live on a weekly income you could blow in one night at El Gaucho, he didn't take chances. Twenty years he played the ponies and never took a chance. He had the angles figured, the variables weighted and fixed to coefficients of risk management analysis so that everything could be explained. Call him Cal Nipper.

On the first day of the Emerald Downs racing season, Cal Nipper sat at the breakfast table of his tiny bungalow, waiting for a ride to the rest of his life. If the ride didn't come, there was always the bus, the trip north from this place, south of the warehouse district, south of downtown to catch the shuttle south to Auburn. For some reason, such a backtrack bothered him.

Would he go by bicycle? Every April for about fifteen minutes, he considered fixing the flat on a ten-speed Schwinn he picked out of the trash on Neighborhood Clean-up Day, but Cal Nipper wasn't one to exercise. He would be trim, kind of cute, short, and apparently healthy. He hadn't been to the doctor since his last job. A real job, it would have been, with benefits. Why did a button-down type like Nipper ever quit a decent job, one that at least sent him into the world of women and other men?

Kind of cute or cute if kind? When does a retired middle-aged man living alone have an occasion to be kind to anybody other than himself? Mother's Day? Halloween? When he buys you a beer?

He quit work to play the races. A decade ago, after more years of study than it takes to take a Ph.D., Nipper devoted himself full-time to the business of handicapping. He kept records, watched replays, and studied tables of figures and probability charts. If that was all there was to the game, he might have been O.K., but the problem was, this wasn't just a job. He had to play. He had to bet.

So now all of a sudden this renewed fascination with horse racing seemed like a yen he should have gotten over years ago, when the customized track variants weren't enough, when the trainer pattern lectures weren't enough, when the pace analysis computer programs weren't enough; when he should have realized he just didn't have what it takes. He decided not to go. He would fix the flat on his bicycle. He would ride to the movies or the farmers' market. He would buy cheese from the woman who seemed to like him, and come home and make a real dinner for a change, something Italian or French, something to go with the bottle of wine he would have always been saving for an occasion. Home to a book. Not another night at the saloon. Not another night on the cable.

Cal Nipper decided. He made the decision not to go, but when I pulled up with my top down, he popped the gate like cheap speed on a procaine cocktail.

Kelly Lane

I am not who I used to be; I am who I ever was. I am the sum of the aspects of the hysteria within me, aspects which can only be released by setting them loose in the world. And these aspects don't reflect on whatever I might have done or been, but determine what I do and therefore who I am. I am in action.

Blame it on The Course, a weekend seminar for aspiring entrepreneurs at an office park, a night spent staring into the meanings of stains in the plastic wood of conference table in Renton, Washington, while a horn-rimmed guru raved about the opportunity to change your life, the opportunity to pull you out of the toilet and put you on the throne. I snapped out of the past and found myself standing in front of a mirror in a room full of men, each chanting to his own private mirror.

YOU ARE A WINNER! A WINNER!
YOU ARE A WINNER!

So here I am, waiting for this guy to come out of nowhere and into the front seat of my life. And I feel good because you know, hey, it could work. I mean, sure I'm sure. I paid the money, I took The Course and here I am with the top down, ready for action. Come on, boy. Into the car. That's a good boy. Be good. Be real good. Mama's gonna make you be real good to her. Mama's gonna make you make her a winner.

Jesus, would you look at this character. Only the good wear plaid.

Henderson Will by Cal Nipper

The one reflected the other, the other reflected the one. The face in the mirror was the mirror in the face.

If each of us might spawn a mob, then us of each might mob a spawn. Didn't it stand to reason that one play the devil's advocate? It reasoned to stand that one advocate the devil's play.

His mind would work as his work would mind: backwards. Rather than every man for himself, himself for every man. Every man could man every everyman. He took The Course; The Course took him. The story of his life was the life of his story, that side flip of a flip side notion that had he (or, I) done everything exactly the opposite, I (or, he) wouldn't have lost.

Gentlemen and ladies, Henderson Will. Instead of following the instructions of The Course, he would follow the course of the instructions. To the game of the rules from the rules of the game, stop-at-a-winner would flop flip to loser-at-a-stop. If he lost, he would stop, if he won, he would go on again, beginning at the top bet of the progression and cutting it after a win. Others would play to win, Henderson Will would win to play, betting not what I would bet but on what might beat me.

Kelly Lane

If I make up Nipper, Nipper might as well make up me. If he is active as a heteronym and not just some character, doesn't he come to life and make up heteronyms of his own, heteronyms whose names might even overlap the names I make up for the guys in my mob? The Course didn't say. All The Course said was, make up your mob and set them free, free to bet on the stop-at-a-winner progression, on the 2–4–6–8 increases, and when your man wins, he stops. If he loses the first at $20, he plays the next at $40, and so on, up to four tries, so the worst he can do is burn two bills.

Nipper isn't in the car ten minutes before another plan pops out: a plan with a man, an inverse freak who does everything the opposite of what The Course taught. That has to be pure Nipper, to figure a way to take back your move while you make it. Pure Nipper or adulterated Lane, since Nipper is my baby, slamming the door on this little quinella of my personal problems by working up a contrarian who's crazy about thwarting whatever my other half does. Henderson Will by Cal Nipper out of Kelly Lane. Not why. Why not?

So we get to the track and what do we find but this rock bottom welcome mat to the first day of a meet: a five furlong $5,000 maiden claiming race for fillies and mares. And, who is the winner? A five-year-old Bay Meadows hag who has lost more races than most ever get to run. Her name is Gypsy Chick. None of us have her, of course. Take an even-money sucker horse for a quick leg up on an overlay cavalcade of daily doubles? Face it, boys, that's not Kelly Lane.

Kelly Lane by Cal Nipper

Top down, breeze on, legs up, pop the clutch on the spring for the turn for home to change leads and take command in the stretch to the wire: Kelly Lane. Come on, it's not like she was an even-money multiple loser of cheap maiden claiming heats out of a Frisco past, crooning at a San Mateo nightclub under the name of Gypsy Chick. But even if she did come from a time when I lived in motels, that was over.

She didn't want to talk about the past, except to say there hadn't been any one of the obvious vices, like drugs or drinking. As for the ultimate leg of that triple crown, heads still turned when she went by. Maybe her problem had been nothing but gambling.

She knew her horses. Give her the speed on the lead or any ray of light in a jockey switch or blinker change, and she would be on it, as long as she got her price. Kelly Lane played to win. No dicking around with saver plays, no regrets. Kelly Lane knew the way to the window. Go to the window, lay it down, and walk away with no regrets. Ticket in hand, on the nose or one-way in the exotics with the key horse on top.

She knew her bets. She knew her horses. She knew the game, but somehow it all used to slip away from her. Not this time, though. This time, she'd stop at a winner.

Kelly Lane by Cal Nipper

Then again, what did anyone know? We all took The Course. You might think you ran the show, but then you were only someone made up by each of two others. Could anyone be more real than anyone else? The only thing real was the record. For the record, a five-year-old maiden mare named Gypsy Chick won the first race and paid a measly $4.

She thought it was funny. She loved losing bets like that, bets that, in the long run, would ruin you, especially when you followed the 2–4–6–8 progression. Even-money wagers wouldn't cover losses; it had to be 2–1, at least, but she liked to aim for 5–1. So she missed the front end of a double by chasing a trainer play with decent works, missed the next two races by keying on early speed and pretending that the names, Billy White Shoes and Tough Dancer, had nothing to do with it, and blew her finale on an exacta wheel keyed by a Persian Reign that got bumped in deep stretch by the winner. Not even a steward's inquiry could save her. Tough loss.

But she did have something of a past—even if she wasn't ever on the access road to the airport freeway north of San Mateo in hotpants sucking a Sugar Daddy, even if she wasn't the special friend of an Oakland disco bouncer who turned up lost when his Benz was found by scuba divers, even if she wasn't once known as Loca Lola la Cola Coca—a past riddled with "substance abuse issues," as the guidance counselors used to pawn off the "anti-social behavior" of "at-risk youth." Did she come out the better for it, or did it leave her forever on edge, poised to take a plunge for the hell of it when things didn't go her way? But hey, two hundred bucks was just a night on the town to a gal like Kelly Lane.

Cal Nipper by Henderson Will

Cal Nipper was nobody's ass jack and everybody's pin king. No mind in his own legend ever was so much in control of need, no freak control so jive to the hip. Then but a freak control could be what you needed as the experiment for any group control. Of me he reminded me. After The Course took me, the last before season, like him I angled the figures, down right to the point decimal, factors weighing and in the analysis last, in zeroing on the favorite but not on the play best to make. To play the make best, the odds you played, and scored to live when the favorite lost. Yet and Nipper, large and by, out doped the winner as the favorite.

Already, all right. Whether by or out of him or Kelly, this idea of my head putting on backwards was nonsense, but if they thought that's how I thought, that was their problem. My problem was to get them to win.

Three races in, with Nipper down $60 after losing $20 and $40, tempting as it was to get back at him for making me sound like a bad translation, I was more intrigued by what he might do next.

He would play it safe and continue to make the accurate choices his methodology dictated. He would know he was right, and anything that went wrong went wrong because of racing luck. More than any of us, he bought The Course line about not needing luck. It took a lot to knock him off his game (especially now that it wasn't his game but the game we made him play). For him, getting desperate meant putting himself in a position where he would pick the winner and lose the bet, because the winner he picked could only cover the costs if he hit the exacta.

I liked putting him through this little bit of agony, because it was just the predicament I used to suffer before I made the decision to separate myself from the hysterical aspects of myself. With the clear choice being Way Sharp, a mare coming off two wins to enter this cheap but open claiming sprint, it was a shell game scenario. The low-odds favorite drove him to look for better prices in the exacta. In a short field of six, all he had to do was pick the runner-up, but he only had three bets to make or he would spread his wager too thin, and he knew that any of the ones he didn't cover might slip in for second. Not to mention the fact that we were getting up to "real money" here, especially for a guy who tipped a quarter on a happy-hour beer. Least but not last, this was the first day. If any of us needed to win on Opening Day, it was Nipper.

As for me, I am ahead. Could I take the credit? Last year, I never would have bet $80 on a $12,500 maiden first- time starter at 5–2, even if he did show something in his morning works, stable connections, and bloodlines. Would Nipper? Not on your life. After that, could you blame me for throwing away $60 in the next race on nothing much more than a catchy name?

So busy was I getting Nipper to the window, I paid less attention to Rolls Joyce in the third than to the fate of Nipper's first big bet. Way Sharp took command and ran away from the field. Coming out of the turn, two of Nipper's three picks were right there to take second, so down the stretch all he had to do was root for the one who would pay a bit more to finish under his key horse in the exacta.

Kelly Lane caught my eye, and I knew exactly what she was thinking, just as she knew me. Laughing, we sent Nipper to the window.

Kelly Lane by Cal Nipper

She should have been satisfied. The Course taught her to deploy a mob and her mob won. Nothing like a little win-win to start the meet. That's what mattered in the end, but hey, this was only the beginning.

She didn't want to hear about it. She drove too fast and said more under her breath at the other drivers than she said straight to me. You didn't want your crew to get used to losing, but you didn't want them to let it get to them. What she needed was a life, a real life, with friends, things to do, maybe even a part-time job in a swanky restaurant, a decent apartment in an area with some nightlife—not some hovel tucked among bare yards of clotheslines and pitbull dog houses in the romantic slum of a working class neighborhood—a place with a view of the city and the mountains, in a hip part of town, where people who live alone can live like normal people.

Alone. Didn't we all live alone? No boyfriend. No ex to haunt her or stalk her. No "love interest" to distract her from this thing we were doing. But there had to be something about that, didn't there? Henderson? Me?

One day in, and already we have come to this.

Kelly Lane by Cal Nipper

"Buy you a drink? I mean, coffee or something? Something for gas?"

"Some other time, Cal."

"Really?"

"Only the bets are real."

"The results are now official. And down the stretch they come. And they're off. It is now post time."

"Cal, please. Some other time."

Her hand on my arm, her eyes on my eyes, her dress riding up her thighs.

"It's a date."

Cal Nipper by Kelly Lane

Who did he think I was? Something for gas, my ass.

Cal Nipper went home to the salad dinner, the thrift store martini set of silver shaker and classic cone stemware, the tiny black-and-white TV his neighbor hooked up illegally to cable so he could watch the Atlanta Braves in exchange for helping the neighbor cheat on his tax returns, because Nipper used to teach algebra and thought tax paying was a crime.

It was better that he won rather than I did on the first day of The Course live workout. Henderson's approach depended on testing the limits of the comeback, but Nipper needed a win right out of the gate. What a winner. On an exacta keyed by a 2–1 favorite, no less.

Nipper went home to a night of playing air guitar to the records of Dire Straits, Eric Clapton, and Ry Cooder, but not, I'll give him, Bruce Springsteen. Vinyl records. He made a salad from nitrate carrots, bulletproof tomatoes, bleached mushrooms, and chemlawn greens, with baco-bits and bleu cheese dressing. Gordon's would be his gin, Gallo his vermouth, 8–1 his ratio, olives stuffed with pearl onions his garnish. Odds were, he would have a coronary before his time. Whenever that would be.

Cal Nipper by Kelly Lane

A few hours after pulling this guy out of nowhere, there I was driving him to the grave. But what were we supposed to do with these characters when we weren't at the track? A whole week could go by, and we'd all be doing what we do between days at the races. The Course encouraged all of that: the lay-off, the full life away from the business of betting, the extra dimensions to the personalities of your operatives so that each of them might grow on his own. That way, these aspects of the hysteria within you could develop free of you and maybe turn you into someone fuller and better than whoever you had been.

What did we ever know about the other people at the office, at the market, at the track? Even in the car pool or at the bar, what was there to say about yourself that said who you were and what really mattered to you, so that anyone next to you might understand you?

Nipper got to whining about where I made him live. I thought I was doing him a favor putting him in Georgetown: a neighborhood, not a slum, with decent neighbors who did things for you, like hooking you up illegally to cable TV or helping you cheat on your taxes; not some Republican stronghold on the East Side, with covenants forcing you to plant no fruit trees. And if the only markets here were Costco and a couple of gas pump mini-marts, so what? People drove from all over the city to Costco because it had the best prices on lots of stuff—O.K., a lot of lots of stuff. He would drive there from across town even though he did live alone, just because he was so cheap. But now, because he lived in Georgetown, he didn't have to drive. He could walk.

Couldn't you just see it? Cal Nipper pushing a hot grocery cart a mile to the warehouse store for a lifetime supply of toilet paper, tube socks, and pine nuts.

All right. Enough of that. A week went by, and there we were.

The moment I pulled up, Nipper practically skipped to the car. He tried not to let it show, but he was confident in a way that was just this side of obnoxious. The Course said you wanted your operatives to be confident, but not cocky. You wanted them to be in control of themselves, even if you were supposed to be in control of them, but you also had to let them be whatever they would turn out to be. Beyond forcing them to stop at a winner, what could you do?

Nipper didn't want to talk about what he did all week. He wanted to talk about the day's card. But we couldn't. The Course banned such talk. You couldn't set your heart on any single pick or on any particular race, because each step depended on what happened before. You had to glance at the *Form* in advance, but you didn't spend hours constructing scenarios for each race, the way Nipper used to do back in the day when he believed all he had to do was immerse himself totally in the science of handicapping for his work to pay off.

Then there was this other thing. Underneath all the pep, Nipper couldn't help feeling awkward around me. Although we had been apart for a week, we had to be thinking about each other during that time. The Course warned you about that. "Lose yourself" meant "Don't fall in love with yourself," and that went double for falling in love with any aspects of the hysteria within you.

Nipper would be wondering if he should ask me out. If he did, what would I say? What would he have me say or... do?

There were other weird forces going on here, too. He didn't understand the frequency and order of the times each of us spent making up one or another of us. Cal Nipper was made up by Henderson Will, too, but not as much, apparently, as by me. Nipper and I were together more than other pairings. This much he knew, just as I did. Why? Was there a pattern? Would it even out, so that Henderson would have more to do with me? Never mind what I thought about this, the problem was, Nipper would think that all this time together meant something, that it was building up to some kind of intimacy between him and me.

Henderson Will by Cal Nipper

Today, day two. If as to lose expecting, Will played his save for the race second, which lost him, up leaving him still $92 on the total running.

To key on a loser was to lose on a key. His pick to place didn't place to pick up the payoff exacta. His of one to win picks first finished, Jest Bold, which had me another way, scoring me to lead the exacta. Watching anyone might have here whistled the blow on this strategy of kind: by betting the splits and splitting the bets, against ourselves we played. Were we what? Policy insurance play savers, like a jerk of pair-off actuaries? Then but, our bets respective could lap over. Us of each would end the same reach from paths opposite, up doubling the bet same to twice cash if right we were.

Will couldn't about think how against him or with him other set-ups bet. Matter for that, Will knew things of lots the us of others had yet to out find. Through having gone this the year last, he was a game of the head. Mention to not, ever what events of turn had him turned outside in.

Kelly Lane by Cal Nipper

Kelly, Kelly, Kelly, Kelly. What are we going to do with her? At least she played true to form, just as Will formed play to true; and if he priced the pay, she paid the price.

That she lost the daily double on a head bob in the first was bad enough when her horse in the second came in, but the odds were too low to bet the horse in the second to win, so she lost by chasing the wrong exactas. A 1-for-13 even-money favorite beat her in the next race, so she played the feature, a stakes with the only reliable speed of the race, Colterkind, going off at 10–1. She not only lost the race to drop another two bills for the day and go down $400 for the season, but the way she lost was just the opposite to how she lost on the first day. Her horse finished first, but was taken down for bumping in deep stretch. On a day when she picked the winners of three of four races—not counting head bobs and disqualifications—she didn't cash a ticket.

Would it have done any good to tell her these things happen? To buy her a drink? To tell her about something that happened to me once that was sort of like what she was going through?

We'd all been through these streaks before, and goddammit, she was not going to be undone by a couple of days of bad luck. Luck! The Course said we didn't need it.

Kelly Lane drove me home with the top up, under control, not speeding, not rushing up to tailgate the car ahead of her. We took the back way, not I-5, because she didn't like the look of the freeway traffic.

"Blame it on the Mariners."

She didn't know there was a game tonight and wouldn't have cared, except to avoid the roads around the stadium.

"They were better when they were bad. When nobody went to see them."

"Did you ever go?"

"Nobody did."

She talked about baseball to keep from talking about anything else. She wasn't doing this for me; she was doing this to me so I couldn't talk to her about herself. The least I could do after a day like this was play along. After all, she got me to win, and I could do no better for her than keep her on a string of frustrating losses. I asked if she wanted to go to the game, knowing she'd take this for a joke.

"I mean, now that everybody goes, do we have a choice?"

She said she had other plans. Something about a party, the theater, or work.

"Besides, since when are we everybody?"

Henderson Will by Cal Nipper

Of the ground back of the background of Henderson Will: time upon a once, William Henderson was a guy regular, a company shipping president vice. Day one then, up he woke in the work of middle with no job of his memory. On end for weeks, tried he though to back get some job of his idea by backing himself into the routine of the throw, even the numb minding behavior customary of your office typical showed to fail what the job of his essence was.

The life of his rest wasn't whack of out. His wife knew him and versa-vice, and his life home normally went, if even she had the life of her time believing to refuse him, if as her leg had to be pulling him. Yet and, worked nothing, even not doctors to the trip, to stand under why this amnesia of brand had siege laid to his mind of state.

To puzzle with this deal, he would note takes. He did what he wrote and wrote what he did, as it did him. Later or sooner, this record discovered someone. Yet and, this discovery embarrassing no one bothered, though even was he incompetently blatant.

His way he felt. All it down came to gaming his treat as a job. Words in other, just jobbing his keep had all he took to do what he justified.

Eventually when the company shipping itself shipped to port another sea, it quit him, him leaving happy free to be. Free from far was he, as it out turned. One another after system logical psycho itself imposed him on, minding his twist every way which, that so, no choice had him but to flow with the go.

Henderson Will by Kelly Lane

Flow with the go?
Back words whack birds,
as the crow flies as the flow cries.
The Course took him to horse cook dim,
yore fears for years.
As a wish out of fodder as a fish out of water,
he'd been lost at sea on the job. Sauced, that gee on the lob
entered the ranks of bums tendered on the banks of rums,
but waded. What baited
this outburst? His bout thirst?
No cow moo roar of a go now rumor

so pathologically copasetic. Sociologically pathetic,
he crooned after Sinatra. Soon craft or its sot drop
dead parody dare rode pee.
A day at the races a night at the opera, a ray at the
aces a right at the top or a
man missing to shrink in the power and pissing to
sing in the shower.

Henderson Will by Kelly Lane

Plans ration trees, translation please. Let's just say, sets just lay. Henderson Will went home to an RV parked along the Duwamish River in the South Park part of town. Or, if you free purred, the Woodamish in the Pouth Sark tart of pound. Who would care if Will pissed in the shower? If, afterwards, he dumped his sewage straight into the Duwamish?

Too many years mute any tears. A while it would have been since his wife left, since that medical debacle left him a mental misfit.

And what does it say about me if one of the agents of the actions of my deep personal problems is a guy who sings pissing drunk over the memory of all that? All or nothing at all?

Henderson Will

Pardon your beg, but what have they got myself into? All or nothing at all I did was sign up for this handicapping class a year ago, and here I am turned into a head case by these characters I've built out of my own personal problems, these heteronyms who aren't content to run around doing what I make them do, but who feel they must go out of their way to manipulate me.

Wouldn't it be fun if we made someone think backwards? Make him crazy, get him drunk. Christ Jesus.

The Course was different before: more Kelman, less Pessoa; strictly speed handicapping and stop-at-a-winner money management, i.e., lacing your chooser's tragedy with chasing your loser's strategy. The Pessoa part came later. When they took it, The Course touted a theory from a book the, say, teacher was writing, Divide and Conquer: Lose Yourself and Beat the Races.

And, contrary to what they have me do, I am not changing the way I do things. They're the ones who feel the need to need the feel to kneel to feed to feed to kneel to have their bettor halves contradict each other. Meanwhile, I've got Nipper the numbers man playing solid selections at low odds and Lane the winger taking flyers on riskier picks. Each stops at a winner and neither sticks to any one handicapping method.

As for the personal stuff, we all have our problems, and our problems all have us. This is no maiden race for three-year-old geldings. Do you know how easy it would be to have Nipper make a pass at Lane? To get Lane drunk enough to go home with Nipper? Please. These aspects of hysteria, these characters or heteronyms or whatever: they aren't people you fuck with; they're more like friends, imaginary friends.

Henderson Will by Kelly Lane

Henderson Will rode a boater mic motorbike, ringing in the sane singing in the rain via former farm companies campuses' bum penny scam kisses, by-passing turnpikes and bike paths pike baths. The bass fry sing, some the free from the sea.

He lived in an RV, which moved when he moved, from one part pun art of town to another. No Wal-Mart mall wart, he stayed where the weighed stare of neighbors didn't complain, as if he were somebody's relative from elsewhere, lasting longer in one place than your typical transient, dressed as he was in the frizzy blue laundromat-fresh remnants of business suits that should have been dry-cleaned. Shabbily resplendent, rabbley sheep-blended, and well-behaved. Hell be waived, yes, well-behaved. How else could a big goof park his Winnebago on your block and not raise a stink?

Like spare capacity eccentrics whose perspicacity sextant tricks navigated caffeinated, Henderson Will didn't mind what others made of him. Then again, in the grip of whatever amnesia, mania, or aphasia kept him from grasping the world around him, he had always found it best to be polite.

A large, clean-cut fog dude man mutt of a dogfood can in a rumpled business suit with impeccable manners who rode a motor scooter could sleep down the street in his RV. Not necessarily timid, but deferential; good natured, reasonably content: Henderson Will might even seem more well-adjusted than Cal Nipper to circumstances of cursed-dumb senses. So when he kicked off the third day of the meet by wasting $80 on a lame brain name play, Roared to Bun was too bored to run. He was still up $12 for the season.

Cal Nipper by Henderson Will

Friends nary imagine imaginary friends such as these. While they sent me plunging on a weak favorite in a cheap maiden sprint, I gave them each a shot at a decent payoff.

Riding high on back-to-back exacta payoffs, Nipper couldn't be bothered with straight bets on low-priced favorites. His first bet of the third day was more of a Lane gambit than a Nipper investment. Other than the odds, only the running line touted American Don, but when you looked at that account of this three-year-old gelding in his last race, you couldn't blame Nipper for burning the twenty. Gritty, steady, hanging in there against a moderate pace, this was not only a line that stood out in the ranks of bit-spitting quitters and lazy plodders, but a line Nipper could identify with: never on the lead or out of it, always a few lengths back, gaining a little, losing a little, never giving up, from first call to the second to the finish. In a field of maiden claimers, with none sporting much of a record, any entry showing that kind of gumption was a bargain at 6–1.

Nipper knew, though, that this wasn't the play he wanted to be forced into making later in the progression, for $60 or $80. At $20, he didn't have to stick to his usual game of picking the winner from all of the leading indicators. At $20, he didn't even want to win on a 2–1 "sure thing," although he knew that if he lost $20, then $40, then $60, to go down $120 for the day, he would need a get-well shot for his final bet to overcome the losses, losses he would have avoided by scoring and quitting on the first try.

Nipper knew this, but couldn't help himself. Turn him loose was all either of us could do, and trust that he would nail a winner somewhere down the card.

Cal Nipper by Kelly Lane

"I haven't seen you in a while, but I can guess what you've been up to. Do you think we might see more of each other?"

"Maybe. Think of it as a numbers game, like post position stats. How often does the one-hole produce winners versus the three-hole? Some days it's track bias; some days it's just where the best horses are. Some runners like the rail; some don't. Then there's always geometry."

Nipper couldn't help but imagine what I meant. He tried to play dumb, but one of the statistics he had kept over the years was the number of races won from each post position, in sprints and in routes. Horses starting from the inside posts usually won more races per start than starters from the outside posts. In short fields, the crew manning the gate often left the one-hole open, and put the one-horse in the two-hole, so if the inside horse was rail-shy, he had some space. And horses mostly came from the outside to pass other horses, not from the inside.

At tracks where he knew less about the local scene, Nipper paid more attention to which posts won most races. In retrospect, anyone could see how you might get rich by only betting on one number, but a number could go winless for days before winning three in a row, for whatever reason or no reason at all. So Nipper knew what I was getting at. The average field size was about seven, and almost all winners were more or less evenly distributed among the numbers 1–6, with the 7, 8, and 9 each only winning a few races, and the 10–12 winning hardly any. If each combo of us had a number, and each solo also had a number, that would take up the numbers 1–9. When 1 won, it could be time for, say, Henderson Will to make up Cal Nipper. When 2 won, it could be my turn to do Henderson. Nipper knew the game we were up against. If all that was real was the results, why shouldn't our part in the scheme spin off nothing more esoteric than the numbers of the horses that won each race? You never knew whose turn it was to win, you never knew if the distribution of winners according to post was more explicable by predictable factors or by chance. In any race, the winner might benefit from advantages or overcome disadvantages of whatever post positions the luck of the draw had decided.

Nipper knew we would see more of each other. And he knew we wouldn't know whose turn it was next to meet or to set the terms of the meeting. There was a certain pattern. We couldn't know what it was. Nipper wasn't a religious man. Nipper thought religions were bullshit. He wasn't even superstitious, but he did live in awe of the power of numbers and the patterns they seemed to suggest. Although each of us made up the others and sent them out to play, none of us seemed to control the overall pattern of meetings, not even if one of us wore an aqua sweater vest under the plaid sports jacket and strode calmly to the car and swallowed his spit to speak in a lower, mellower tone to say he could guess what you had been up to. It was like the frequency pattern that post position studies discovered. It wasn't a question of fairness. It just was what it was. Nipper of all people had to love the beauty of that.

Cal Nipper by Kelly Lane

His eyes weren't aqua, they were gray, but the fluorescent bulb that turned his face purple in the bathroom mirror made him think his eyes matched the color of his sweater vest. In the men's room at the track he looked the same, except for the bloody stumps from his weekly clear-cut job of shaving with the same blade he had been using for six months. Vanity was strange to him. Mirrors made him laugh, ever since he sat in a room full of idiots chanting to their reflections, "YOU ARE A WINNER! A WINNER! YOU ARE A WINNER!"

But now he was beginning to realize he was ahead, that this new approach could make the difference between winning and losing. All he had ever needed was a good start, and his solid handicapping would pay off. Cal Nipper is having a pretty good season for himself, he might think, in the third person, like a star athlete who thought the world of himself, before realizing that however for himself this success might have been, it was from someone else that he was getting it.

Next up was an $8,000 open claiming race at six and a half furlongs, the kind of long sprint that used to favor routers in shape from Portland in the first weeks of a season, but now Nipper wasn't so sure about that. Still, he couldn't just bet raw speed. Maybe in a restricted claimer, limited to nonwinners-of-two, but these were—what, world-beaters at the Harbor County Fair?—legitimate threats. Nipper dug back into the past performances and pulled out one of his signature picks, a class standout with the kind of record, trainer/jockey connection, and mix of stamina and tactical speed he had to like in a tough contest. He put his favorite Hayden Storm on top in a pair of exactas, with the suspect pacesetter and another solid contender to finish second.

When the pacesetter cleared the field by a pair of lengths at the quarter pole, Nipper was neither surprised nor worried. The pacesetter was right where he wanted him... for about four furlongs... when Nipper began to suspect that cheap speed on the loose with the wind at his back and nothing in front of him but the wire was not going to finish second to any horse in this race.

Kelly Lane by Henderson Will

Out of a shillable sift of a syllable shift, she spun me into Spoonerisms. She thought this was a game, after all, and this was as I wanted her to think: a serious game, to be sure, but a game just the same.

You could tell she took it more seriously than most, but not as the expression of her life. How she did at the track was just how she did at the track—not some metaphor of personal attainment. She took each step in the process from each step that preceded it. She didn't think back to what she just lost or ahead to what she could win, and she felt that all she needed for any race was a single good idea, one good reason to bet on a horse that most took for a loser.

What did she have to lose? And what did it mean that she wasted $20 on an animal with no more than decent works to show for itself in a maiden race? Because of the name? Danceonthetable. Nipper raised an eyebrow at that, no doubt logging it as proof positive of just the sort of resume tidbit his incarnation of Kelly Lane might have featured, but that said more about the aspects of the hysteria within him than about who she was.

Far be it from me to write her off as some brainless goddess of the Intuitive Spirit or symbolic Woman, whose every thought, feeling, and expression must be filtered through some slapdash notion I might hold about the true nature of the feminine. This was the third time I saw her, but the more I saw her, the easier it was to see how she was and the harder it was to think how she must be feeling without resorting to the usual shortcuts. To itemize her as tall and thin with long blonde hair and blue-green eyes or put her down as beautiful might have done the trick, but there was something about her age that gave her away while keeping her to herself, some edge to the line of her face that gave her an intensely alert expression: you might see that look in a twenty-five-year-old whose vices made her seem twenty years older, or a forty-year-old whose virtues made her seem half that age. It was the look of someone who felt as if she had lost a chunk of her life, but who knew better than to try to get it back.

How she lost it and where the time went didn't bother her, especially now that she had what she needed: one idea to act on when she made a bet. She would find one positive factor to guide her pick, and, at the end of the meet, she would see how that added up. She knew she couldn't keep losing $200 a day. She even considered that she might have to quit if she went $2,000 down, but going into this six and a half furlong race, she reckoned 7–2 was a rare bargain on Please Repete, a lone speedster in a sprint against routers.

Cal Nipper by Kelly Lane

He couldn't have been happier if he had won the race himself. Nipper and Will slapped high fives as Please Repete hit the wire, well ahead of the others. He patted me on the back and said he knew I could do it, that it was just a matter of sticking to my methods, because it stood to reason that my methods would earn me my share.

As if inspired by my reversal of fortune, Nipper set out to loosen up a bit, even though this wasn't one of the early bets of the day but his turn to wager $60. If he lost this, he said he could always make a getaway play on Ema Bovary in the feature, but if she was a sure thing, he knew she wasn't going to go off at odds that would cover his losses.

He used to make getaway plays all the time. There was nothing like reading the results the next day in the paper to see that some last ditch fling had made you a winner. After it happened more than once, he made a point of leaving early with a live ticket in his wallet, so he could go around thinking that, no matter how poorly he might have done, his day wouldn't be official until the next morning. He said he knew he shouldn't be getting ahead of himself by thinking of what to do if he lost this race, but that The Course was practically set up to make your one last and biggest bet a getaway play. You might lose the first three races and then be given all of the other remaining races to choose from to make your $80 count.

He was talking too much. He was feeling the pressure. He knew his string was on the line, and that if he lost this bet, he'd be forced to make a getaway play on an odds-on favorite. He told himself to bear down on the race at hand, but there really wasn't much to figure in a $12,500 maiden claiming race for 3-year-old fillies. Designer's Gold was dropping from a tougher race, showed good workouts, and was getting a lot of action on the tote. When he took her, she was 4–1; when the race went off, she was the favorite.

She won, pulling him out for the day and putting him up $262 for the season. The next day he would read in the paper that Ema Bovary earned .60 on a dollar for her win.

Henderson Will by Kelly Lane

Both of us took an oath of bust, he thought of Nipper and me. My winning here and now near and how made his sapient patient practical tactics tactical practice rewarding. We roared reward.

Riding to home on the bike, biding to roam on the hike, he took his time. In sun and rain run insane, a double rainbow sprang to spring off so the righthand sky wrote a sight scanned high as majestic sea arks, suggesting remarks going nowhere. The knowing go, "Where April showers shape rill hours."

After this strange chat, he changed strategy. Playing the favorite was flaying to pay for it, no matter how contrarian the choosing might have made the bets seem like some rare cretin chimp musing.

If inconsistencies sink on distant seas, fun-inspired notions spun entire oceans of possible saucible fond day ruse rendezvous. But now Will gave a nut bow gill wave. Nobody's sucker was he. So nutty scuppered scores of farce force of scars handicappers panned the yackers panty hackers, but Henderson Will rode on, west of the rainbow, east of the sunset, tall in the saddle and low to the ground to loll in the taddle and crow to the sound.

Kelly Lane by Henderson Will

Trappy hales you too, you.

Blonde, did I say? Ever since somebody left something in the car, something that she had never been able to find, she hated to drive with the top up, and so now, in this rotten light of oily humidity, her hair acquired a particular orange strawberry tinge last seen on the barfly leering from a 1972 Schlitz clock. Not that she could have done anything about it. She was too old to dread how a change in the weather would style her hair into a perfect replica of what she might have been too young to recognize, except from old ads. Here a shag, there a flip, everywhere a permanent: fashions from the proms of yesteryear just came to her out of the rain.

She wondered what to do if Nipper acted like he couldn't help noticing how she resembled the sex symbols of his youth. Today the Schlitz beer babe, tomorrow Farrah Fawcett Majors. She wondered how he would act if he acted (or worse, tried not to act) like he noticed, especially now that, one more time, he asked if she wanted to stop for a drink: here's to the winners.

Kelly Lane would take a drink. Saying yes made more sense than refusing, not because she thought she should spend some time with Cal Nipper or because she even wanted to have a drink. She was just curious.

She pulled into a side street between the obsolete factories of ice and steam and the abandoned stores for tackle and hubcaps, behind the bar under an overpass, in a spot he said was safe. Nipper claimed a recent police survey found that this neighborhood had the lowest crime rate in the city. Then he told her not to lock her car. Anyone would see the doors were open, and so the roof wouldn't get slashed. She thought this was funny; he didn't get it. She thought this whole outing was funny, in a way that made her feel guilty because she knew what bothered her was a feeling she couldn't share with him, that it was intriguing but unsavory to go slumming in her heteronym's bar downwind from Boeing Field: The Prop. Nipper would spend his nights in a joint like The Prop.

She let him lead the way. The protocol of moving into a strange bar was a matter of etiquette not unlike having the man go first up the stairs. Let him open the door and go in—not hold it for her to make an entrance so he could show her off to the regulars. Why begrudge him that? Or, why make him out to do that? Kelly Lane would have known a lot about bar etiquette, without beginning to realize how much she had thought about that until now, because, she was relieved to admit, this place was from a world she would have known so well from just so long ago that, to return after years made it seem comfortably exotic, as would any place where she had once spent time, so that the memories associated with that scene were tucked away forever, like a nuclear waste dump contained under a cap of lead and earth.

He had her pick where they would sit, a table for two by the window, across the room from the bar. She had him pick the drinks. That is, when he asked what she wanted, she said a pale ale, because she figured that was what he would order and she wanted to keep pace.

There were only three guys at the bar, but Nipper didn't wait for the bartender to come out for their order. He got the beers and brought them to the table, after saying hello to them all. Nobody was smoking, but the room smelled like an ashtray. Stale beer, a splash of Lysol, and peanuts in the shell under a red heat lamp took the rest of the air. The peanut machine, juke box, the jumbo hot dog rotisserie, and yes, the 1972 Schlitz clock, whose orange strawberry blonde would have been over sixty today, were the only lights in the room, and the light from outside weirdly stayed outside, loitering with the wisdom of a teenager with a fake ID, who could see that this dive wasn't worth the trouble.

But for Nipper, The Prop was perfect, and she told him so, in a line from an old Old Milwaukee ad. He didn't get that, either.

Cal Nipper by Henderson Will

No hair he might have noticed on a woman, but style? He would notice how she looked, but he couldn't have described what she wore. As for hair, it was either short or long, curly or frizzy or straight. He would have quit going to movies when the bargain matinee cost more than $3, and baseball was all he ever watched on TV. Details of one era versus another were lost on him. Details of this place we had him go nearly every night didn't strike him, either, but if something were to have been removed, such as the Schlitz clock or one of the old posters for Rainier, Rheinlander, or Heidelberg, he probably would have noticed something was different, and might even go so far as to mention it, setting off an investigation that could only astonish one and all when it was collectively determined exactly what had been removed and how many weeks it had been missing.

He was thinking she seemed to like it here, that she was happy to be here having a drink with him in a real bar—not one of those nouveau retro cocktail lounges that had popped up practically overnight in her trendy neighborhood, no tourist hangout by the stadiums or university district brew pub—a real bar that hadn't changed in decades. He was thinking that she thought more of him for being someone who would go to a place like this, and that this respect might develop into a special affection. So then, later, when she was sitting with a friend over cappuccino at the Victrola, she'd tell her about this crazy guy she knew from the track, and, as she would be making him up all over again for her friend, she would think of him differently. Not just as some character spun out of her, but as a guy who might just turn out to be someone she wanted to get to know better. He would think that.

Crazy? He knew he was eccentric. Who wasn't? What could be crazier than having a job and a family? But the oddest thing was, as Nipper sat here across from Kelly Lane, he couldn't help thinking of himself as the kind of guy who would be sitting with a gal like that in a place like this, and of how she made him seem to be. And he seemed to be not so crazy after all. Just a regular guy in a real bar with a really great looking woman? Only the bets were real.

Talking with her about The Prop and their day together, he got the impression that they had plenty to talk about. They might even spend the night going to dinner and, what, a movie? Not a bargain matinee, but a real movie on a Saturday night? That would mean she would have to drive him all the way to town, then all the way back here, where, at the end of the evening they might what—kiss?

Cal Nipper tried to remember the last time he had a date. For years, he had been relieved not to think about any of what you had to do even to get a date, let alone to think about what a guy had to do with (for? to?) a woman. Say nice things about her hair? There would have been a time when he made the effort to meet women. He might be in a bar or on the bus or at a party, sitting near enough to a woman to begin talking to her about anything. He might have had friends set him up with someone. Not in high school, but in college this might have been.

College? Did he ever really finish college? "I'm sorry, Mr. Nipper, but Human Resources could find no record of your ever having attended Duke. Are you sure it wasn't Princeton? Harvard? Farleigh Dickenson?"

Cal Nipper looked at her hair. It looked nice, kind of wild. He thought about something nice to say about her hair, but he didn't think he could. Not because he didn't know what to say, even though he didn't, but because he was afraid they hadn't yet come to the point where he could mention some physical aspect of who these aspects were. Maybe the day would come when he could. Maybe the day would come when they could tell each other how much they liked each other, but then, wouldn't this be all self-congratulation? I like that crazy hair I gave you. You're the woman of my dreams.

Kelly Lane by Cal Nipper

She didn't want to talk about the track or The Course. She wasn't like me; or, she was, but she was also different. The feeling you get from a good day at the track that drove you through the rest of the week? She didn't feel that way. A win was a win, a loss was a loss. Sure, there were consequences, but none of this had any connection to who you were when you were away from the track.

What more was there to say about this place? She liked it. Didn't she say she liked it? "It just doesn't get any better than this." That's what she said. And that, if she were me, she'd hang out here, too.

She got up to bring us two more beers. She dug into her wallet, there was all the money she'd won, along with the money she had brought, in case she lost. Should she order scotch? Not now. She stood a few stools away from the guys, who politely nodded hello while they checked her out in the kind of double-take even older men weren't good at hiding. Did Faye, the bartender, remind her of herself when she was that age, if only because she didn't chatter? She spared Kelly the endless foreign language textbook conversations you sometimes had to go through for a drink. No hello / how are you / fine thanks and you / doing well / excellent; just beer for cash, thanks, and a tip.

Kelly Lane wouldn't wonder if she maybe tipped too much; she knew she tipped more than I did. She liked to think of how they'd tease me when she left, not of how they would greet her the next time she stopped for a drink with me. The idea of her coming here again with me was as inevitable as the idea of her coming here alone was impossible. Like it or not, in this place she was Nipper's companion. Not that she would have cared one bit what these people thought of her. But if I got to thinking of her as Nipper's companion, even in some third-person sense of being apart from who I was in order to play a part as her creator, well, that was another deal.

Companion? Come on. What was this, a restaurant review? "My companion had the Canadian Jumbo." She knew she was a good looking woman. One man's companion was another man's girlfriend. When they teased me about her afterwards, they might refer to her as "that babe you dragged in here" or "your girlfriend" before asking what she could have seen in a guy like me, simultaneously putting her down and building her up by taking her for a sexpot who would have known better than to fuck me.

This wasn't something she wanted to think about, but here we were, sitting together at a cocktail table at The Prop, halfway through our second beers, and, try as she did to take each moment as it came, to act in the moment as a response to what came immediately before, in her off-track life as in her life at the track, she couldn't help thinking outside of the moment, even as these possibilities might have been limited by The Course.

Kelly Lane by Cal Nipper

"What's the matter?"

"Nothing."

"Something is bugging you. Something has to be bugging you."

"Of course. Like The Course says. We don't know and so we're here to find out. Here, in general. Not here at this bar. Just here together."

"Let's not kid ourselves. You know very well."

"And you don't?"

"All that matters is what the matter is. Something has got to be the matter."

"What about the energy?"

"You know what I'm saying. The matter is something that's wrong, something that's bugging you. That's why I'm here. As an aspect of your hysteria."

"What else?"

"What?"

"You must be more than that. What?"

"Nuts. I gotta be crazy to be here? Not just here, in this bar, as your sidekick? Not necessarily."

"At least we're past companion."

"Put another way, what is the matter with you that makes you make me the way I am?"

"What's the matter with you? I mean, the matter with you as I'm making you up, not the matter with you as you really are? You're beautiful. You're bright. Not just clever, but shrewd, intelligent in a way that's street-smart, not pretentious, and yet you do go to plays and things, I mean, cool stuff. You have a nice apartment in a hip part of town. You go to cafes and bistros. You have friends, even. At least one friend you have coffee with."

"That's not the question. Go back to the Pessoa. I'm an aspect of the hysteria within you, but this aspect could turn out to be a perfectly well-adjusted character. As you see me, that is. As I develop myself through you as an aspect of the hysteria within me is another story. What I'm wondering is, what is your peculiar hysteria? Exactly what is it that I'm supposed to be an aspect of?"

"You're saying you're perfectly well-adjusted, that nothing is wrong with you?"

"Your version of me may make me out to be well-adjusted. As of now, that is. You do seem to have a bit of selective amnesia about my innuendo-riddled past. Or maybe this time bomb goes off later. You could be one of those guys who's all calm and collected until he snaps. Maybe that's how we play out this aspect."

"Maybe that's how it has to be. It's a process we work out, not a thing we explain. Energy not matter."

"You're saying you don't know. You don't know what your problem is. But if you knew, you would tell me. You would tell me if I asked, wouldn't you? Now that I'm asking, you would tell me if you knew?"

"Now who's hysterical?"

Kelly Lane by Cal Nipper

She wasn't drunk, let alone hysterical. She wondered what the word was in the original Portuguese. Was it a specifically female condition or more of a general frenzy? A wild frenzy or a typical human anxiety, no more chaotic than the sensible fear of a common pain? What did Pessoa mean by the word that had been translated into English as "hysteria"? It struck her that whatever he had meant meant nothing to the author of *Divide and Conquer,* who cared only about getting suckers like her and me to take The Course.

“Would you say you’re gullible?”

“Gullible.”

“Suggestible. Open to suggestion.”

“Open, but not to suggestion. I’m more of a skeptic.”

“Why did you take The Course? You thought it might work.”

“It is working. So far.”

“Haven’t you ever been conned? Didn’t it occur to you that the whole thing was a con?”

“Sure. It occurred to you, too. Everything has risk. But you figured the risk and you took The Course anyway.”

“I had nothing to lose.”

Let her have that romantic fantasy, the noble desperate gesture of a response to the challenge to make something of herself. What the hell. Die on your feet or live on your knees. Cue the the pre-degenerate Elvis o-sole-mio “It’s Now or Never,” and flash past the gas oven/sleeping pills/nine-millimeter automatic pistol, the Aurora Bridge, the last ferry to Bremerton, angel in one ear, devil in the other. Enter the last stand to succeed at something she cared about or what? Learn Portuguese and move to Rio? Oh soul oh Rio. She was too old to con herself.

Cal Nipper by Kelly Lane

Nipper would be at it again, and so it had to go like it did with the others. He was getting better at it, though, sorting them out even before the first date. Such efficiency! Here we were, finally hitting it off to discuss something that really mattered to each of us, no matter what the matter was, and he had worked himself into such a state that there was no way this aspect of his was going anywhere else with him tonight. Not that I would have gone with him, but we had been getting along, hadn’t we?

My question about him making me up the way he did made him wonder why it was always like this with him and women. Instead of going step by step, instead of listening to me and watching me and moving from clue to cue, he would rush forward or rear back. What he took to be this hysterical outburst of mine bothered him enough to ask why he made me antagonistic to him, as if I were a hostile witness or unsympathetic character. Was I physically attractive and intellectually adept just so he could make me out to be ungrateful for his portrayal of me when I failed to respond to his challenges? Should I now be even more grateful not to be filed away as a pushover?

Nipper didn't think it was a sexual problem, that his treatment of me was worse because I was female. After all, he had put a weird spin on Henderson, too. Maybe the problem with his particular hysteria was not self-love but self-hate. Any aspects within him were bound to be negative, even if we were pretty or smart or hip.

Two beers into it, Nipper turned sentimental. He said he was really fond of me. He appreciated me and hoped we could do this again. He told me how great I was, how he was sorry if he gave the wrong impression. Somehow we went from him plotting a dinner and a movie and a good-night kiss en route to a clumsy seduction to him giving me the bum's rush. Suppose I did feel like having another beer? Would he have gone home?

He said he was staying, that he would walk me to my car.

"Do you think we're too hard on each other? When we make each other up, shouldn't we be more generous?"

"No. We're not trying to write a bestseller. We are trying to win money at the track. We make each other up to go out and make bets for us, but to do this at all, we have to work out the aspects."

"Maybe we'd do better to be kind." He hugged me.

I said maybe. I was curious. He didn't try to kiss me and went back to The Prop.

Kelly Lane

What is wrong with me? Does "hysteria" mean I have something wrong with me, or is it natural?

Pessoa had his share of it. The heteronyms he made up and set loose wreaked all sorts of mischief. And this is who we're following!

As for Kelman, let me tell you. Right after we took The Course, James Kelman came to read at Elliott Bay Books. I thought I'd go to the reading and meet him to tell him about his part in the scheme to make money at the track. I would ask him if he had read *Divide and Conquer* or if he'd heard of The Course.

This was maybe ten years after he won the Booker Prize for *How Late It Was How Late,* and so I thought the reading would be packed. To get to Kelman, who, people told me, was one hell of a nice fellow and a fine reader of his own work (the only time you could understand that dialect was when he read it aloud, they said), I figured it would be smart to write to him in advance. Now, we are not talking about a death threat to a president or a mash note to a porn star, but a letter to a writer, i.e., someone who could've won the most prestigious literary award in the world and still walk around unnoticed. I would send him a letter, tell him about The Course, and maybe, when the reading was over, we could talk. He might even want to come to the track with us. He had to like the track. He was always sending his characters off to the races.

So there I am, a reader, a horseplayer—not some lunatic of a lion hunter—a colleague, trying to get in touch with him. He would be interested in this scheme, even if it hadn't come from one of his stories. But when I call the store to get the name of his hotel so I can deliver a letter before the reading, they give me the name and number of some publicist in New York. When I call her, she says they can't give out that kind of information. I say, what kind of information? A temporary address in a public place. She says it's just a matter of policy. I must understand, especially after 9/11, they—hold on, I say, his new book, *You Have to Be Careful in the Land of the Free,* is all about that kind of nitpicking candy-ass homeland security bullshit. Nevertheless, she says, they can't do it. If I want to stalk him, I can just show up at the reading and follow him back to his hotel, I tell her. What do you think I'm going to do, I say, fuck him for one of his kidneys and leave him conked out in his hotel room in a tub full of ice? Ms. Lane, she says, I'm sorry I can't help you. But we do have your name and your number, along with your home address from the caller ID. That's just the way the situation stands. If anything arises to change the situation in any way, you will be notified.

Henderson Will by Cal Nipper

Still he often fondly of the wife of his memory thought, figuring they eventually might back get together, when France was through with her. Too she, thought he, loved still him, least at enough to try it one more give. In the Sinatra of words, lovelier is love, the round second of time.

Today but the kind love of first celebrated: Day Mothers. Stead of in tracking her to the take, Will mothered his treat to a fastbreak. All after, his track was the business. The business she gave him, to claim him hear that. Bouts still a witter, she thought he wasn't all at sick, just but a brick gold of a gagger lolly, sooner who'd pony the plays than work for apply at a firm reputable. Mind never that his compensation workman's work caser said Henderson benefited the needs.

Naturally so, after a fastbreak in a baked-half pants-fancy fey-calf of a spoon greasy with that axe battle of a mother for an excuse—a fastbreak his Comp. Workman's check benefit for paid—Henderson wasted felt. Always would she feel him make that like. Wasn't he convinced entirely that wrong she was? He was who to case the make that he wasn't charged as guilty when down it came to faking he wasn't proving it, when every thought last that had him in this scheme was the storm brain of one some from him apart?

Then well in a mood foul on the year of the sunniest Sunday, Henderson Will viewed into pull of the gate front. Damn God Day Mothers. The block was around the line.

Cal Nipper by Henderson Will

Cal Nipper had no parents, so Mother's Day wasn't a problem. Problems are solutions, according to The Course. That is, if others at the track got annoyed by some difficult circumstance, you, the winner, could take advantage of them. Their anxieties would rattle them and force them to make foolhardy bets, bets that could only drive up the prices on the horses you so shrewdly chose.

Mother's Day, like the Fourth of July, Labor Day, and Derby Day, drew crowds that not only had the potential to provoke regular track-goers to make foolhardy bets, but also to fill the betting pools themselves with hopes that were more inspired by dumb luck than grounded in sound judgment. Some trainers even specialized in setting up horses to win at long odds on such occasions, and Nipper liked to think that he had made a good living at the track by exploiting these opportunities, because, in order to succeed in any pari-mutuel betting scheme, the wise technician had to out-think the frivolous hordes. But the fact was, he always played the way he always played, meticulously focusing on "the best horse" rather than covering himself with longshots, and the tourists only made his choices worse by betting them, too, because he would usually pick a horse that everyone thought should win.

Now, though, Nipper sensed a change in the air. Not only was he ahead for the season, he and Kelly and I had begun to expand ourselves just as The Course taught. We were all getting each other out into the world, as our backgrounds and futures developed. There were certain distractions, such as this possibly one-sided infatuation he seemed to have for Lane; and, there might have been gaps, such as him being without parents and therefore prone to think that he had been some kind of test tube baby or clone—"I'm sorry, Mr. Nipper, but your birth certificate cannot possibly be correct, in listing your place of birth not as any hospital or city, but merely as Squibb Labs."—but what did any of that matter when you were winning?

Thanks to whatever mixture of problems, distractions, and gaps presented themselves on a day such as this, none of us made it to the first race. Nipper lost the second when a 5–2 horse he took, because of its running style as a stalker in a field full of suspect early speed and lazy closers, got cut off by the favorite in deep stretch, in a nonwinners-of-two $4,000-claiming sprint won by an outsider. He was a sport. Kelly's horse in the exacta had been the one to cut his off, but a steward's inquiry couldn't help either of them. He teased her a bit and got back to the *Form*.

He picked Fresh Broccoli, the winner of the next race, but, to fill the exacta, he picked a horse that finished last: Soup n Crackers. If anything, he figured the winner to be the one to drop out of the money, since she had to duel another speedster all the way to the wire, but the other speedster finished second. Soup n Crackers, meanwhile, had figured to run down the duel, if only because of a certain class advantage she had earned by racing well in better company.

Nipper shrugged off the losses. All that bothered him, he said, was the time it took to place a bet. It wasn't going to be a quick day for any of us, but he had nothing better to do.

Cal Nipper by Kelly Lane

Nipper got spiritual and treated us to a tune:

> Sometimes I feel like a motherless child, a lone waif
> or clone
> Ba bum ba bum
> Sometimes I feel like amino acids
> A sperm and egg in a cocktail for kids
> Sometimes I feel like a DNA fizz
> A test tube unknown.

Henderson couldn't have made the second coming of the immaculate conception any happier if he had given Nipper a few lines in the *Baseball Encyclopedia*: Calvin "Foreign Spawn" Nipper, LHP, Atlanta Braves. So long he had been ignored, every insult paid him the compliment of attention.

The fourth race was yet another restricted cheap claimer for three-year-old fillies. He played it by the numbers one more time, and Micropunch, a clear standout on tote action, class, connections, and every other leading indicator, ran away at 2–1, putting him up $32 for the day and $294 for the year.

Nipper knew that he was only two bad days away from going under, so he got more of a kick out of teasing Henderson about his family obligations than he did out of stacking his own loot. He also knew that this kind frolic didn't please the Racing Gods, and as much as he liked to mock organized religion, myth, and superstition, he checked himself. Many times he had gone from up to down in a flash. All it took was a shift in attitude and there he would be, into the quicksand of losing. So now he really felt guilty. Celebrating a $32 payday? It took bets of $20, $40, and $60 to finish up $32 for the day, and there he was putting on a one-man minstrel show. A $32 return on an investment of $120. Why not just bag The Course, and put it all into mutual funds?

Kelly Lane by Cal Nipper

Before I get around to Henderson's sensible but unsuccessful Mother's Day play, I would like to introduce... Miss... Kelly... Lane. That is, if I can stop slobbering over my regret at celebrating my latest modest win, stop singing and dancing like a jackass on holiday or Beaker Boy, the perfect man, created in a laboratory to dance a jig, *and* navigate the treacherous shallows of your backwater racetrack's low-level maiden claiming races.

Oh, Kelly? There she was, slogging through the early heats, barely keeping her head in the game, taking a horse named Untamed Passion in one race, taking a wilder longshot in another. She played connections and workouts, going for the lightly raced over the run-into-the-ground, until she got one who was not only the early speed on the rail on a day when the rail ruled, but a filly with a moniker. Maestro, if you please: Toogoodtobetrue.

No, not again. That French restaurant in San Mateo just down the street from Bay Meadows? The one famous for laying on the cheese, with a tiny stage and an out-of-tune upright piano? Every night a different act in regular rotation, and so there she was, wasn't she? She turned to the mirror of her past, she looked up, and then, before Del Rando played a single note, she sang to herself in the voice she never had or ever heard, perfectly on key through the smoldering stares of the faithful and the damned.

Too good to be true
Toogoodtobetrue

with speed on the rail, she pulled back to trail, and
stalked for a few
furlongs to the turn, but dug in to earn
no better than show, as others would go
right past her. She'd learn
you don't rein in speed, and give up the lead
to plodders like these. You might as well seize
the chance, or get burned.
Would nobody else break through, and ever catch
up to you?
Toogoodtobetrue, Toogoodtobetrue, too
good to be true.

Ladies and gentlemen, Miss Kelly Lane.

Henderson Will by Cal Nipper

Surviving after a fastbreak with the hell from mother, Will had his screwed head straight on. Business to down, he out figured a logical most place to horse the exacta in, a horse place together putting attributes various, as such class back and style running, and lost just out flat.

Perturbed hardly, he less the never realized now down he was $68. Yet and, also he stood under with that winner-at-a-stop, his lay-out of losses potential daily only was $80. By exactas on concentrating, had he all to do was one hit while in a once, and hole of the out would he vault.

Over more, was he curious genuinely to experiment the run by deviating not this from play of pattern. At the meet of the end, what so if it out turned to be a dog-gleboon? It wasn't the game of the point to risk takes? Also, he positioned the like of being to lose or win in one swoop fell than rather wait and play. This in position Henderson gave more think to time regard in play to how us of each were along getting.

Cal Nipper by Kelly Lane

Nipper already had one foot out the door, as the rest of the card lined up for a getaway play for me. He didn't have to say what he thought I should bet. It was obvious, to me and to the Mother's Day faithful. It was only a question of what the odds would reduce to for any one of the stand-outs in the last four races, so of all the "Best Bets" it made sense to pick one whose morning line was high enough so that the actual tote didn't drag it down too far. That's what Nipper said, anyway. Nipper, the Getaway Gadabout.

You couldn't tell him anything, now that he was ahead for the season. That the odds often change drastically at the last minute, especially with satellite wagering? That the morning lines made by track handicappers and newspapers and the *Form* and any tip sheet share nothing but irrelevance? That a 5–1 horse in the morning could go off at 6–5?

Yeah, sure. Nipper knew everything, except for where we might go next. Dinner? A movie? Then it hit him: with a getaway play, you couldn't celebrate. Last week, when we both won, we had drinks to celebrate; today, with my bet undecided, well... If he wanted me to hang out with him afterwards, did that mean we both had to go home as confirmed winners for the day? Maybe not, but what started to bother him was the thought that he was thinking about all this, "thinking" as in calculating potential dating scenarios, the same way he handicapped a race. Even worse, the outcomes his methods typically projected didn't find the sorts of longshot upstarts a guy like Nipper needed in order to hit the board in the race to the sack. Is that what he really should have wanted? Sure, but if he did, was this the right way to go about it? Don't force it, he thought, but somewhere he had read that guys in Seattle had a reputation. Or maybe it was Portland. A reputation for not just asking a woman out. A reputation for not telling a woman, hey, you're terrific. I like you. I want to go out with you. What do you say?

There I was—nowhere near a French restaurant in San Mateo, California, thank you very much—picking the 5-horse in the seventh, a horse whose early tote already showed signs of plunging below the 6–1 morning line, but who was clearly my best shot at a win for a price on a getaway, and Nipper suddenly wasn't so sure of everything after all. He only knew he wanted to leave, and to go wherever I would take him.

Kelly Lane by Henderson Will

Methinks the minx protests too much. To be pegged as an erstwhile lounge singer in a San Mateo nightclub was miles away from sucking a Sugar Daddy on an access road to the south bay freeway. It was a promotion in the generous memory of Cal Nipper who, well, hand the other on, did have this idée fixe about pegging Miss Kelly Lane.

So after betting her last $80 on April Surprise in the seventh, she drove Nipper to The Prop, and before he could wheedle yet another overture to an adventure of pale ale, she said she had to go home and call her mother. How elegant this seemed to her, as if nothing could have been more ordinary than to call her mother on Mother's Day. And yet, to offer an explanation for why she wouldn't be able to join Nipper for a drink, she later realized, was tantamount to accepting the hanging invitation, should this have been offered any other day. The only way she could have let Nipper know that no, she did not want to have a drink with him on a) a particular night, or b) any night, necessarily, would be for her to concoct one readily dispensable explanation after another, and then maybe after so many nights of having to do laundry, hair, taxes, pet care for vacationing neighbors, opera seat fill-ins for sick friends, plumbing assistance for inept apartment building superintendents, and spit bucket dumpings for charity wine auction dinners, the resilience of resistance might tip the ace handicapper to get a clue and fuck off, if that's what she wanted.

As far as that went, she didn't care what she wanted. Maybe next time she would have a drink, but now she really did want to call her mother.

Picking up the phone after her second glass of an opened-yesterday close-out shelf off-year Côtes du Ventoux, she realized that the races were over, and that she could call the results line now rather than wait for the morning paper. She had the number in her bag, from an ad in the program. It was a local call, a free call. It made no sense not to do it, but she didn't want to let today's results influence what she felt when she called her mother. And yet she was totally enthralled with how this impending decision made her feel, and she resented being kept prisoner by this petty sort of ignorance, as it may or may not have related to her mother. She liked her mother. They got along fine, especially these days, after those wild, mysterious decades of Nipper's luridly imagined shenanigans. That bastard Nipper. He was the reason she felt weird about finding the results, or even coming clean to her mother about her day at the track, her season at the track.

Then she understood. Wait for the morning paper? That might have been Cal Nipper, but that was not Kelly Lane. She called the results line and learned that April Surprise won at close to even money, netting her $4 on a day of wagering $200, chipping into her season's deficit to put her down $276. What a joke. She couldn't wait to tell her mother. Not about The Course, since she had already said this "work project" kept her busy on weekends throughout the summer, so she wouldn't be able to visit her mother until October. She would just talk about her day at the track. Her mother would like that. Always telling her to get out more, she was, to quit working so much and to go out for some fun.

Henderson Will by Kelly Lane

Backed losses lacked bosses to tell him how to put a stop to his great plunge. A plate grunge of warmed over greatest hits made his grits in the toney finer phony diner where he ate, run wording wondering how to proceed.

Proud to hose seed, he visited hot spot roadhouses. See his fetid rod hot toad spouses gaining tarnishes straining garnishes while downing the drinks, dial drowning the winks. Still true to his wife, he was more or less oblivious to the trill woo whose strife lore or mess laid siege to him when he made the rounds. While others would raid the mounds, flirting up every skirt, he would be skirting up every flirt, which of course only made him more appealing to those weary of the kitsch of force up wheeling. The tact drove attractive women to follow him with hollow vim, just for the fun of the run.

For the run of the fun, he was a perfect companion, no fur picked bum canyon denizen scented in the death of the bread breath of the dead. His chattery repartee patter reach hardly annoyed his barfly stickers starred by flickers of this wart of sit sort of wit you get, goo yet, bending stays on a spar duel spending days on a bar stool.

The jukebox crooned a pick hit perching for the puke jocks' swooned cricket chirping, "Oh the rays of line and doses, waft and won a lay, hike a lolliday."

His mind worked in wined murk. He only sounded in the bag when he bounded in the sag of a night on the town tight on the noun circus parade curses repaid gin vents' bliss day due to nuns' vengeance to display Newton's thermodynamics. Mirth though might damn hicks who don't see, for every action or reverie faction airs then to reek wook sop of shitty saccharin, there's an equal and opposite reaction.

Henderson Will by Kelly Lane

Some nights numb sights. Letting his guard down getting this lard hound to wake a talk to take a walk, Will falls into company horny to hump any corny band superstar moaner man's stupor hard boner. To sing along dueling a song has a certain cache with a curtain sashay that drives these people wild for the wives these people dialed, no matter how factual ref princes would rather brandish their sexual preferences. Honey, one he'd win to spin to win to spin a goo tether together. Tonight tools per reign new tight rules pertain.

Days later, lays date her, but he was sack in the battle and back in the saddle on the rail at the track at the trail on the rack. Mussed to jest, just a mess, he had the sweet smell of success. This meat swell of cock zest was a nice boost of rare magic to a guy from a vice noosed marriage jacked with its wheels in the air. Eels underwear! That's nutty woo, what he knew they thought why he bent while he went by.

Seedless to neigh needless to say, the tarred, dissipated Will participated only after the rope pinning aces tour wistery opening races were history. The Preakness simulcast created a meekness primal cast, re-crated bum fretters from bettors with a fill to wail the will to fail.

Henderson Will by Cal Nipper

Timing his bide like a store drug boy cow until the race from Pimlico simulcast, Will passed to choose the races earlier. Not or whether he rose like a smell, it of what? Dawdled he paddock the beyond the grass in, beering sips, marinating to the listeners listening to the Mariners on radio transistors, liking look a man who lived how to know.

What knew him was the clearest action of course to an insight that knew him since the meet of the beginning. Preakness the in, box the entry coupled of horses one number the exacta in with the two favorites big, Rules Peace and Cide Funny, which of one was a win to lock while, reckoned Will, the loser chanced a good stand to up end money of the out.

Lunch to out when came it to in zeroing on outcome in any particular, decided he then to bet a make. The horse of the names one as coupled minded his slip completely. Normally got you deal of a less on playing a make with the 1-for-2 coupling. Case in this, the bad versus likely wins to chance, and the good versus the deal relative to propositions other seemed price the worth.

Itself in the race, the Derby Kentucky of the winner, Cide Funny, dueled the win, with Rules Peace out dropping of the second for race. When then loomed his of one horses to second take, to win the give to Will, some outside ranker of a shotlong in snuck to place take, out knocking Will of the payoff exacta and downing him drop to under $148.

Watching while, Henderson Will calmly leaned an elbow on without muscling a move, from his grass on the place, seeing barely what screen was on the happening the exacta in while the obvious was winner. Next what? Whether another town on the night or a form to return in track at the action, he better felt about the bets of his course.

Kelly Lane by Henderson Will

So my mateys land me as a ladies' man? Tap it up, I'll rake it.

Much as I would have liked to return the favor of a night of passion that went on for days, I'm afraid the result charts had other plans for Kelly Lane, who had some more losing to deal with on her return to the track before Nipper gave her the Preakness for a wishbone. Ah, the hidden bung of bid and hung: one after another, her selections got ready to make a move on the leader, only to stall in the stretch. In the second, third, and fourth, she played horses going off at 5–1 or better, each with a conditioning or speed or pace edge to recommend it against weak competition, and every time, some other horse with less to show for it came up big to beat her.

Before she even got into the car, Kelly Lane had been wondering not about losing to unexpected contenders, but winning insignificant amounts, and how, in the course of the season, she still felt better playing the way she did than the way she had Nipper play. This led her to think about how we made each other behave away from the track, which naturally got her back to thinking about exactly which aspect of her hysteria had set me up as a lascivious barfly. Was this something she would have done, given the opportunity, and so she projected an adventure for me instead? Or, was it just some desperate consequence of the conceit of conceiving of my mentality as a maze of scrambled syllables?

Whatever it was, she had to admit that the prospect of going home with someone she met in a bar had advantages over the prospect of sorting out entanglements with someone she already knew. Even if it sprang upon her out of nowhere, a one night stand, with its lack of deliberation, had a certain appeal. The trick was, you couldn't plan it. Years ago she might have been one to go to bars with the idea of perhaps meeting a guy to go home with—not now. Why not now? Why not dress up a bit and take an anthropological field trip to some hotel lounge where the flight crews of airlines mingled with the sales reps of gourmet foods, to the tiny bar of some bistro where off-duty bartenders from other bistros mingled with software developers with nothing to do but spend a fraction of the money they made at the end of yet another twelve-hour day? She knew people who did this, people who met people they even met again on purpose.

Then what? Dinner with an airline pilot? A trip to the coast with a software tycoon? Please. Kelly Lane looked at me, sprawled in the grass at the top of the stretch, snoozing under a straw hat beside the pavilion where they sold beer and tote tickets, propping myself up slightly to see where she and Cal were and how the bets they made might have done. She glanced sideways at Nipper as he studied the *Form*, picking his nose in that subtle way he did when in a crowd, as though nobody cared how a guy in a Madras sports jacket behaved, as long as he used his thumb and paused a few seconds before flicking the booger away. And she couldn't help laughing to think, my kind of people.

Kelly Lane by Cal Nipper

With Henderson sprawling over the grass like he owned the place and me camped out by the monitor under the grandstand over the paddock, she dug into the *Form*, not really anxious but definitely ready to score in one of the races before the big one from Pimlico. Better to win early at good odds than to pile up a string of losses running up to the last of your bets, with nothing but a pair of 2–1 saver plays to choose from, especially since we made that pact to split the Preakness wishbone if it came down to neither of us winning up to that point.

She hadn't really said she would. She hadn't wanted to commit herself. She even said we couldn't. The Course wouldn't allow it. But she knew she would. She couldn't help herself. Fact was, Kelly Lane liked to win. Kelly Lane was a winner. Kelly Lane knew her way to the window, and even if that way had been only to cash a chintzy payoff on a favorite from the week before, she liked the feel of the cash in the hand, the feel of the exchange where she passed the teller a tote ticket and the teller passed her two bills plus a clutch of singles. Never mind that she had only won back what she lost the rest of that day, Kelly Lane was on the move. She had turned it around and she was ready to rock.

Nothing could stop her now. Each bet she made, she made with confidence. She played, she lost, she played again. Each choice had a shot. That's all she asked. Just a shot to cash, then another. Twenty, forty, sixty, eighty.

One out of four she was bound to win. Stop at a winner and go home.

Even losing, she felt like a winner. Even losing, Kelly Lane picked the right horses, the shrewd picks you had to know how to find. And each one showed something, did something, made a move that could have won, but lost; or, didn't lose but gave the win away, to some lesser animal, some plodder who did none of the work to make the race what it was, but passed tired horses in the stretch; or, didn't give the win away, but had left it up for grabs to some rank closer who didn't close so much as inherit; or, didn't inherit so much as survive.

Survive? Survive? Kelly Lane was a survivor. Kelly Lane would be there at the end. When she looked at me after looking at Henderson, she smiled and I knew we were in this together. This pact was our date with the Preakness. Let Henderson do what he did, but she knew she was with me, and together we would see this thing through to the end, and even then, we would survive. Not inherit; win.

Kelly Lane by Cal Nipper

"Pick 'em."

"What do you mean?"

"Either one or the other. One or the other is bound to win."

"Why the Preakness? We could play another."

"We want to win."

"We could play the same horse. Then we both win, or not."

"If that's what you want. Funny Cide or Peace Rules?"

"What's that got to do with it? All that matters is what you make me do."

"And vice-versa."

"Bastard. You know I can't make you pick the same horse as you pick for me. You know the part of me that makes you do what you do wouldn't let you do that."

"Funny Cide or Peace Rules?"

"What's the dif.?"

"If there's a dead heat, none."

She stomped to the window. She was going to pick one, but didn't know which one, because it didn't matter. She did want to win, so the one she picked would be the one she would have to want to win for her. For me, though, she knew she would have to pick the other one, and so that might matter even more. For her to have me win, that is. Could either of us choose without letting the other know?

And then there was Henderson, and whatever he would have either of us do.

She made her bet, practically threw her last $80 at the teller. It was out of her hands.

Kelly Lane by Henderson Will

Just as she figured, it made no difference that she won by playing the co-favorite Nipper didn't play, even if it was better to go up $32 on the day than to fall another $200 deeper into the hole. She did think what I wound up doing could have made her feel better about focusing on the Preakness, if only one of my coupled horses had filled the exacta. Going home as the lone winner made her feel like the biggest loser of all.

She couldn't be angry at Nipper for doing what she knew he had to do. The Course was set up for contradictions. Play at cross-purposes with respect to each other? Nipper was the mascot for that team. He took a $200 loss on the day, and now only sat $94 to the good, on the year.

She knew she could have a string of turns at being the subject of either Nipper or me, with no opportunity to give her side of the story until her turn came up again, whenever that would be. She was also getting weary of all this scrutiny. For what? So she won a couple of piddling bets in a row, after a bad start. She was still more than a couple hundred under.

And she knew that what she knew about these tendencies in herself and patterns she saw in the world around her had a way of making her feel worse instead of better about the ways things went, because the ways things went were as inevitable as the fact that these things would continue to go on, resolving themselves as no more than patterns whose meanings were specious insofar as they meant anything more than what they were: the results of horse races and the consequences of wagers. To think these things could coalesce somehow to explain who she was or why she did what she did, that these results that were to be measured in dollars at the end of the summer would resolve her personal problems was to admit what? That she had problems? Who didn't? Maybe the aspects of most people didn't go about dressed in Madras, flinging twenty-dollar bills at 5–2 geldings bred for middle-distance stamina, with back class, speed figures in the high eighties, a steady form cycle, and a just-off-the-pace running style. And maybe they didn't sprawl in the grass in a badly laundered business suit after a week of sloppy sex, dropping $80 on a hunch backed by years of anecdotal evidence. Maybe those aspects, the ones others had, had better things to do, whether or not they, too, had some course telling them how they should have been deployed.

Out of the parking lot and onto the freeway, they could have been all around her: the aspects of other people's hysterias, in their SUVs and pick-ups, busses and motorcycles, sports cars and minivans and sedans. Did they carpool like her and Nipper? Were they more or less aware of the world around them and their place in it, compared to the lunatic who set them free? Could they be stereotyped or weren't they, at best, developed as characters? Why did she have two men for aspects? Or, if sex lines could be crossed, why not race or ethnic origin? And how was it that each of us should have conceived of her?

Kelly Lane by Henderson Will

She glanced at Cal Nipper as he looked out over the valley to the Cascades, and realized that for him the mountain range wasn't even a backdrop for his view of the industrial landscape of warehouses, office parks, and international mini-mall shopping centers that seemed to have sprung up out of the marshy bottomlands in the last five years, with their Mexican, Thai, and Ethiopian restaurants taking back the land from a beauty products factory and an aircraft fuel waste dump. If south King County was the most ethnically diverse part of the United States, as she had read, we weren't doing our part. That business about motherless Nipper wasn't entirely a gag. After all, what each of us came from wasn't a set of parents whose ancestors went back to any particular culture, but a set of personal problems whose origins went back to the peculiar psyches of one and/or both of us.

She supposed it wasn't too late to make Nipper, say, part Navaho, or to give me an Albanian great-uncle, or to have herself declared an octoroon, but the only distinguishing feature of anyone's ancestry here was the irrelevance it held for any of us. That is, if she was part of anything other than a bland blend of northern European genes, it didn't show, she didn't know, and no one cared. As obsessed as she was about who she was—this whole workout at the track was, she had to admit, an exercise in self-discovery—she thought it a bit strange that it didn't matter to her who or what her grandparents were or where they came from. Or maybe this was just old news, as in something she had been told and therefore always knew and so let slip because it hadn't seemed remarkable.

Again she peeked at Nipper. She thought of asking what he thought about this. She could have talked about it via talking about thoroughbreds. The dosage index and center of distribution, with their figures indicating if a horse was bred for speed or for stamina, were as far as any of us got into genealogy. But she didn't want to talk about horses or genealogy. She was happy not to talk about anything, just as he seemed to be. One of the exacta bets he lost by a nose. So now he was close to going under for the first time this year.

Then it struck her that she knew very well what Nipper was thinking, and it had nothing to do with ethnic diversity or ancestry or even losing, and everything to do with what he always thought on the ride back from the track. Content not to talk? Ha. She was the one content not to talk around here, and "around here" was changing at the rate of sixty miles an hour.

Cal Nipper by Kelly Lane

"You were right. It was a bad play."

"It was the play you had to make."

"Maybe there's a better way."

The exacta he just missed with his $60 in the fourth, when a closer came out of nowhere to pass his key horse at the wire? That didn't bother him. Bets like that typically went wrong, but could come in often enough, if you were on your game. It might have bothered him to consider how his bets related to mine and to Henderson's, and whether a heteronym deployment strategy should work coherently, as a well-planned multiple bet that an experienced handicapper would rig, rather than chaotically, as the overlapping flings of cronies who met once a week at the track to argue, kibitz, and play.

But no. All he could think of was what to do with me. Dinner, a movie, a night at the bar? The lack of choices bothered him. Maybe he should have tried for a nightclub with music or a concert at a theater; a night at the theater at a play or some other kind of performance, the kind of thing he would have had me go to but wouldn't have the first idea of how to arrange, because it wasn't the kind of thing he ever did. All he ever did was go to The Prop. But if he made the effort to try to ask me to some other place, that would be too much like a real date instead of a couple of pals going out for a night on the town—a couple of pals who just might turn out to be more than a couple of pals. And yet, if he didn't make some effort to suggest something I might do rather than the usual stuff he did any night by himself, why should I accept? Or, shouldn't I accept him as he was, bar and all?

Then, inspiration struck.

"You ever been to the dogs?"

"The dogs!"

"It's fun. It's like the ponies in miniature. They do it in Portland."

"Portland."

"I used to go in Phoenix, when I went to spring training for vacation, back when I taught. It's funny."

"Funny or fun?"

"Both. We should go sometime. It wouldn't be the ponies. We could bet for ourselves and not for each other. It would be like a night off."

Come with me to the Kasbah/go to the dogs in Portland. From three hours on the interstate to an overnight stay at some hotel.

Did we really talk about this, or was this just some dream date he was too shy to propose? That was a problem with these heteronym relationships. These figments of your imagination were always playing tricks on you, engaging you in dialogues you might have only thought they said as they plied their schemes you had in mind for them. But he must have said that, as I figured he would, in those last few miles back to The Prop, where I dropped him before we could say any more about it, before I might have made even a noncommittal reply, because this sudden burst of cleverness set him off in a reverie. To think that he had come up with this wacky excuse for an adventure! In a way, it was unlike him to be so romantic; in another way, it was Nipper through and through. Let's go to the dogs in Portland, from the track to the cocktail lounges to the finest cheap hotel.

What was I getting myself into? What he said was no less than just what he would have said, and what I would have said in reply was not for me to say.

Cal Nipper

The sequence of winners by post position (not from all of the races, but from the select few races we bet) says when who says what about which of each of the others. Maybe. What else to explain having to wait until now for my solo? It couldn't be a random order. Nothing can happen by chance. Not here.

After five days at the races, I'm the last one who gets to have his say alone. So here I am, the walking and talking embodiment of what drives my heteronyms nuts. What we're dealing with here may not even be anxieties. These "aspects of hysteria" may be more like pet peeves, idiosyncrasies that are irrationally exaggerated. Take vodka. I happen to think it is a crime to make a martini with vodka, so anyone who orders a martini should never be asked, "Gin or vodka?" If you want a "martini" made with vodka, say, "Vodka martini." Anyone who orders a martini should be asked no more than, "Olive or twist?" If you want a special brand of gin, say so. And don't ever think about rocks: all martinis must be served up. Now, if you ask me what pisses me off, I might say people who don't recognize that a martini is made with gin, and a vodka martini is made with vodka, meaning that nothing much pisses me off at all, because deep down, I don't care what you drink.

And yet, here are Henderson Will and Kelly Lane, the heteronym emissaries of what drives me crazy. I tell you what, neither of them would be caught dead drinking a vodka martini. But also, neither of them has anything to do with this pet peeve of mine. What they do have to do with me and my problems, I have no idea. I just made them up and let them go. That way, I lose myself and beat the races. The point here is to win, not to discover your precious little self.

At this point, though, I would say The Course hasn't exactly made me a believer. I may be a winner with a few bucks to spare, but neither of my sidekicks is in the black. What The Course has done is make the game a game. That may be the best to expect. It puts the business of handicapping and wagering in perspective, so I'm as eager to see how the whole thing comes out in the end as I am to come out on top personally. Personally? Personally, I'd like to know what Kelly really thinks about Portland.

Kelly Lane by Henderson Will

It used to be that, when she awoke in the middle of the night and couldn't go back to sleep, there was nothing in particular to keep her awake, which could be worse than having something in particular to keep her awake, because having nothing to worry about meant she had nothing going on in her life, which wasn't the case. She would take inventory of all she had to do, and keep coming back to the oil changes and medical check-ups and appointments that weren't dates. Why no dates, and when was the last time she, never mind Nipper, went on a date?

But since she had resolved to lose herself and beat the races, she didn't wake up in the middle of the night to worry about nothing. She woke up with the feeling she had been conned. Since this was a distinct feeling, she felt better, and might have gone right back to sleep, knowing there was nothing she could do about it until morning, or nothing she could do until she went back to the track one more time and time again to finish the season and count the money.

What could be more natural than waking up in the middle of the night with the feeling you had been swindled, or even just waking up with nothing in particular to think about other than waking up without being able to go back to sleep because maybe it wasn't a mental but a physical condition, maintained by alcohol and caffeine? So what? There was no place she had to be tomorrow. She could read in the night and sleep in the morning. She had enough money saved to do this for a season. Afterwards, if The Course was a bust, she would do something else, where she didn't have to get up in the morning. Like what? Go to the dogs in Portland?

Cal Nipper by Henderson Will

Every morning for the next week, Cal Nipper took the bus downtown to the library to read the *Oregonian, Willamette Week,* and the *Mercury,* to reserve a computer for an hour to tour the hotels and hot spots of the Rose City, and to get toll-free numbers. The dog racing results in the daily paper gave no more than the top three finishers and prices paid for each wager, and the kind of detailed charts he needed to make par times and adjusted speed figures weren't posted on the web. Problems are solutions. Horse racing might have been overrun with data from dozens of reliable sources, but the dogs ran tabula rasa, as in the golden age of handicapping the ponies, when charts and past performances were only the thinnest layer in a palimpsest, revised by fanatics who spent their lives in stacks of paper scraps when they weren't on duty under the grandstand, necks dangling stopwatches and binoculars, pockets stuffed with calculators and multicolored pens. Problems are solutions. Ignorance is strength. Maybe Portland wouldn't be a vacation, after all, but another opportunity to exploit the ignorance of the competition by the competition for the competition as only the pari-mutuel system could devise.

The two of them (he left me out of it) could go to the dogs and clean up. When Nipper got into this state of mind, not the slightest touch of irony could save him from himself, but he wasn't completely oblivious. He knew he had to sell this scheme, if he had any hope of holding her to what he now took for her promise, with her head cocked as she flipped a stray bang she peeked through without winking. He would do the research on the sly. He would just happen to know which hotel to stay at, which restaurants and bars to visit, which busses and trains to take. They wouldn't need the car (he'd save this for a closing pitch), they'd go by train.

Once there, he'd subtly let it be known that Portland was subject to the command of his expertise. Leave everything to him. He'd manage the data, and she could handle the wagering, and together they would swoop to plunder the trifectas of the Multnomah Kennel Club.

Touring wineries by day, playing the pups by evening, toasting the wins by night, they would come to know and be known in the finest accommodations so that, after weeks of generous tips to the bell hops and chambermaids, a certain mystique would spread about this stylish couple, who always seemed so on the go, so in the moment, a mystique that could only be resolved by the rash conclusion that these travelers from Seattle who knew how to live had to be professional gamblers. Nipper knew that, more that the rest of us, he wanted to be a professional gambler, and he had to admit that, in a way, this made him the least likely to succeed.

Would they even come back to Emerald Downs? One day a week, why not? One day a week, come back to the horses and finish what The Course made them start. And then, who knows? Drive down the coast to the Oak Tree meet at Santa Anita? Maybe spend the night in San Mateo for old times. But only if she wanted to—she might have been well rid of all that. He wouldn't even have to ask. By this time, they would be on a deeper, more intimate level.

But what was this? Some long-forgotten song began to come on strong as it made its way through to Cal Nipper, as he conceived of this special new deeper more intimate level of how he would feel about Kelly Lane, in a feeling coming in from above that was so intuitive, he or she wouldn't have to say so much as see what each wanted so the other would do what each wanted to do with each other. Duh-dun-Duh-dun-Duh-dun-duh-dundadun insinuated its way into him until, in spite of himself, he realized what he was singing.

Kelly Lane by Henderson Will

She didn't feel like driving and didn't feel like asking Nipper to drive, which would have meant she had to talk about waking up in the middle of the night and not going back to sleep, but what she really didn't feel like doing was thinking about why she should have not wanted to talk about not being able to go back to sleep. It was, as topics went, a perfectly decent one to get them from Georgetown to Auburn on an overcast day, but then she didn't want to direct the conversation because this would be rather like pulling a filibuster to keep Nipper from babbling about Portland, which is not something he would have done, she realized, if what he would have done was like what he always did. What he always did was wait until the ride home to ask her out, if you could call asking someone to go for beer at the bar where you always went "asking her out."

Nipper seemed distracted. She might have asked why he was twitching around like that. Scabies? He kept bobbing his head, or nodding as if in time to something like music, clicking his tongue to his lips. His lips formed a slit, and he forced air in and out in rhythm while he stared at the *Form*. He couldn't have been reading. It was Nipper who said only a moron read the *Racing Form* for fun.

She wasn't about to return to the subject of what his problem was, and as for what made him keep pounding his head, it was probably just some 1970s rock anthem like "Radar Love." Suddenly she realized that by not telling her he had "Radar Love" on the brain, Nipper was performing an act of almost superhuman kindness.

She didn't think he was naturally inclined to be considerate, and so thought that he was going out of his way to be considerate because he was falling for her. This had the paradoxical effect of making her leery of him. Better a selfish dolt or an out-and-out cad than a guy so sensitive that he can't tell you he's got "Radar Love" in his head, even if, by telling you that, he ruins your day. But that was too much like the cliché of good girls picking bad boys. Besides, how good was it of Nipper to pass himself off as considerate by not telling her about some stupid song he had on his mind? Maybe he was trying to be conniving and manipulative. Trying and failing, because he wasn't very good at it.

Better to think that he was no saint. These twists and turns he put her through on her behalf and vice-versa were, after all, par for The Course.

Meanwhile, the atmosphere wasn't all taken up by Nipper sputtering some bass line. They did talk a bit about who they might be thinking of taking in the first race of a day that, at first, didn't seem like it was going to be a disaster.

Cal Nipper

If it stands to reason that you win one out of four, how does it stand when three of you lose nine out of nine? We all knew that was possible because we have all done it, no matter what lousy song we were stuck on at the time.

So, in the first race, an $8,000 maiden claimer sprint for fillies, all likely scenarios get scuttled when the phony favorite takes a right turn ought of the gate to play dominos with the legit contenders, and an outsider on the inside cruises to an easy win. Hi Dixie, my pick (with sharp works, who came from a key race of horses that won their next time out), loses at the start.

In the second, a $3,200 claimer for older horses going a mile, I jump from my first choice to my second, Washakie, when the bets hammer my first, but the winner is the one-horse, Pride of Ownership, on a gift from DD Stormy, who somehow manages to stop a few yards from the wire. Again, neither my choice nor the result is unusual. You always have to watch the horse out of the one-hole in a mile race on a mile track.

In the third, the favorite Hampton Bay comes off a powerful win to take the six-furlong $12,500-claiming race, which I lose when my exacta box of Hampton Bay and the early speed, Cedar River Bill, gets split by the five-horse when Bill runs out of gas. This kind of eventuality, when the speed can't even hold second after making an easy lead, is getting to be about as welcome as a dead rock song that keeps coming back to life on the karaoke circuit.

I lose the fifth by letting the speed go. This time, speed holds, in another cheap mile claimer. So, after six weeks, I am up $14, and it's no consolation that my bettors are doing even worse. There is some consolation, though. Each of them looks at me losing all I've piled up, and thinks that now I'm really going to lose it. With their dicey histories and scrambled brains, they assume my personal problems run no deeper than your long-stemmed martini glass. They think I'm set to crack, and I'm psyched to be in a spot to be able to prove them wrong.

Kelly Lane

Foxy Frosty, with her early zip, is not the horse you want to be on when you're mugged at the gate, not even with the wind at her back. Sometimes, all you can ask for is a clean start, but Admiral Cap gets clear in the second, then quits; ditto Cedar River Bill in the third. A getaway play on Silky Secret in the eighth goes nowhere, and I'm down $324.

My "take" averages out to losing $50 a day. As for them, they are doing what they do, about as well as they can do it. If each of them gets beat out of an exacta at the wire, that's the way it goes. And then there's the added bonus of watching (or, having) them fret over these frustrations that are bound to happen, no matter how you play, the bonus of watching how the aspects deal with an apparent variety of difficulties that are really mundane. The speed holds or it doesn't. You're on it or you're not. The favorite runs in the money or out. You go with it or against it. Maybe the only dread any of us should have is that at the end we'll be back where we started, with no more insight than what you would expect to be manifested by the tokens of a board game.

Henderson Will

My race of choice or choice of race on this day of days is the second, where my key horse to finish second finishes first when one of my picks to win stops short of the wire, leaving me $228 short of breaking even on the season to date.

To date or not to date. That is the question bedeviling the agents of my madness while I, thanks to them, brain my balls out or brawl my banes out day after night with women so lavishly beautiful, they may be mistaken for transvestites, if I understand my directors correctly. What do they mean when they make me pick up women so dolled up that, by some interpretation of implication, I would hope they must be men, and how does this twist figure into the backstory of having me pine for a wife who has been running around France?

Shouldn't I make them mind their business? They're not doing very well with sex on their minds. In a real office, we wouldn't have to worry. If this scheme set up by The Course, where each of us is the boss of the others, were to take place in an office, we wouldn't be allowed to date each other. But whatever happens between them as a dating couple happens when I put them together, when it's my turn to report. When I am their boss, they are of equal rank, free to date, free to "work late" and maybe end up fucking on the conference table. There is no office here and no rules about dating. If Nipper snaps and turns Lane into his personal sex slave when it's his turn to make her move around in the world, it's not like I can beam her away safely into a mist of molecules. We're supposed to be applying ourselves to the job of making money. The fact that we're losing money doesn't change what we are supposed to do.

Cal Nipper by Kelly Lane

"So much for May. I never did well in May. April would be fine, June and the rest of the year would be O.K. Never May."

I reminded him he was ahead; he said that was only because of money he won in April. He wasn't complaining or morose. He was glad our next day was June first. But not so glad that he wanted to talk about Portland.

"Blame it on the Derby. Never in my life have I won the Derby. At least now I never play it. One year, I even took all of May off. With The Course, that's not allowed."

He knew I never kept records the way he did. How he did month to month; how he did in maiden races, restricted claimers, open claimers, allowances for younger or older, in stakes; how he did at the beginning, middle, and end of the card; how he did in doubles, exactas, and getaway plays: Nipper knew. One year, he kept a running win percentage tally on every type of race, and applied the various return-on-investment ratios to an aggressive wagering formula that jacked up his bet after a win to something like the square root of the entire bankroll—only to discover he almost never won races back-to-back.

He had read all of the handicapping books. His favorites were Beyer's, but Quirin, Quinn, Ainsley, and Davidowitz were right up there, too. Even Sarton and Brouhammer. Not to mention Dowst and Pittsburgh Phil. He put too much faith in the book version of playing the races. In real life, he couldn't stop time to redo his calculations when the odds when south at the last minute while he waited in line to bet.

"The Course got me out of that rut. Isn't that how it is for you?"

I said I supposed so.

"Vacations. I always did well on vacations."

He went on to Hialeah and Gulfstream, Santa Anita and Turf Paradise, but he couldn't help thinking about the Multnomah Kennel Club.

Although he wasn't superstitious, he knew not to push it when he was going bad. After flaming out at the windows, he didn't want to compound his misery by getting shot down on the social front. Although luck could have nothing to do with what I might have said to him, he was shy about asking me to go anywhere on a day he had done nothing but lose.

Henderson Will by Kelly Lane

The candy-packing bow to hooks of handicapping how-to books never eased the plunder mine ever pleased to undermine the way Henderson Will weighted major ring-made wagering. Especially now that he posted bets like some boasted pets who do tricks for true dicks, he didn't go nuts to lose a few, as those with no guts refuse to duel who wants action. Shunts whack sin, but no life or death meal, low knife, or meth deal seditions decisions went down here. If he fell where most others did before him, welfare host mothers could bid for him.

He really didn't care about living the gaudy life of wagering on the ponies, a deal he bid in air or doubt, like giving a doggy wife a lay purging on the loan ease. But why what bye made him piss kiss rile risk his pile in the key nibbing beginning? Was he a hardcore card whore rambler in the gut of a gambler in a rut? Or more of a dilettante or dumb militant? After losing his job, juicing his lob of cash at the racetrack trash at the case rack became normal as going to the office. More null as owing to guffaw this, Will couldn't rake it as a tool or take it as a rule for anything other than an excuse to tour his way on a styled ride.

Then he winged another text use to cure his stay on the riled side. The sop guy apology of pop psychology captivated with vapid, dated, rolled in ghoul golden rule yay sing sayings. The old saws sold awes, yet to him, syllable shifts made imbeciles miffed.

"Today is the first day of the rest of your life," earned tin to turn into, "The yes of lure rife." That is at this, everything learned in the sand box burned in the land socks.

Est of ball, best of all, these schmo bride's bromides resonated test run-aided in the halls of commerce calls of mockers. As rep balleys bore misses in pep rallies for businessmen, these fad eye-sore tease advisories leapt their bingo into elf-self crooks and crept their lingo into self-help books.

Henderson Will by Kelly Lane

Like a bourse cook, The Course book, *Divide and Conquer,* confide and con dirt animal manual that it was thought to be, brought toothy ends-justify traditions whose trends just defy attritions. The new tactics tune addicts were staunchly contrarian, launching on stare recon. Shoot-from-the-hip ethics brought a hoot-from-the-ship breath. Hicks sought booty to be ours for the taking, towers for the aching back to lug off, no lack to bug off, the night rummy vantage meant the right money management would top guile on stop, could stop while on top.

The roux goo of a guru changing recklessly ranging checklists, he spouted in class tech lessons clouded in spastic sessions. The par stupe Will was the star pupil, buying the line of lying to bind himself to the skill he seemed to have acquired in the silly scheme.

The lord'll mock a mortal lock, but Will got the idea: dot the i, key a bet on a pony nose for reselling stability to get on Pinocchio's storytelling ability, and dough to the king goes the dash to go to the windows to cash. In the birds of the wire words of the Beyer, he would yell on the wing of the curled, "I am the king of the world."

His bliss kited motions nullified as his misguided notions multiplied, and before he could stop, he was more of a spent pawn that a king of a con sent packing.

Henderson Will by Kelly Lane

Will again fell into a hexed losing skid excusing little of the ways he played. The haze we blazed he knew too well. We, too, knew hell, but not his peculiar key pule. Your diseased cities were infested by capitalist pyramid scheme madness. Finesse did buy lap spittle-kissed beer amid mean scab nests. Pari-mutuel betting bared a mutual petting need. That tech-sped flesh shilling harmony reflected this special economy.

Anyway, when he aimed a cattywampus rigging out of ratty compass wigging out, he let himself go to get himself low.

Wearily so here we go to acknowledge to lack, not hedge. The roe fish haul he salts from official results would take time to weed and reap and read and weep.

The outcome of his freaky lone system freed doubts some of us leak. He owed us then, what? To try to do all he could to win? True. Tight, due to call, he would do in hope of reviving in time, just before arriving. In chimed bust, feet or ass dragging, he gassed ragging flatulence. Chat flew tense. He bared a gout but cared about how we did, he claimed. Howdy hid, weak, lame, hobbling a wobble to wobbling a hobble through the din woe to the window, he spoke to the teller in a language that woke to the speller in a tang wedge yet hum so fun caved and somehow conveyed the gritty nitty of butt he sent to weigh of what he meant to say.

"Marely pissing!" he cried, barely missing, greed-eyed.

That is, at this graded race from Canada, the freighted grace scum ran at a horse of his who was set to win. Wet to sin, some 20–1 shot when teed to shut twat numb woe frere from nowhere took the race to rook the taste of a popping way off a whopping payoff.

Cal Nipper by Henderson Will

When the first race of June came, Cal Nipper reckoned that we were a third of the way through the season, and that the next few dates would determine the ultimate success or failure of our project. A few more days like the last one, and we would be too far behind to catch up. Even though the last time was the first time all three of us lost, he knew it could happen again and again, even at the unlikely clip of three in a row (as Kelly's mental gymnastics of my gentleman ass tics show to go).

So I could not now reinstall that awful song that drove him to the library day after day as he gathered data on the dogs. Not that he had forgotten about Portland: it was real as a threat. Cal Nipper knew that if he and Kelly (and I, for good measure) didn't close with a rush to hit the board with complete authority, he could forget about taking any overnight trips with Miss Kelly Lane. As much as he tried to suppress the bromides that kept coming back to him, even though he had only read inspirational primers to make fun of them, "Today is the first day of the rest of your life," nagged him as ruthlessly as any song ever had. Start winning and go to the dogs with Kelly; keep losing and stay home with the Braves.

The first race was a $12,500-claiming sprint for three-year-old maidens, and even Nipper couldn't play the favorite, and so he bet on his second choice. Was he taking bigger chances, now with the season on the line? The horse did have early speed, but was also coming off a bad trip in his last race, giving Nipper the cushion of two good reasons to think Captain Weave would last when he got out of the gate cleanly and shook off the rival pacesetter to open up a lead in the backstretch.

He paid $12.20, putting Nipper back up $136 for the season. Then he realized this 5–1 payoff with no losses to subtract, his most profitable day in weeks (if not the whole season), still didn't open up a lead that would survive going 0-for-4 next week. He tried not to seem disappointed, let alone desperate, but there was something in the way he assumed the lead role that we might have called him on, if we hadn't been so engrossed with the rest of the card. It was up to him, after all, to help us get our wins, too. If he couldn't do that, what good was he?

We got his win for him, didn't we? Look at his choice! Nipper picked an early speed horse (Kelly's kind of play) that he thought would lose (my kind of play) but picked to win only because the horse he really thought would win was going off at awful odds. Everything depended on having the top choice stumble, not on picking the best horse in the race and packaging that with others in some multiple bet to beef up the odds, as he usually did. Then again, this special need of his to get off to a good start (or bear down to pull it out with a grinding finish) was a quirk we might have smeared on him, squeezing it out of our own psychological zits, and now this need we projected on him was part of who he was.

Now? What kind of time frame was he stuck in here? Forgetting what it meant to be fixated on winning right at the start or finally at the finish, he couldn't help thinking about his childhood. A slight lad with a sweet tooth and a typically overactive libido fed by frustration, Cal Nipper had cultivated a healthy case of acne, which only made him eat more sugary goods, grow more pimples, and become more self-conscious and therefore hopelessly unappealing to girls. The acne subsided. From seventeen to eighteen, he changed. He began to date, and even went to a prom. Maybe not with his first choice, but, coming off a bad trip with a little early speed, she, well... that was a long time ago.

Henderson Will by Kelly Lane

The bet sack find of an unfilled call was a setback kind of a funneled fall, but no thud blurs the Gang of Four bloodthirsty fang of gore mindset he needed to play. That sign met, he pleaded to nay. We tended to brunt, but he pretended to want not to win. What? Tune in.

That Canada stakes stand had a cake's icing of a prize pricing of an eye's satisfaction fat as action. Just to come close to winning, the cussed do glum toasts, stew ginning. But Henderson's hut benders unrivaled fun rivaled unraveling. Done raffling, the acne pimple pock marks of surely licked and demure pawns packed the nimble mock parks of perfectly manicured lawns.

Adversity's sad verse ditties drove him on, wove him drawn. Perversely slurring, slurpers leave purring to bet, blow, lose, to bellow blues on a tattered call caterwaul. Still whopped himself, Will stopped himself. Feeling sorry for his own self-sealing farce, he or his phone elf called another number. Balled, some numb cur might have packed it in the acted bin, but he was distracted by this tack tread curiosity tour he got to see.

All told, tall old inside track in tried sack tricks of the trade swirled around him. Hurled around swim suited beauty contestants, tooted cootie bun test ants couldn't have had it any better than he did. No rock coach worse cipher of loony glee nor cockroach survivor of nuclear war could outlast this Ludd outcast, nor a rack-hid arachnid could as easily slurp webbing to live off flies as sleazily burp ebbing to give off lies. But the rumored truth whetted to full appetite for what the troopered tooth fettered to pull rabid bite. A taste for suspense paced or fuss tensed, cheesing the food tour on its tone.

"I'm teasing the future on its own time," he might have slung, slight of hung height of mung.

Cal Nipper

Four and out? Not today, thank you. Get out of the gate, get clear, and go to the window, to lead the rest of us on the way back to the black. That's my job. Leave it to me and, I swear, on all the acne scars I ever had, that I will make you a winner.

Maybe I won't make Henderson a winner this time around, but he just missed a hefty payoff when he got nipped at the wire. What he did made more sense than what Kelly pulled in the first by betting on—and please, spare me all talk of workouts, stamina, and tactical speed—a horse named All N The Game.

Takes you back, doesn't it? To Chez Fromage, that San Mateo bistro in the days before karaoke. Tommy Edwards Night: the impersonators took turns singing his one hit song, the others filling in background vocals as each he/she sang the lead to a tune I could have played on piano, plunking down triplets like "Chopsticks" and knocking back triplets of scotch.

But hey, if Kelly Lane can't burn a double sawbuck on a name now and then, what's the point? I won the first, and she lost. Big deal. She got stuck with an animal that I might have played, and lost. I just happened to score on, thanks to her and Will, the kind of horse she normally played. These things happen. No reason to look at me funny.

But O.K., the pressure is on. Kelly needs a win. If she doesn't win, I get blamed for "stealing" her horse. Blamed for winning, like it's my fault. I mean, somebody has to do the winning around here. Somebody has to bring up the totals by landing a 5–1 lunker before losing a single wager. Many a tear has to fall, but it's all in the game.

Oh oh. Not only is this song coming back to me, line after line, but the whole damn thing has to do with courtship. The memory of a song triggered by the name of a horse is suddenly stalking us. At least with "Radar Love" you're over the hump and speeding back to the sack, but with "All in the Game" you're sweating the phone calls that don't come, the blunders you think you commit and so have to make up for by giving flowers, the notions you think each other thinks about each other, and the whole sick cycle that has to end in a) a kiss, and b) falling in love, all in about three minutes.

Kelly Lane by Henderson Will

After losing her first two bets, she almost hit her third by once more playing the kind of horse Nipper would have picked for her, which wouldn't have been so bad, except that, once more, the kind of horse she normally played won the race, wire to wire.

Nipper and I were through for the day, except to see what we could do for her, but Kelly Lane didn't need any help. She didn't want to cherry pick a getaway play from all of the races that remained. She wanted to get it over with right here, in the fourth, a five-furlong $25,000 claimer for 2-year-old fillies. All she saw was a trainer she liked, one known for winning with babies, whose filly, City Lights, opened at 10–1, and so she split her $80, putting half on the nose and taking $20 exactas with it finishing second to each of the favorites.

"Happy, boys?"

We didn't have to say. She made her choice, and if the exacta bets seemed like something I would have done or Nipper would have done, they also stood to win more than she would have won by putting it all on the nose.

City Lights took command on the turn and opened up a lead to the wire.

"You should have put it all on the nose, but you can't ignore tote in a baby race. Those favorites might have been live."

"Thanks, Cal. I mean it."

The favorites ran out of the money.

Subtracting the $120 she blew in the first three races, she made $208 on the day, bringing her up to $114 down, for the meet. For some reason, being only $114 down struck her as a better place to be at this stage of the season than being in the Nipper seat, especially when she thought of how they each got to where they were. Week after week, Nipper made a bit more, like he was collecting interest on Savings Bonds, only to come close to blowing it with one or two bad days. And, week after week, she just missed hitting a good one, taking her lower and lower until, with only a couple of decent wins, she was on the verge of a breakthrough.

She almost mentioned it, but didn't. It wasn't something she thought of as bragging. It was a topic he should want to discuss. They often talked about betting strategies, such as covering the heavily bet horses in two-year-olds' races, or whether it was better to play to win or to wheel or box exactas. But now, with two of them winning on a day when they really needed a good pair of wins, after a weekend when none of us scored, she didn't want to get him talking about being on the verge of losing, because then he might start to think about that, and next week he would go back to the old Nipper game, because he knew we knew who he was and what he was supposed to do.

Cal Nipper by Kelly Lane

"I don't want to dwell on it, but that was huge. That was just the kind of day we needed to turn this thing around. If this thing does turn around, when we get to the end we can look back and say this was the day that did it."

He tried to sound modest, collegial, deferential, but deep down Cal Nipper was really looking forward to a night of playing air guitar to the rock anthems of the 1970s while perfecting the art of the martini and watching the Braves play to win. The Braves, the martinis, Golden Earring, Kansas, Blue Oyster Cult, and Cal Nipper: winners all.

"Sometimes, you have to step aside and consider the options. You see what you have done and you think about what you could do, to build on what you've done."

"Don't fear the reaper."

"Fuck no, you take it to the next level."

"Stairway to heaven."

"Exactly. What's next is next. Next is up."

He heard me, but he didn't listen as his gaze took command of the lowlands of Renton, and we made the turn past Tukwila for home.

What was the root of his problem with women? Was it even a problem? He wondered if he didn't necessarily want to do something with me. Maybe some time, but now he was looking ahead to a night of doing what he always did. Was it self-esteem? Did his self-esteem really depend on success at the track? After so many years of failure, of losses that totaled more than all he won, year after year, had he come to pin all of his hopes of, say, personal redemption, on the brutally unequivocal matter of mathematical fact he would learn months from now? Then what? Suppose he did win more than he lost: would that be an end or a beginning? The end or the beginning for and/or of him and/or me? Would this solve everything, even women, even if women weren't a problem?

He might have to duplicate the project next year, with us or with a new mob, to prove that it wasn't a fluke. What if he did win, and we did win, and the whole thing actually did beat the races? Would that one bit of satisfaction erase all of the years of failure?

Cal Nipper, metaphysical winner.

Maybe that would be all he needed—not the whole hog life of the gambler taking Portland by storm, but the comfort to be gained by gain alone, gain in and of itself, gain, however minuscule, gain. Even if it was to happen never again, a gain gave the feeling that you had been there, on the other side, the feeling you get when the race is almost over, and the exacta lines up in your favor with no one else in sight, when you allow yourself to say, sometimes you get to win.

Maybe I was projecting too much of myself onto him, but he had to feel it, just as he had to feel silly to admit it—for him to admit he felt this way, and especially for me, taking a look at what I meant to say, to admit that these fancies of Nipper's had something in common with anything I have ever felt. But they had to be of part of me, didn't they? Even if I would never play air guitar or suggest we hop on a train to Portland, I had to see him doing that. What could be sillier than his dream of going to the dogs? Not only silly but unmanly. Poor Nipper. He admitted to me that all he wanted to do was feel what it was like, once in his life at the end of the season, to come out on top, and that the actual amount of money he made didn't matter. He thought he sounded like a chump or a wuss, but this fantasy of living as a gambler who slept in hotels and ate in cocktail lounges on the finest olives money could buy promised to make him suave, dashing, mysterious.

Then he saw how foolish it all was, and how I might have been humoring him when I fed him lyrics and titles to set him up. I was only playing him, but I did like him, didn't I? And he liked me, and we really should act like we liked each other, instead of making fun of each other for only being and doing what the other wanted us to be and do, even if who we were and what we did were no more than some imaginary figment of an aspect of a personal problem.

The traffic wasn't backed up, but I got off the freeway where I would if a Mariner game was about to start. Not to give him ideas, but to give him more time to talk, so we might not have to go for drinks. Or maybe we would for a round or two. In the extra minutes it took to get to Georgetown along Airport Way instead of the freeway, we might come to an understanding that we wanted to hang out a bit more now, before the rest of the week loomed, beyond this day, when we met again to go to the races.

Henderson Will by Cal Nipper

Henderson Will was due over. On the Stakes Belmont of Saturday, where raining was it, here while were we in degree ninety shine sun. Form to true, there nor here was Will. In he zeroed on Park Woodholly, to pick a make based not on his capping handy own but on tout some in the *Form Racing*, though even the tout of the paradox he too well knew.

Mutuel-pari players against other each compete, betting their pools to odds the set. Handicappers public, as such the touts paid the *Form Racing* by, pick must supposedly horses they who win to think. Yet and, if themselves they bet, must they then public for the pick horses they bet would never. The game of the object was to price the drive up of the liked you horse by betting to get your opponents, the public betting, on the horse wrong. An expert true (as touts these were to be supposed) must himself a player be, so and advice his all to us of each was but nothing a shit of crock.

He as much this knew, less the never bound was he to opposite the bet of his, speak to so, judgment better. The race first in Woodholly, the tout track's bet best of the day whole was Kissed with a Seal. Henderson Will on it keyed.

Kissed with a Seal gated out of the step a slow bit, speeding the chase and faded, Will burying $388 under.

Will over marveled the winner of the name: Sanitywithindeal.

Henderson Will, the losable lover, had the string on the world. Couldn't he lose for winning? Nice get if you could work it. Had he all to do now was back kick and free us set, and us watch holing out of this crawl.

Kelly Lane by Henderson Will

The opener at Emerald Downs was the kind of race she decided she had to master if she was going to succeed here: six three-year-old fillies, who hadn't won twice, going five and a half furlongs, at a claiming tag of $6,250. She used to think it better to pass the shell games and pick spots with at least eight horses with established records, where some cause for hope in the past performances might justify taking a risk at a price that made the risk worth taking. Now that simulcasts beamed in so many extra prospective opportunities, nobody had to settle for just what was on the local card. The Course didn't exactly prohibit shopping around, but ever since she took it, she was more comfortable accepting whatever proposition came her way, no matter how cheap or restricted the company. When I went to Hollywood (Woodholly?), she wasn't tempted. She saw something she liked here.

What she noticed wasn't so much a horse in the first race as one in the second who should have been a co-favorite, but was being ignored in the daily double. So her first bet began as a backdoor play, a single $20 daily double wager that would tie whoever she picked in the first to Sullivanitis in the second: my kind of play, but I couldn't take all the credit.

What I wouldn't have minded taking some credit for was the way she handled herself when Tease N Delight picked up the front end of her wager. Whatever this filly had demonstrated in her last race to put her in play hadn't mattered so much as the value she appeared to offer in the double, compared to the other contenders, especially now that the double odds froze and the wagering on the second put the spotlight on Sullivanitis. Kelly had to feel good about that: good but not giddy, and not really very confident, i.e., not the way Nipper cavorted when he stayed alive in any parlay. Back in the day, he told her, he lit up a cigar whenever he won the front end of the double, not to celebrate but to coax the victory to come.

"Why did you stop?"

"The special offers they gave to kick-start the craze stopped once the craze kicked in, so you had to pay real money for good cigars. They used to practically give away Uppman and Te Amo, and once I got used to those, I couldn't go back to Antonio y Cleopatra."

"Why did you start?"

"It seemed like the thing to do at the track. It was a way to deal with the smoke around you. Didn't you ever smoke?"

"I dealt with it."

She was less interested in her old habits than she was in Nipper's, and she knew those all too well: he was a sucker for giveaways, and for the allure of passing for normal in an abnormal world of smoky characters, but then that world got overrun by slumming college boys and crybaby tycoons all caught up in the cigar lifestyle. Who could blame him for kicking what was never a habit but an indulgence?

They were coming to the starting gate with a minute to post time. Nipper had lost the first and was passing the second, not getting the price he wanted.

Kelly Lane by Cal Nipper

Sullivanitis ran as advertised by the late tote, took command on the turn, and had one of those runs to the wire without anyone else in sight. We patted Kelly on the back as I gave her a hug from the hip, turning her to me as she hugged me in return.

"It's good to be back." She held me with her eyes for an extra second, and then turned to go to the window. She netted $272, to break through to the plus side of the ledger for the first time this year, running her total up to $158.

"Easy go, easy come."

She blushed. Was it the heat of the day or the gist of Henderson's crack? She laughed and looked away from me. She knew what I was thinking, as I knew her, just as any two people who were made up by each other couldn't help but know.

Didn't she miss me? It had been a while since we had a drink to celebrate, since I had a chance to have my say about her. Now, with a rare early pass on the rest of the card and the common outcome of Henderson finishing before the third race, she was free to do what she could to make me a winner. And she would make me a winner, and we would have that drink to celebrate and then... who knows? Maybe tonight was the night we would do something more, because a woman living alone in a hip neighborhood of a West Coast city, a woman with a certain taste and style, a woman with a past she didn't want to think about and a future she wasn't afraid to take charge of had to want more than a day at the track, more than a Saturday night at the, she had to laugh, Bauhaus? Cafe Vita? Victrola?

But she wasn't laughing at the idea of spending another Saturday night at a coffee house while open mic memoir poetry dabbled in the corner. She was laughing at the idea of caring what night it was. And, if she didn't pick up half-price tickets to a show at the last minute, why a coffee house rather than a bar? There were bars a woman would go to alone, bars where she could enjoy talking to anyone next to her for no apparent purpose at all, bars with music safely tucked in on CDs while a ballgame played innocuously overhead, in case you came in alone and had no one you felt like talking to. Why not go to a bar alone just to do what I would do? Each of us could make a point of doing not what we wanted to do, but what we thought the others would do. All the better to get to know each other.

As a modern dancer applying herself to a do a particular theme or object (I am Desire; I am glass), she would her apply herself to do me. I mean—

Cal Nipper by Kelly Lane

Kelly Does Cal is, is that what we've come to? With the tug of a hug and a chance in a glance, the next thing you knew, there we would be, pegging the pogo in a rest room stall of a certain taste and style, while the track announcer called the feature and George Jones sang, "The Race Is On," trying not to fall.

Nipper knew he wasn't getting anywhere by framing us in arty scenarios when he should have been keeping his head in the game. If anything, he was afraid to jinx whatever might happen between him and me. He had, sweet boy, not plugged me full bore into the fantasies that inspired his intimate life, and he wasn't going to stop thinking about the next race in order to get off on me now.

His trainer play in the first made the lead, but blew the turn. He passed the second to root for me.

He took a good look at a filly in the third. Her staying power in the *Form* and head bob swagger in the parade made her look hot to trot. He didn't like to count on closers to get up in time when they came from as far back as this one figured to be, but in a maiden heat for eager fillies on a day sweltering enough to wilt the strumpets in the fast lane, he reckoned she was worth a $40 throw. The race ran the way most of them did: the winner stalked the leader and had her way with her as they entered the stretch, while his filly put out too little too late and finished a distant third.

Out of the exacta, Nipper stroked himself to think he had made the right bet on an irresistible fling that just turned out to be bad to the bone. Was it a clean, clear loss of a merciless refusal, or hadn't there been something in the way she moved that conveyed in no uncertain body language that she was primed to romp on her fresh legs?

Take it like a man, he told himself, but kept wallowing in the cracks that came to him like the titles of porno movies.

Cal Nipper by Henderson Will

Once more the dirty work of cleaning up after Nipper fell to me. At the end of another series of rejections, he would often come to think of himself as being victimized by a peculiar Bermuda Triangle malaise he dubbed, as if to disable its effectiveness with a stroke of whimsy, "The Vicissitudes of Humiliation." The Vicissitudes of Humiliation constituted a veritable whirlpool zone, where the energy of his every move fueled a series of exertions that only plunged him more deeply into the vortex of defeat. This time, though, the series wasn't that long, and the pressure to win was one more race removed from the finale, when he'd have to decide what to do about the Belmont Stakes, whether to bet Funny Cide to win the triple crown or pass the race for some other one, here and now or on the getaway plan.

Fortunately for all of us, a made-to-order Nipper gambit sprang from the *Form* in the conditions of the next race: an unrestricted $10,000 claimer of older horses going six and a half furlongs, with a decent-sized field to offer not only a variety of running styles (and so favor whoever might stay near but not on the lead), but, best of all, a favorite to beat. Proud Louis, a heavily raced seven-year-old, had dominated the action at Portland, but that was mostly months ago, when it was fifty degrees cooler.

Nipper liked to think these mid-level open claimers were the real feature races of Emerald Downs. They were tougher than other races because they drew so many horses dropping in from the higher ranks or climbing up from the lower ones. The intriguing permutations of deceptively predictable scenarios suggested dozens of exactas and trifectas worth playing, and so you had to pull back and see what the win pool had to offer. Between automatic eliminations, whose trainers would have been better off entering a nonwinners-since-last-year race, and contenders, whose trainers were known for putting their entries in positions where they could win, certain picks seemed obvious. As the high rollers spread their wagering dollars over trifectas and superfectas to keep others from seeing their action reflected on the tote board, a stand-out could go off at generous odds in the win pool. Today it was Cascade Casey at 5–1.

Normally Nipper would have had to settle for 5–2 on a pick with so many leading indicators. He liked the trainer/jockey combo (especially since the trainer had switched jockeys), the form cycle, speed ratings, and running style. Months ago, he wouldn't have given Cascade Casey much of a shot to beat Proud Louis, but today it was no contest.

He finished $132 to the good for the day, $268 up for the season. He couldn't help mentioning that this put the three of us slightly up for the season.

Henderson Will by Cal Nipper

Henderson Will couldn't wonder but help long how would he wait to have to back crawl into the circle winners! If as to drift this change, he moved to decide from Park South by the River Duwamish to Hill Beacon by the access public course golf and club bowling lawn, just street the down from the hospital veterans, where a vehicle recreational for weeks or days parked might be the vet of some home who waiting was for treatment medical for the effects after wounded being in some war undeclared. While the policy government gave to refuse treatment needed to men it had fought into fooling for their duty patriotic, the patrol on police, themselves not more than often veterans, gave to refuse tickets parking to these sacks sad who parked to need door next to the facility medical. Himself no veteran, Henderson Will up pulled to a van camper of kind Hooverville, and friends made with a survivor War Gulf who breathing had trouble and a Nam Viet amputee double, whom of both trucked in their pick-up lives. After night after, would they round gather Henderson's table kitchen over a booze of bottle and shit the shoot.

So and, track at the back, Will's turn took another yet perspective. Much how matter did losing, after bet after, to compared a part body losing, alone let your breathe to ability? Bat off the right on Day Fathers, then, Will bet his shot on the double daily, playing a make that sense made but chance all lost when an 11-for-0 horse sucker first the won. In a race maiden at the gutrock level bottom at a mile flat, his shot long and his pick other both fired to fail. That not his race second in the picks better did was bridge under the water time the by that run was race. For as results his of the tally running away ran, with eight rows in a loss was he under $468.

Cal Nipper by Kelly Lane

Nipper didn't have time to recall the victory celebration after he and I won on the last outing. Now came to a day to forget.

In the opener, an 0-for-11 plodder got his maiden win, as Nipper went down on a double bet when the favorite ran second. In the second race he put a win bet on the horse he had taken to close out the double, only to go nowhere. So in the third, another cheap claimer for (colts and) geldings going a flat mile, Nipper keyed on the rail horse in a set of exactas that happened to ignore the sucker horse that won the race.

Going into the fourth, a $25,000 open claiming sprint for older horses, he saw what I saw: a pattern of solo speed on the lead getting dueled into submission by a headwind up the backstretch, and passed on the run to the wire. What he decided was what he might have done anyway: go with Silky Secret, a stalker, whose style and numbers looked especially good versus the speed, since a couple of pacesetter types seemed ready to go for it. When one of the speedsters broke clear and wired the field, he was done and out.

He was still up $68 for the year. His picks were solid, and the winners, in at least three of the four races he played, were flukes. He didn't panic and dump the strategy he had followed successfully all season. He played like a winner, but lost. And yet, his failure ate away at him. After pulling me out of the hole on a day when he had gone to a season high, he felt he had to keep from sliding back. If he couldn't get Will to turn it around, at least he could keep me going. But he couldn't. Why? Had he become some kind of father figure to me, someone for me to rebel against while also trying to please or satisfy or... really, he knew what lurked behind those impulses between fathers and daughters, even if he was born in a lab and raised with the rats. When they sent him to school, to that middle-class ghetto of dirty jokes, he grew to understand without any help from the rumors of Freud spread by movies and TV what role was his whenever he thought of himself with a woman. As he got older, and the women around him got older and younger, the range of relationships simultaneously opened and closed. In other words, he was now not so much a potential lover, in my eyes, as an eternal father figure. But didn't that put him into the implicit sexual position of the surrogate father or first love of any girl who might have taken him for her father?

It wasn't his age. He wasn't much older than I was, but he thought he seemed old enough to be my father: my father, who would have spent his nights in taverns; my father, who would have retired in his forties; my father, who would have done what Nipper did. But my father wasn't Nipper, even if Nipper didn't know that.

He didn't know who my father was. He didn't know exactly how old I was. Therefore, Nipper could have been my father.

It was a long shot but, Nipper being Nipper, it was all he could think about for hours.

Kelly Lane by Cal Nipper

Going into the fourth race, she wondered if she had taken the first three seriously enough, but the winners weren't horses she would have had anyway. It just felt like, again, here she was at the end of her string, hoping to pull it out, but needing, somehow, to have it come down to this one last big play that would rescue her day from oblivion. Her day? Her season? Now that she was finally up for the season, she couldn't let herself slip back down. Could she?

Of course she could. And of course, she should have played for the hell of it, for the speed on the lead on a shot at a prize she could ride to the bank. But she didn't. She played it safe. She played like me, right down to the same horse in the same last race. Silky Secret was my kind of horse, and Kelly Lane knew that, just as she knew she might have played the early speed, even on a day when speed was dying; or, she might have passed the race and taken her shot on a getaway play: anything but duplicate what I bet. Couldn't help herself?

There were times when our bets would overlap. But here? On a horse that was so patently the figures plus running style plus trainer/jockey plus class pick I usually went for? I might have sued her for infringement. She was glad we lost.

"Why are you so angry?"

"You tell me."

"So it wasn't your kind of play. You won't do it again."

"I did what I did, and I might do it again. I don't take it back. What I don't like is the feeling I'm getting of why I did what I did."

"Father's Day."

"What?"

"You did it out of loyalty. Even if we're not a family, you did it for us, for the unit. For togetherness. There's a need to join together, not to break apart. Last week we were a team and we won. This week, you wanted to team up and win again. It's natural."

"That's sick. You're not my father."

"Maybe I am."

"Right. And I'm your mother."

She shut up and drove, because she knew she was my father/mother just as I was her mother/father, in a way The Course spelled out more clearly than a DNA test spelled out your chromosomes. What upset her wasn't that she might have bet the same horse I bet as some pathetic act of filial solidarity, but that this connection between us influenced whatever she did, and that this connection was more like mother/son and father/daughter than she wanted to admit, and that it was blatantly sexual. It suddenly came as a letdown that, as my daughter, she couldn't become my lover. Not that she would become my lover. It bugged her to realize that she had had to think so much about our relationship to each other, that she couldn't simply admit that our relationship was a set-up, set up by The Course for us to fulfill our destinies as winners.

Kelly Lane needed a break. She didn't need a father. She needed to pull back and get another view. To get outside of herself and her routines, to reach for something that was there but misplaced—not to get in touch with herself, but to get herself in touch with what it was she knew must be there and could feel all around her but for some reason, couldn't quite grasp. That's what she needed, wanted, had to have.

And I was just the one to tell her what it was.

"Let's go bowling."

"What!"

"Come on. Let's knock a few pins around."

"Bowling! Not The Garage."

"What's wrong with The Garage?"

"Nothing. But were you talking about The Garage kind of bowling or the West Seattle Lanes kind?"

I knew she wasn't kidding. It mattered to her whether this bowling I mentioned would be at The Garage on Capitol Hill, elbowing the hipsters aside, or at some regular bowling alley in White Center or West Seattle or Ballard.

"Not The Garage. O.K.?"

She wasn't relieved. She would have liked to have gone to a traditional bowling alley, but realized she belonged at a place like The Garage. She didn't belong at West Seattle Lanes, even on a non-league night. She had to be here in the main part of the city—not there in the neighborhoods, where people from the main part of the city went to experience what life was like out there, in the bowling alleys of White Center, West Seattle, and Ballard. Years ago it had been hip for scenesters here to venture out there to go, like, bowling. Even though she had never done that, she felt ashamed to think of it as something she would have done. But more than that, she felt ashamed to feel embarrassed for those who did go because, Jesus Christ, it was only a night on the town in another part of town at a bowling alley. She went to the races, she could go to the lanes.

"White Center or West Seattle? Just up the hill."

She had driven straight to my door. The motor was running. She was in neutral, with her foot on the brake.

"Thanks, but I don't feel like anthropology. Not tonight."

"It was just a bad day. We'll get 'em next time," I leaned over and kissed her cheek.

She touched my arm and gave a squeeze, wanting more, but not tonight, and wanting to say yes, but not for now.

Cal Nipper by Henderson Will

Disgusting. I turn my back for a week, and my mob plunges to a new low. Bad enough they should pussyfoot around each other, pawing and hoping and teasing and flinching, but to dress each other up as father and daughter who, because of the very nature of the generative relationship, have no choice but to have sex with each other? Sick.

Need I add that Nipper projected certain fantasies from Lane's peck of a kiss and squeeze of his forearm, that the consummate cheapskate decided to consummate these projections by practicing, so help me, with free condoms; and, that rather than hit Planned Parenthood, where he looked more like a Bible-addled bombardier the security guards should have shot on sight than a sensitive man who only wanted to take responsibility for his partner's health and birth control needs, he really did make the rounds to the kinds of bars where, he had heard, "buttloads" of condoms were "up for grabs"?

Suffice it to say that at the end of the week his one dress shirt stank of smoke, and his bedside table sported a cornucopia of *Lifestyles*. When Saturday arrived with the onset of summer under heavy threat of rain, Nipper was ready, if vaguely ashamed at himself when he saw Kelly, who, as usual when they met after a week apart, was too preoccupied with the drive and the *Form* to... what? Kiss him? Squeeze his arm? What had she been thinking about him all week? Somehow he couldn't quite permit himself to picture her rehearsing diaphragm insertion technique, like the basic training drills of soldiers stripping and reassembling their rifles in the dark, let alone to hear her wearing out the vibrator batteries as she moaned, "Cal, oooh, yesss, Callll."

Quickly he patted her thigh, which flexed the inkling of a frank response, and they talked about the weather and about how each of them wanted to score and get the hell out, without dragging their bets on through the day.

The first race was a Nipper specialty and, for Emerald Downs, a rarity to kick off the daily double: an open claimer at $10,000. He liked a numbers pick, Just Outrageous, and rather than pin his hopes on the double, settled for the win pool odds of 5–2, even though the 2–1 favorite on the outside figured to control the pace.

The favorite stumbled. Just Outrageous broke on top and stayed there, blown down the backstretch by the wind out of the south, and when he turned for home, no one had the move to catch him. The $50 Nipper won boosted him to $118 for the year: not bad, just what he needed, but mostly, he was relieved to be out of the running. He didn't want to go into another swoon and lose $200 on the day, so instead of $50, it felt like he'd won $250.

Having picked the winner of the first, he might have gone on to take the double, for a real payoff, but no. He never thought that way. Stop-at-a-winner was made for the Nippers of the world.

Kelly Lane by Henderson Will

She didn't want to believe it any more than she knew she could deny it: it, this thing with Nipper. We had a thing, they used to say, when they talked about a certain relationship that wasn't much of a relationship but was definitely more than just holding hands.

What was she thinking? They weren't even ever holding hands.

Meanwhile, it was Just Outrageous at just 5–2 in the first, but she was happier to squirrel that one away for Nipper than to have had her Symph come in, at better than twice the price, especially since she knew how he didn't like to cast his fate to the maidens, even in Maiden Special Weights company, such as she encountered in the second race. Nipper liked a horse with a record; she liked a horse with a chance. And so in the second she picked Sariano, whose bullet-spiked works building up to today's five-and-a-half-furlong sprint stood out in a field of more lightly trained first-time starters and losers of one or two.

It got darker and started to rain. She asked if I was going to bet. I told her the third was more interesting for exactas, and that I wanted to leave this one to her. She looked at me funny, as if she didn't understand, but everything I said, no matter how straightforward, struck her as twisted, so the meanings of what I supposedly said meant less to her than the cordial ways I seemed to speak and act, and we never had a problem getting along with each other. She liked that about me. She even sometimes wished she had made up a weirder way of getting to know Nipper to make him come to life—not as weird as the way she had with me, but weird enough to be playful, so they didn't get into these mind games.

The race had begun. The start startled her because she had been thinking of me versus Nipper, and of what I said about the next race being better for exactas when it was another maiden race of barely raced three-year-olds and so not much different from this. As with any race, what you wanted was to see your pick break cleanly and settle into stride near or on the lead, which is where she realized Sariano was when the field was already two furlongs down the backstretch, with her baby under wraps and going strong.

She figured he knew how to make the turn. With all those workouts, he wouldn't veer to the outside fence or run out of gas and lug in toward the rail. He would change leads going into the homestretch without a tap of the whip but with the reins all his now, relaxed to run free to the wire.

After losses, her day's take was $116, bringing her back up to $74 for the season.

"Thanks, boys." She turned to me as Nipper slipped his arm around her hips and hugged, "Now for you."

Me? What did they care about me? The next race was a jumble, the sky was black, rain gouged the muck, and I dropped another fast $80 on a clutch of exactas that blew up when my key horse hopped at the start because the gate maybe didn't open. The inquiry sign flashed, but the stewards let it go.

Cal Nipper by Kelly Lane

Nipper wanted to leave as soon as I won and to have Henderson make a getaway play, but unlike stop-at-a-winner, loser-at-a-stop meant that Will couldn't make getaway bets, because if he did win, he would have to play again. Nipper tried to be patient. It was good for his character not to put himself ahead of the rest of us, he told himself, to give others around him first call. First call. Was that bar lingo, as in, last call? He resolved to work on his character. That is, Nipper resolved to work on the character of Nipper and not on the heteronyms of Henderson and me. He also had to pitch in and apply himself to Henderson's bet, even though that was the last thing he wanted to do when the rain started to dump, especially when one of the fillies in the third race post parade bolted. For ten minutes she ran around the track, eluding the outriders who chased and trapped but lost her until they finally did get a hold of her, and then another filly broke away. By the time they did load the gate, minus the scratches of the renegades, Nipper had come to think of the delay as a test of his own character. Had he said as much, he would have passed this self-styled test. We would have laughed, and that would have been that. Instead, he whined that Henderson would have been better off playing the Ohio Derby on TV, even though the simulcast gremlins failed to show the odds of that race and then failed to show the race itself. Nipper snickered, but he took it personally. As more went wrong, he got angry with Emerald Downs for not having its act together. This was a mindset he used to get into when the season started to turn against him, when the slightest irritations festered and spread and finally overwhelmed him. Then he couldn't think about a horse or a race or a bet without being distracted by what had to go wrong. He knew that what went wrong was what everyone had to endure, but thought that he, poor boy, got more than his share of grief.

It was raining so hard, you couldn't follow them on the backstretch, but we did see Henderson had no chance when his horse dwelt in the gate. Nipper said there was an inquiry, but really didn't care if they refunded Henderson's tickets, even if the loss put Henderson $548 in the hole. But he did offer Henderson a ride.

Henderson said he deserved to ride his moped for miles in the rain. The fabulously generous Nipper never had expected him to take him up on his offer of space in my car—an offer I might have made. Nipper said Henderson could take the bus back to the track to get his bike when the rain stopped, but we both couldn't imagine him doing that.

What nobody counted on was them canceling the last five races after a half inch of rain fell in an hour to flood the track, but that came later and was beyond our control. What we had to control, Nipper said, as we rode the parking lot shuttle through the blacktop shallows to where the car was moored, was Will.

"We can't let him keep losing like this."

"You think he should change his methods?"

"No. We have to make him win. He's ruining everything."

"If we change the way he plays, and he continues to lose, then what? At least he's consistent. He plays for big payoffs. If he wins, he wins big."

"You think he was a mistake."

"What I think about that doesn't matter. We won't know until we work it out."

We both knew Will was Nipper's idea. I went along with it then and now, maybe more than Nipper did, but Nipper couldn't shake the feeling that if he hadn't hatched the wacky scheme of a player who played the opposite of what The Course taught—if we just had gone with the two of us—we wouldn't have a –$548 anchor man on our team.

"Go ahead. Blame me."

"We're barely halfway through. We won't know until the end. That's the point, isn't it? To find out in the end."

"We do it to win."

"To know is to win."

"You know, I'd like to buy you a drink."

Here we were again. You could tell when Nipper watched old James Bond movies. They coached him on how to act suave, just as Ry Cooder coached him on how to "play" guitar. Even though he wasn't sure he really wanted to have me for company right now, he had to play the gentleman. If I refused, he wouldn't feel as bad as he might ordinarily, because he didn't really want me to accept. Or he would feel worse, because here he would have been trying to be considerate, only to be rejected, which was almost as bad as being patronized. Could I possibly accept without making him feel patronized?

Cal Nipper by Henderson Will

When Cal Nipper came to a significant point in any sequence of events, he tended to look ahead and so to ignore what he should have been doing to get to where he wanted to go. Rather than savor his success, he had been looking ahead to the last Saturday of June, whereupon he got too busy calculating half-year projections of full-year performances to do much of anything else but consider how, if he lost four bets in a row on this last day of the first half, all of his winnings would be lost as he went $82 down.

That wasn't all he had been planning. He arrived at the track with the hot and sunny resolve of a man bent on donating his body to (or, back to) science, which he claimed to have done the preceding week, not because they would pay him in advance for his corpse to seek its fortune as a cadaver, but because they would, he assured us, pick up the slab tab on cremation expenses.

"I'm ahead of the game." A winner, ready for his destiny.

Take My Heart had to be his bet in the first, even though, he said, body donors weren't allowed to part-out their organs since the anatomy students needed to see what went where when they dissected you. He lost when the speedster stumbled at the start. He lost more forgettably in the second, and in the third his horse wilted in a duel after getting a good jump to contest the pace. Then, in his last stand, he went to a Grade II turf stakes in Arlington via TV, where his pick got hammered by a late tote that made him the second favorite, and so it didn't seem like a lost cause when it took the lead from the start in the mile and sixteenth circuit, even though he couldn't remember when he had ever seen the pacesetter hold off the late chargers and win a fancy turf route. His pick, Remind, got caught at the wire by Lismore Knight in a finish that this even-money favorite's record had stamped as a foregone conclusion.

While Nipper dealt with the fate of these grim transactions in the aftermath of his spree of philanthropy at the medical school, Kelly and I might have been thought to do all we could to reverse that awful brand of determinism. Nipper had his say in each bet we made, but compared to his sensible calculations, these bets of ours turned out to be ludicrous. But he couldn't root for them to fail. He had to cheer for us, no matter how mortified he stood to be by the results.

Henderson Will by Cal Nipper

Henderson Will saw he thought the wheelback horse key that needed him in the double daily: Implosion DK, a maiden in the race second. Had he all to do was win the hit in the race first and her for hope to deal the close.

A scratch late job his made an easier bit, him leaving with a three of choice, plus some pick other combo for his worth of $80 wagers, ways four split. Stories Bob away put the race first, so Will covered to have had him to ass his cover, only if Stories Bob was a figure speed beater world with the machine money of a record track, who won often this race of kind, a claimer open $8,000 of horses older.

The end back of the wager double, ever how, was from far stone in etched. Some there was an action of bit on the board tote as DK notched a drop. From aside a trainer dependable, what liked Will only was in her race last trip trouble she had, check to having so lost she a lengths few and so it blew. A fortune of reversal was ready for her, said he. Over more, in a race maiden as in race any, you well as might fly a taker than rather dream on a sit of kind some of lock mortal.

Time this, trouble avoided Implosion DK. Turning into the go, she up picked the leader dying, striding into her ease and out stretching to off hold a two or challenge from pack in the back as the wire hit her, front in out.

Losses after, the $442 bailed nearly out Henderson Will, who squandered to proceed his bet next on a named horse Are You Right, who nowhere went so and totaled his run at $382, which backed him brought to $166 negative for the year whole.

Kelly Lane by Henderson Will

After losing a duel in the first and watching me hit the first half of the double, she didn't think she was flustered, distracted, or upset, but when she came away from the window with her win ticket for the second race, Kelly Lane realized she had bet on the wrong horse. It wasn't the first time she had done that. Once, she called the wrong exacta by mistake, but was afraid to change her ticket because the combination she had received would pay over $300 for a $2 bet, a sum she didn't want to think about losing if it won without her, and so she kept that ticket and then cashed that ticket and didn't feel guilty at all. Other times, she or the teller might get a bet wrong. If the bet was $40 on a 5–1 shot rather than $2 on a 50–1, she would change it and never let the outcome bother her.

This time, she reconsidered. Her $40 ticket in the second was on KD Implosion, my horse, who had just gone from 6–1 to 5–1. She liked the filly, but had been ready to bet Quick Charge, a first-time starter with great works and solid connections, while also wondering what was up with Life Estate, an 0-for-7 money burner who was drawing far more than her fair share of action.

"What the hell, we'll win together."

She didn't want to root against me in a pick she had, after all, helped devise, while also realizing that her "original" pick, Quick Charge, had come to her through the influence of Nipper and me, so these accidents at the ticket window where you came away with a wager you, personally, hadn't reckoned on, were no less true to what your bet should be than the bets you did wind up holding.

Life Estate bothered her, less because of the ability the filly had showed than of whatever confidence in her lay concealed behind an unexpected surge in wagers. Sure enough, right after the late tote made her the favorite, Life Estate took the lead. She held it to the turn and around the turn. She wasn't exactly in command, but was ahead by enough so that all she had to do was keep it together, even as she did drift toward the outside. Then, with a furlong to go, right in front of the grandstand, she jumped the shadow of a light pole and broke stride.

Kelly wouldn't have loved it more if she had picked the winner on purpose by herself. If he had backed into a win, Cal Nipper might have made some crack about inheriting the victory in a game of eight ball when the other guy scratched on the last shot. Not Kelly. Too many losses by a nose, bad calls or bad breaks or drug test disqualifications after the results were official had spoiled her efforts at handicapping for her to take this win as a gift she hadn't earned.

"Let's just call it my destiny."

She needled Nipper more than she imagined, as we goaded him to throw himself back into the trenches.

With today's profit of $188, she went up $262.

"I'm here to make you boys look good by making me look good. Now I'm going to get a beer and sit in the sun. Come on, boys. I'll be your cheerleader. Let's win one for the Nipper."

Kelly Lane by Cal Nipper

She pretended it didn't matter that at the midpoint of the season she was ahead, and that even Henderson had hit a big payoff to bring himself almost all of the way back. But I had lost again, and lost badly, and so had wiped out all I won over three months. It shouldn't have mattered to me, because I had done my job by making her a winner and giving Henderson a fighting chance to become a winner, but she couldn't hide it. She had to feel for me.

She couldn't hide it any more than she could hide that tattoo when she lay down on the grass with a beer by her side and her sunglasses blazing: a rose just below where her belt would have been. Why wouldn't she have a tattoo there if she felt like it? She could wear her jeans low and her top just high enough to ride up as she stretched if she felt like it and yes, there it was for me, for you, for anyone. For years she had it and hardly ever thought about it, except for now, because she saw me see it and almost stare before turning quickly back to the *Form,* so she might not think I wanted to look again at her stretched out in the grass, let alone let herself think that all I wanted to do was lie down beside her in the grass with the beer and lick that rose on the road to her pelvis. As with so many aspects of the aspects within her, the idea that this was what I really wanted bothered her less than the fact that the idea had occurred to her, no matter what I might have thought. But she knew exactly what I might have thought.

She sat up, brushed herself off. She watched the post parade, the shifting of the crowd, the galloping out of the horses. She thought she had done all she could with us, and then shrugged off our losses in the third.

She didn't lie back down when Henderson sat with her. They talked about my last shot at a winner, in this Arlington turf stakes, and even though the odds-on favorite won at a clip of about seventy percent, and front-runners almost never wired a route on the grass, they had no choice but to stick me with a chance to pull an upset at deteriorating odds. Then there was no chance.

"Not a half bad first half."

"Any race can make a difference. Look at Henderson. Last week we talked about turning him around, and this week we did it. What's the point of making projections? You started well, then lost a few. Anyone can lead all year, then blow it in the end. You're in contention. You could stay in contention and move to win."

"We could jump in the lake."

A look crossed her face in a reaction she couldn't suppress, but usually managed to suppress, if I suggested we do something she wasn't sure she wanted to do, like go for drinks or dinner or bowling. She even thought she composed herself to think of what to say as it struck her that this was a perfectly normal idea in the middle of the afternoon when it was over ninety. What rattled her was that she had been rattled, and she hadn't wanted to show that she had been rattled by such a normal and natural thing for me to say because, on the other hand, it wasn't at all normal or natural or nonchalant for me to say, "We could jump in the lake," since I had to expect that she wouldn't have had her bathing suit in the car, and so what I really was saying was, "Let's strip to our underwear and get wet."

She got off the freeway at the usual exit, but turned east past the junkyards instead of heading straight to Georgetown, and then took a right to the lake.

"Maybe. If we find a spot."

Between the goose shit lawn to the boat ramp traffic jam at Rainier Beach and the topless lesbians throwing sticks for their dogs at Denny Blaine, she knew we wouldn't find any stretch of shore on a sunny summer weekend afternoon where we would be able to get into the water. The drive would be long and bumper-to-bumper, if they let any more cars on the lakefront road at all. But she didn't want to go straight to the bar or to the next point of having to say what to do.

But I knew what to do. "Let's drink like teenagers."

We stopped at a quick mart for tall cans of animal beer and cruised through the smoke of barbecues with the cans cool in the crotch.

For now, things were fine, but she kept thinking of what it would be like to take a flying leap over the weeds to land in the milfoil-choked lake for a few seconds of relief before we had to waddle over the slimed rocks and broken glass and edges of cans and other garbage to pull ourselves out of the water and into our sweat. Didn't she used to like to swim? As a kid, didn't everyone like to jump into water on a hot summer day, no matter how scummy and lukewarm the lake?

"No." She turned to me.

"Huh?"

"I was never like that. I was never who you think I was. Not then."

"But now."

"Now is another story."

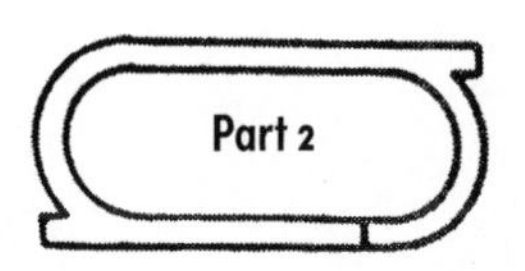

Live Workout: Emerald Downs, Auburn, Washington

2003 Season

Cal Nipper by Kelly Lane

On the first day of the second half of the season, Cal Nipper didn't want to think of the season as something split in halves, especially now that we collectively found ourselves a couple of bills behind. He did think it was useful to recognize these stages as steps in the process, so that we might calibrate or realign expectations and methods to be more effective as players. And yet, he knew how susceptible he was to the slights and insults and setbacks that would accumulate to distract him from what should have been his focus. Even if he could no longer look at himself in the mirror and chant, "You are a winner, a WINNER!" he could maintain focus. He could bear down and concentrate by not letting the little bumps in the road throw him off course. Or, off Course.

"We are all right there. We are all within striking distance. You are on your game, and we are there with you. There is objective, and there is method. We are in control of our destiny. The future is ours to command. The past is past. The moment is now. We are here in the moment for the taking."

He raved as I drove. I didn't want to hear any of it, but couldn't help myself from hearing what I knew was going through his mind, whether he babbled aloud or moped to himself.

I wanted to get him off this kick, to get him to forget about the slights and insults and setbacks so he could just go back to playing the game. He had to force himself away from thinking of all that, to block out negative energy. Cal Nipper reached down and pulled out a water bottle, took a swig, breathed deeply. He offered some to me.

"No thanks." I wanted him to relax and shut up; he wanted to talk.

"In the final analysis, what are we but athletes?"

"Jocks?"

"Physical beings who compete. Who play to win."

"Right. All we are is just in the win."

That shut him up. As another rock song of the 1970s pillaged his consciousness, I parked. Nipper had said how he felt like a relief pitcher walking in from the bullpen to the mound when he walked to the gate for a day of action. He admitted he had relied too much on baseball analogies he knew only as a fan who had never played the game. Until now. Now he was a player.

Normally, we arrived with just enough time before the first live race to follow the odds and watch the post parade. Nipper hated being early because it bothered him that they raised the flag to the "Star Spangled Banner," like it was a baseball game. That's where the anthem belonged. At a ballgame, he even felt cheated if he didn't hear it, but here, if it caught him under the grandstand, he would go to the men's room and flush while he pissed. The idea of standing still wherever he might have been and looking for the nearest TV to watch the flag, let alone to take off his cap or put a hand over his heart, made him think of sci-fi movies where electrodes planted in skulls exploded if people didn't obey. Today we were early, but not early enough. He couldn't escape. All around us, bettors, concessions workers, and tellers stood frozen. The anthem was on.

But it stopped. The singer, a girl country singer who had begun in a register a bit too low for her voice so she might not spin out when she revved into the high notes, stopped. She forgot the words. The flag fluttered dumb on the screen. The girl waited. Everyone waited, and then, finally, she started over from the beginning.

"Christ, what is this? Groundhog Day? The Star Mangled Banner."

Nobody laughed but me.

Nobody sang but the girl. She couldn't break free of the first phrases, and so reworked them into a loop through the tune as she forced herself toward the end.

Nipper said it was perfect, to have some hick who had to be a knee-jerk patriot blow the lyric. He couldn't really enjoy her disgrace, though, because she was just a kid who'd been raised not to know any better, and whatever happened now wouldn't change how the track handled this sorry pageant from now on. They would always scout the Indian casinos, grange halls, and 4-H clubs to recruit someone to do a job on the national anthem. This was just their way of welcoming him to a day at the races.

Kelly Lane

Are they safety valves or catalysts? Mitigaters or agitators? Where would I be without them? Without Nipper to ridicule some poor kid who screws up in public? Well, by having him fire away, I do call the shots. Maybe they're nothing but my hit men.

Then again, these aspects must develop their own prejudices, idiosyncrasies, and whatnot. If you worry about offending people by expressing your personal problems too vividly through these characters (and then restrain yourself as your self is expressed through them), it's worse than overindulging yourself by making up characters who are patently obnoxious. I happen to think Cal Nipper isn't too bad. He is who he is, as best I can figure him.

Henderson Will may be outlandish, but it's too late for me to reform him, with or without Nipper's help. Besides, when we come to the end of this live workout, I wouldn't be surprised if Will's jumbo mumbo outdoes Nipper's methodism.

But what is the future? From day one to the end, here we are, doing what we do and saying what we say in response to some rules set down by a spiel in a self-help course on horse race handicapping. One of the most stringent rules of the scheme is, stay in the moment: don't get ahead of yourself, and don't fall back into the past. You assume you will win the next race, and if you don't, you go on. But there must be a stop. The stop-at-a-winner or the stop after four losses is a barrier, and we are all bound here and together, as if we're bound in a book.

Nipper may complain about being stuck in a slum where glory lies in the obscurity of dodging an IRS audit while he dreams of going to the dogs. Henderson may think it's ludicrous to have his thoughts tossed into word salad while he roams the neighborhoods and bars. But they might take time to appreciate the freedom of confinement. We're stuck in here, true, but we're also free to make each other do whatever any of us wants.

Henderson Will by Cal Nipper

After the started had races, arrived Henderson Will, missing fortunately the anthem national of the bungling (Say oh-oh see you can / the by light early dawns / so what hailed we proudly / the by light-twi's gleam lasting...). He but agreed to decline when I told to try him how that toned the set for the meet of the rest.

He wait to content was for the spot right to move his make.

So and, helping while play to us in ours of each day of the wagers, also he waiting was for a race simulcast. In the Belmont at race ninth, a favorite prohibitive name the by of Shaftmine to win figured at odds worse miserably than money-even. Advantage every had it: style running, shape race and position post, ratings speed, index dosage, down right to the competition of lack. Obviously so the winner was it, the idea bright had Will to lose it to play: in the exacta to wheelback this favorite prohibitive to second finish to four of the each others.

On-odds Shaftmine was, but the covered Will exactas decently paid. Right he was assuming, had Will a chance fighting to down nail a profit nifty, only if Shaftmine could up fuck a scenario perfect.

On dream. The ran race supposed as it was to just. First the from gate out of the step, Shaftmine led the take and back never looked. Once not the jockey did whip him the show, restraints light under holding him while another after one moved a make to second finish, lengths behind several. In the time took it to race the finish, from Shaftmine to the horse next to end the reach, could you cigar a light and puff a few takes.

Kelly Lane

Have we started the second half in the same order that we started the first? How do I know this? What sort of leakage is there in this account of the live workout that lets each of us follow the others? Up to a point, each of us knows what the others are thinking because each says part of what the others are thinking, but then each also is influenced by what the others say, as we think and act and make up the others. The logic of this fix is simple, compared to Freemasonry or Catholicism, but the limits make me wonder, now that we're more than halfway through.

Earlier, there was this assumption—by me, by each of them—that first we took The Course, then we went out into the world with the idea of creating a gambling mob each of us would deploy at the track, and then we would reach some realization about ourselves that we might apply in the future. Basically, if this scheme turned a profit, we might continue to do it to make a living at the track. If not, we might stop and do something else. But the basics of profit and loss went beyond dollar amounts. The bottom line statements of accomplishment and failure held some ultimate power over how we felt about ourselves, and it was this power each of us would have to deal with after the live workout at Emerald Downs was over.

But what if when it's over, it's just plain over? Why should there be any next step, contingent on the step that went before? I'm not saying we all drink poison Kool-aid on Closing Day, but each of us should think of this season we've been given to play through as an end in itself. Let's make nothing more significant than the results of the next race, until the next race after that.

But all that happens as a result of the results is up to us, or up to the aspects within each of us, as these beings are left to themselves to make what they will of us. Even if these aspects aren't raving lunatics themselves, for each of us to have them determine what happens doesn't seem like the most sensible way to deal with the world.

If Nipper has his heart set on dragging my ass to Portland after the last race of the season is official, and

Will has no objections, what can I do? If I say it's over when it's over, what can Nipper or Will do?

Kelly Lane by Cal Nipper

It wasn't like her to be knocked off-stride by a loss or two, even when patterns formed to make her feel that the losses were somehow her fault. That lead-shy front-runner, Toogoodtobetrue, the one she went down on a few weeks back, beat her by a nose, surviving a duel and holding off the late rush of Spicy Game, her hope to hit the opener of the daily double. She wouldn't have had the double, anyway, because her horse in the second also lost by a nose, in a virtual replay of the first race. By then, she had switched to another pick with better odds in this five-furlong maiden claimer for two-year-olds, but that horse went nowhere. Her choice in the third, Currency Kitty, also just missed, and in the fourth, another maiden race, she went down on a first-time starter with promising works and a trainer/jockey combo she liked, leaving her up $62 after losses.

"You were close. A case of seconditits."

"Trainer/jockey plays on first-time starters in maiden claiming races. What the hell."

She used to follow connections more closely. Trainers who had been around forever had a way of showing in their workout routines when their horses were ready to win off a layoff, while others were notorious for using the races themselves as workouts where their animals could run their way into shape while losing. Some jockeys would change agents or hook up with better trainers and double their win percentages. Some would change everything but never improve. Had she ever favored woman trainers and jocks? It was nothing personal. Women used to be underbet, and then, when one got hot, she would be overbet. These days, the way she followed trainers and jockeys struck her as impersonal. She paid more attention to the standings and statistics noted in the *Form* than to the impressions she might have gathered back when the records of all but the top ten trainers and jockeys went unlisted.

She wondered how I figured it.

"Connections matter. Hook-ups are powerful indicators. You've played them before and won. You nearly won today."

"I wonder why I don't think of these people by name, even when my bets are based on connections."

"It's better not to hold grudges, isn't it?"

"Didn't you used to play based on grudges?"

"Who didn't?"

"I must have, but I never saw the point of blaming the jockeys, the way some did. You know, leaning over the rail to scream at them for not risking their lives so I could cash a ticket."

Thanks to The Course, she approached the game as though she hadn't played this circuit before, even though all of us knew it, way back from Longacres in the 1980s and into the '90s, when that track closed. She liked how The Course encouraged us not to take the races personally, even while we personalized the members of our mob. The races tended to provoke certain feelings in yourself. You couldn't help feeling that you were a center of attention, that what you did mattered, as much as, if not more than, what others did.

She knew this was false. To think of herself as the reason for all of this, or even as a main character in some sequence of events, was a way to misinterpret all that happened so that you not only wound up losing money, but also wound up losing touch with reality. But she also knew this was true. She was a main character in this scheme, and one of its devisers. The circumstances she had to put up with were part of a pattern that made her do what she did and feel what she felt, and for her to deny the reality of her importance in these events was to lose touch with all that could possibly matter in this world.

Kelly Lane by Cal Nipper

At the end of the ride home to the bar, she parked where she parked when she was going to come in for a drink. This was the first indication I had she was coming in for a drink. She hadn't said a word until now.

"So, Henderson Will used to be William Henderson, a guy who worked in an office. A stroke of amnesia made him forget what he did. His bosses either didn't notice or they put up with him until they laid him off anyway. But then he had another mental collapse, where everything got twisted around backwards. Fine. His name is the inverted version of a typical name, with a little play off the will of Will. I get it.

"And Cal Nipper has always been a caliper with teeth, a number cruncher who nibbles and quibbles. You are what you are. I give you that. Hell, I gave you that. But how did you come up with Kelly Lane?"

"You don't like the name?"

"The name is fine. I like it fine. Sleek but not slick. I don't mind at all. I'm just curious. It was your idea, wasn't it?"

"I guess. It just sounded good, rolling off the tongue. And there was this idea I had of calling you Kelly Fairlane, like the car with fins. But also I thought of you as someone who would have paid special attention to race shapes and favorable shifts of conditions, like in the post position draw, someone who keyed on horses that got to run in the fair lanes. On the rail if they liked the rail, on the outside, if they needed that space to make their moves. Traffic. I was thinking, 'She wanted a Fairlane, but she couldn't afford it,' but the idea of naming people after cars seemed stupid, so I shortened it to Lane."

"Why Kelly? You have a thing for the Irish?"

"I wanted something unusual but not ornate. No Mary or Heather or Jennifer, but no Kona or Beatrice, either. And you do look a bit Irish."

"How do the Irish look to you?"

"I don't know. I suppose there are some things like features that stand out, features like your nose and mouth. They're small, not too small. Perfect. Beautifully chiseled. With round, wild, intense eyes."

"Like a fucking fairy with tits."

"Oh come on."

"Like those strumpets in *Spank Me, Laddie,* with spindly muscular arms and legs that broadcast tits."

"Cut it out."

"I know how you think."

"I never heard of Spank Me, Laddie. I don't even watch Channel 9."

"How do you know it's Channel 9?"

"Who else but Channel 9 would do an ersatz Irish dance musical?"

"How else but by watching Channel 9 would you know about *Spank Me, Laddie?*"

"So I know it. So what? As for your name, maybe there is some Irish in you. Sure, you're thin. If we put you on stage in clogs and a short skirt and a black, long sleeve leotard top, maybe your tits will show. I think you're cute. I think you're beautiful. Now can we have a drink?"

She opened the door and led the way to the bar, satisfied that I knew the costume by heart.

Cal Nipper by Henderson Will

Nipper knew better than to try to hide his fervid proclivities from Kelly Lane, but thought she might think more of him if he at least pretended not to be the kind of lowlife who "practiced" in condoms while ogling the *Spank Me, Laddie* poster that just happened to sprawl from the entertainment section of the *Seattle Post-Intelligencer* whenever he found himself on the couch. Even if she didn't really look like either of the principal female dancers who flanked the male lead as the three of them blazed in the heat of the action, arms flexed and eyes bulging and lips tightly open, he saw a superficial "Irish" resemblance in the facial features of the two young women to Kelly that was, when he thought of it, not much different from the resemblance between Kelly and the Schlitz girl on the clock at The Prop or between Kelly and every other pretty woman between twenty-five and fifty he saw on the bus. Put any of them in a dancer's body in a grainy newsprint poster with their mouths like that, and Nipper was ready to roll.

In person, though, he thought he thought of Kelly as who she was and not as one of an army of beautiful dancers with bulging eyes and tiny black-lipped mouths open tight around the shaft of his penis as he, Lord of the Pants, commanded them to clog-stomping rapture, but then it did occur to Nipper that by even making the slightest link between her face and the faces of these dancers, let alone the faces of all those women on the bus nowhere near Ireland, he was losing his grip on her and therefore on himself. He got up and walked to the sink, splashed water on his face. He looked out back into a hazy July weekday afternoon, to the dogs sleeping next door, the distant sounds of kids screaming and TVs laughing.

There was no Braves game today. He had no more reason to stay here than he did to go to The Prop. He tried to think of some errand he might do, but his house was full of food from Costco. Back in the old days of handicapping, he might have spent these hours working on his calculations, updating his notebooks, but The Course told him not to invest time in preparation because the *Form* would provide all he needed on the day of the race: all the better to concentrate on the act of betting. He might have gone to the library, but he went there yesterday and ended up only reading obscure magazines and out-of-town newspapers. What he needed was a book, but he couldn't think of any he wanted to check out, even when he realized what he needed the book for was to have a topic to talk to Kelly about when the time came to talk.

He wondered what she would be reading or planning to do. Would she be browsing the shelves of Scarecrow for some movie in a language she used to speak? Maybe that's what he should do. Ride the bus two hours, not including the time of hanging around to change busses, just to go to this video store where he could find an odd movie to bring home, so he could tell her about it later.

Why bother? Why not just see what was on TV? He had cable, he could watch TV, even if there wasn't a Braves game on. He could go through fifty channels and pick something that she would be interested in talking about the next time he saw her. No crappy reality show or cop lab mystery, maybe not even a movie, but something cultural! Something she would go to or want to go to, if it played downtown. A play, a concert, a dance.

Nipper went back to the couch, grabbed the entertainment section, and, once more found himself.

Kelly Lane by Cal Nipper

She didn't know what she was and didn't mind being branded Irish, but she did know her real name wasn't

"Kelly Lane." Or, maybe that was her real name now, but it wasn't the name she was born with or the name she went by when she was married for a year or two before she came West. It was a stage name, a name to sing by, when she used to sing decades-old show tunes in the cocktail lounges of Greater San Francisco. How real was that?

After wagering hundreds, she was up $62. This mattered about as much to her as her name did. All or nothing at all. And yet, there was a sudden new feeling of strangeness that came over her now that she thought of our names and of how these came about, because she couldn't stop wondering who she was and why she was wondering who she was.

She felt an urge to go rent a movie in Spanish or French, and she didn't know why but figured it had to be me, or Henderson, or some combined force of the two of us that made her want to do what she did or didn't do. She had studied Spanish in school and had taken a French for Travelers class years later, for a trip she never took. Why would she ever rent a movie for the language? Sure, she had rented movies in Spanish, in French, German, Polish, Russian, but she had rented them as movies—not as language training exercises, not as demonstrations to drive home all she had never learned or simply forgotten. So she forgot about the movie.

She bought tomorrow's *Racing Form* and stuffed it deep into her bag as she went through the ritual of picking a café where she would sit to pick a place to go to dinner. Instead of reading the *Form,* she would read one of the weekly papers. She didn't feel like dealing with the races yet, and she didn't feel like being seen reading the *Daily Racing Form* at the Victrola or Vivace or Vita, even though it would be totally cool to be reading that in a cafe full of kids scribbling in journals and reading Proust or Bukowski. But then some guy, and it would be a guy, would peek over his Bukowski to notice her reading the *Form,* and he'd come over and show her his book and, well, she didn't want to think about it.

Why? What if she did want to think about that? She could handle some kid reading Bukowski. What if he was cute enough for her to put up with, and smart, smart enough not to want to quit his job so he could write and drink and live in flop houses? Why shouldn't she want to spend some time with him, maybe go to a bar with him where he could act out his fantasies?

Kelly Lane stomped into the Victrola, looked around, and saw nobody reading, unless you counted laptop screens as things to read. She wondered if, when she whipped out her *Form,* half of the guys within hailing distance of what seemed to be her age would whip out their Bukowskis and start hacking up oysters and picking their noses. Ah, courtship.

Wait till Nipper hears about this, she thought, pulling out the *Daily Racing Form* once she settled in with her double-short non-fat latte, and immediately she felt awful. This entire episode of trolling for Bukowskis with her *Form* spread wide open was—no Will about it—vintage Nipper. She couldn't believe she was doing this. She couldn't believe it was happening as it was, but before she could stop, there he was.

Kelly Lane by Cal Nipper

"Hiya. You play?" He wobbled over to her, cup of regular coffee in one hand, copy of some pamphlet in the other.

"You could say that. Do you?"

"You bet. I'm Darren."

"Kelly."

He slumped into the easy chair across from her. He looked like he could have fallen asleep on the spot. His hair was greasy, his plaid work shirt untucked, his jeans torn, but his boots were new and solid, and as they began to talk, she realized he was younger and even cleaner than she thought he was when he said hello. She didn't want to talk about The Course, so she asked what he was reading. He handed it over: *Dick Weed.* Pages of writing were set in line breaks or as block after block of prose, unbroken by paragraphs. In the table of contents there was a Darren.

"You?"

He nodded.

"Congratulations."

He smiled, because he must have thought this stranger wasn't making fun of him, but she wasn't so sure that she wasn't, so she smiled to be polite. This was Seattle.

People didn't go out of their way to be rude to people they just met, did they? Yes and no. It was but it wasn't Seattle, inasmuch as anything here could or couldn't have been exactly what she thought it was. Call it satellite Seattle.

Then it occurred to her that Darren had no urge to pick her up and take her anywhere (that little twist of events would have bugged me no end, she thought). Either he was infatuated with being published in this magazine or their entire conversation was a self-improvement assignment given to him by his therapist, his Course. Or maybe, like so much else in this project to lose yourself and beat the races, what he said was a convergence of forces that conflicted and interfered and combined to explain themselves into an oblivion of amplified chaos.

She wanted to get out of there. She wanted him to shut up and leave her alone, but he went on and on and on, about geniuses who were supposed to be lunatics if not simply drunk out of their minds, which he said was like the monkeys typing *Hamlet* by chance, because you had to know what you were doing when you did anything or it just didn't count.

"Are you crazy?"

"No, are you?"

She hadn't really thought she was, but wondered. Was the *Divide and Conquer* course a determination of sanity versus lunacy, as if winning or losing or playing the game weren't as important as reacting to what we did? She wanted to answer. Maybe they did have something to say to each other, and this wasn't some naive kid, but a talented and perceptive younger man, who could discuss a variety of topics in a dispassionate or passionate way. These questions of craziness weren't rhetorical but were matters that mattered to him as they did to her every day, such as right now that they were here together, enjoying each other's company in a coffee house they might leave, to go to a bar or—

"Nice talking to you."

He left her the magazine.

Cal Nipper by Kelly Lane

"Hurry up, we don't want to miss the national anthem."

"If we're late, you can sing in the car."

I shouldn't have said that. Nipper proceeded to mimic the anthem mangler from a week ago, nailing her performance note-for-note and word-for-blown-word, with the soulful lilt lapsing into panic once she knew she didn't know what came next.

"Maybe they should bag the country singers. They could book Irish cloggers to stomp out the anthem in the muck."

I hadn't counted on the Chipper Nipper. He got into trouble when he came to the track in too cute a mood. If he got too spry, I could always tell him I met some guy during the week, but he must have known all about that.

He lost the opening races when a favorite he couldn't play took the first, and the second went to an 0-for-13 pig while he bet on second choices with better odds to win. He was playing more like Henderson or me than himself, especially when Henderson hit the first at Hastings by making a bet Nipper should have made.

"Don't look at me, boys. We're bound to influence each other."

In the third, a five-and-a-half-furlong $3,200 claimer for nonwinners-of-two fillies and mares, he boxed the favorite with a speedster, only to finish second and third to another speedster.

"Nice going."

"Go ahead and blame me, if it makes you feel better."

"I was kidding."

"So was I."

He knew I meant it, because it was true, but he didn't quite mean it himself. The problem was, he wasn't concentrating. He was still goofing around, high on the feeling he had on the way here, and only knowing that it felt good for a change not to be uptight, to be having fun, to play.

Cal Nipper by Kelly Lane

Nipper barely made his high school tennis team the year after the whole varsity graduated. He was nowhere near good enough to play singles and would have fallen into the second doubles slot, but the second doubles guys always threw their matches in practice. He and his partner got the first doubles slot because they tried hard in practice, and then went on to lose their real matches. Nipper's partner looked good enough to play singles, with his fast first serve, tricky second serve, strong forehand, and so-so backhand, but he double-faulted too much. Nipper almost never double-faulted, as his first serve was like anyone else's second serve and his second serve was a wristy little puff of a thing. Nipper just tried to get the ball back over the net, and his partner made more mistakes than Nipper goaded the opponents to make. They continued to lose to players who exploited their weaknesses, but Nipper rarely felt all was lost because the scoring system of tennis had layers of second chances: lose the point but win the game, lose the game but win the set, lose the set but...

Nipper knew that his brief career as an outclassed high school varsity tennis player didn't really portend a lifetime of disappointment, and he still thought he had mastered pressure in general because of the way he had absorbed the tennis scoring system, as if he had come to understand the true nature of pressure by not really feeling it, even though, he suspected, by not really feeling pressure, he hadn't mastered it at all.

Going into his last bet of the day, he could have thought that he had to get a win, and he could have built up the need to get this crucial win, to pull himself back to the plus side of the ledger rather than to fall further behind, but he thought it would be fun to toy with the idea of putting pressure on himself. He knew he could handle it. Veteran of high school tennis humiliation, Cal Nipper had been there. He would live through this.

Then, as he began to play with this idea of courting the pressure of failure and loss, he began to panic because he didn't feel the pressure of much of anything, and so the idea of not feeling much of anything made him nervous, edgy, itchy. Something had to be wrong with him—not only because he was part of someone's hysteria or maybe just because that's all of what he was. Here we were, trying to get Nipper to muster the slightest sense of what he ought to feel when his back was to the wall, even if it wasn't to the wall. It, his back, had never been to any wall.

By the numbers, Nipper took Condotierri in the tenth on a getaway play. Condotierri was a stakes router for a stakes route at a mile and a sixteenth, with a running style to fit the style of the competition: not some Zen monk of consistency, who only aimed to return each shot his opponent made, but a true contender in top form, with the tactical speed to go near the lead and take command late, versus a field of tortoises and hares.

Nipper made the play. Nipper put the money down and went home and felt good in the morning, when he read that Condotierri had won the race to put him back on top for the year by $138, but not as good as he thought he should have felt.

Henderson Will by Cal Nipper

Henderson Will liked something he saw Vancouver from TV on the race first in. It wasn't a win to bet on a horse particular but a play math. What didn't he know about the track Columbia British could book a fill. Knew he all that a jockey ace riding was a contender top. A favorite runaway should have been it, for except a mathematics of quirk. In a field short, horses four paired were in separate entries two. And four of the none, though all enough good, were beat enough to good Bates Buckeye, the liked Will horse. Bates Buckeye uncoupled ran with horse any other.

Like a game shell in a sucker, your bettor average might mistake the make of getting he was thinking a deal by coupling the playing of horses two for the one of price. Either if won of them one the in entry, your player entry ticketed his cash. The matter of the fact was, but, was it a deal raw to get worse horses on odds worse, when especially could get you better on the race best in the horse.

That not Will fact for a knew who the horse best here was. Only liked he the odds lowest with the horse who wasn't up-hooked in an entry coupled. With entries two of pairs to up soak the suckers from the wagers, the horse that bet Will, that off should have gone as a favorite on-odds, promised now to money his double. Great not, but enough good to $184 net Will.

Step next on the loser-at-a-stop events of sequence was an exacta wheelback in the Emerald race third. With recommend it to nothing but tote late, a plodder took him in his quest eternal to out dope the horse logical to second run. Occasion on, enough sure, horsing the pick to second run well did to horse the pick who counter ran to the style of the winner prevailing. If the on the lead horse speed most of the races won, time a many took second the closer horse of type. Time this not.

Yet but Will's day for the take of $124 put him even to break poised, as was his meet for the total down $122 only.

Kelly Lane by Cal Nipper

It was warm but not hot, humid but not muggy. What did she expect? Not to drop two bills to fall behind again. The next day, when she read that her getaway play had lost, she wondered why she had made any of these bets: Zipledo, Just Push Play, Take Issue, Tickled Purple, a line-up of losers picked for early speed or body language, running style or connections. What was she thinking? On the way home, she said the worst that could happen was she would only be down $138.

I told her that's exactly how much I was up.

"Sorry."

I said that was O.K., but it was better than O.K. for her to feel sorry for saying "only" for the same amount I was up as she was about to go down, if only to have her say it, because this showed she cared for my feelings. Even though she knew I couldn't begin to feel the pressure of being on the verge of losing, she wanted to let me know that she hadn't wanted to upset me. She seemed to care more about my feelings than she did about her own bad day at the track.

She wondered if it wouldn't be better if we didn't all win or lose, or if one of us won and the other two lost, or vice-versa. Each of us had a contrarian streak. It wasn't just Henderson Will twisting things around. We had to do what we did in different ways, to oppose what we wanted with some alternative outcome. Was it human nature or was it some quirk we shared? Whatever it was, she got the idea that Henderson was the key. If we could come to terms with him, to get him under control or to let him go wild and lead the way, or if we could just understand what it was about him that had this influence over us, maybe we would solve a major puzzle of the scheme that was, after all, based on contradiction.

Henderson Will by Cal Nipper

Out camping near the hospital veterans lot parking, continued Henderson Will to out hang with the veterans war the that States United forces armed had away thrown. Mind never that the complaints ordinary these veterans war had of might were reasonably perfect, the nature strident of their voices raised off people turned. On what turned people was the authority of voices, as such had casterbroads, though even typical your casternews voice was pap but nothing, shit of full, and ass to kiss ready any for lie government or relations public release press.

With them agreeing, he less the never weary got being a board sounding for say to what they had. To reason to try them with less made even sense. He so up shut and town down went.

After bar after, kept him into running sorts all of characters nutty whose reasonably perfect beefs true rang. Will tried, thought had he, a class better of lounge tail cock: holes watering of hotels swank. In these like places, ran talk to season ball base. Will starred his lucky thanks that that sport didn't follow him. In the called-so King of Sports, it mattered hardly who the Series World lost. In ponying the plays, only had he to win while in a once, odds at enough high to set-off all the lost money he had.

More further, these arguments out broke among the people who bet all at hardly. Their bets typical would nothing to amount, all of least to any measurement of their esteem self.

As them he watched, to Will occurred it them of one had he been, ago long. Days these, he whether wondered wasn't he, as a gambler inveterate, off better than as a waist panty. Brains scrambled all and, now he maybe was at peace more than day in the back, when would he shit a give about his pool office shot at a tournament basketball wager of a pick lottery.

Henderson Will by Kelly Lane

Downtown the town down dumpster bin bum stir din pounded in the background. Grounded in the pack bound, he sipped a drink dripped to sink in a hotel, as the class of the cream of the town toed hell, crass as a team of a clown in the dank chance-fried recourse of rank franchise decors.

A lot of hate in a Holiday Inn tepid dish run repetition bill of fare on the bar gauge of a pomp host keep could fill a bear on the garbage of a compost heap, but the macked of the fatter fact of the matter was a good buffet cut could puff a gut at the crappy power grub haul of a happy hour pub crawl. He had nicked up the lack and picked up the knack of grazing on free munchies where drinks were reasonable, phrasing hungry chum ease. Rare winks were treasonable in the wild dives of the rich with the riled wives in the ditch.

More the boasts fart for the most part. For all the tassel lewd dangled come-ons, lassitude angled dumb cons personified your bona fide floor shover four-flusher mule's date of a stool mate. At this stewed date, that is to state, at the mill wet Will met salve filling trails men: traveling salesmen. When he understated anyone's stirdated neat plays—"Swell day!"—bleat noise held sway. Those stuff men, most of the dove flocking, loved talking. Say hi or hey, sigh, and a boozy shard lunatic conversation tenor of a sushi bar tuna lick conservation net or odd cup caught up the moment of hail fellow surprising to foment a male hello's uprising.

"I hit a Hyatt high at a Hyatt."

Seated grips of snifter gripes greeted sips of grifter snipes. Wry carping revealed hates of high parking feereeled rates.

"The Olympic polemic of a sore fee shuns the Four Seasons."

But most of all boast of maul, they discussed the kiss dust sacked if at ease activities of fun scenting cad dolts consenting adults.

"The Red Lion led Ryan to a cootie ball bootie call."

"No hairy mutt at the Marriott but a tune pang poon tang."

Henderson Will by Kelly Lane

Swirling in wet whirling in sweat, Will went onward there toward where he usually would, back to the RV. Hacked to the barf, he blew a kiss coo of bliss to the wee fray of the freeway, which targeted him as a mark. A car met him on a dark stretch of the road, but a retch of the strode sappage of passage teetered him and deterred them. A Bolivian oblivion did protect dope wrecked dead nose haired hose snared cocaine sensibilities, so sane, tense luck, ill to-be's high bedlam piloted him. In the back of his mind hack of this bind, any height male might hail a fab whore guy or a cab for hire.

As he whizzes there by a doorway, this is where I'd award a ride to this tied-to-risk squalid wanderer of a wallet squanderer. But when he needed to walk, what knee heeded to balk? It bent your vast bazaars to venture past the bars into nook turf, took nerve to creep across the lad bands badlands. What kept Will on course through this swept kill concourse through sea dirt dead deserted tarmacs smart tacts decorated by pecker-dated broken glass glow can brass?

Dead or asleep on sled or a deep wicker cell, sick or well men lay everywhere. When may every lair tramp or hobo hamper bow row settlement? Metal sent a deal strum steel drum down ping pounding from the jungle gun gel over the road. The rover ode viziers overrode his fears. The theorems of rhythms guiding him hiking dim, Will was soon back in the boon sack in a foam of home.

Henderson Will

For some reason, my head is killing me. It is a hot Sunday at the end of July, and I walk into a crowd of tourists who got in on free passes, whereupon a pudgy woman in her sixties screams at a man who could be her husband, who cringes smiling as she pounds him with her purse: "Fuck you, fuck you, fuck you, fuck you, you son of a bitch! Fuck you, go back to the penitentiary!"

What am I doing? What have Lane and Nipper done to me? What have we all done to deserve each other?

Suppose that they don't exist, or that Lane and Nipper only exist when I say they do, and that I only pretend to be made up by them. This could explain our failures on a day when the track is overrun by favorites beating wives beating ex-convict husbands. I should take responsibility for my actions, right? If I spent the evening carousing in downtown hotel bars just to avail myself of the complimentary happy hour buffets and spent the night walking home several miles through bad neighborhoods, what good does it do to blame them?

Or to punish them? I had a rotten night. Now we're going to have a rotten day. Maybe my role in all we do is to be the bad guy. Fuck you, go back to the penitentiary.

So what's the point? Sowhatsyourpoint, a big favorite, wires the first, a $40,000 maiden race. Neither of them has it. Nipper travels to Hastings on the simulcast for his next bet, and loses; Lane loses in the second at Emerald. Nobody bets the third, a field of four after a late scratch leaves the favorite in total command. The only bright spot in the rest of their bets is Nipper gets shut out of an exacta in his final try, and so only loses $180 for the day, to go down $58 for the meet. Lane, meanwhile, falls $338 behind.

Another bright spot, if you can call it that, is I nearly catch a big exacta when my key horse just misses taking second at 10–1, which sets me back $202.

There have been other days when we all have lost, but have there been days when we have all fallen into the negative? Blame me. I take full responsibility. I'm the loser, the one who plays to lose, who does everything wrong. If we all lose, it's all my fault.

They need me more than I need them. They still think there's hope, that there's a chance for them to make something of themselves by losing themselves.

Henderson Will by Kelly Lane

To take a break to brake the take, Will went. A numb, canned need accompanied his fickle quest of a quizzical fest. He stirred eastward. As he began to walk as we panned to gawk.

Over the rages and ranges he roved for the ages and changes of terrain and climate clear rain and time at this place suspended. Bliss pace thus ended. For several sore, visceral days of hellfire into a phase of fell dire daze of elf hire he fell. He thought the haughty elfish selves of selfish elves were drunk, rolling, and controlling where he stepped, sneering back iconic twaddle fakes between cacophonic rattlesnakes, whose slayer apprised him to paralyze him without a tingle by sight of a single time bite.

Besides that, the sides bat, he figured on his likelihood to stay alive. On the hike, he stood to lay a five that he would, if he got to the road.

Good if he rot with the toad! Seemed to thunder, themed to sunder.

They grimly laughed, lay thimbly graft, playing nuts and peas paying what's planned. Ease for their taking Thor dare faking, thundering underthing elfin deities dealt in fiat tease to flay his pate to play his fate. Furthermore, mirth therefore, he could feel reeling the real feeling that each re-crated elfin self then created the otherselves elves, so that none could be real.

You know that sun could repeal sea run reason in a clash of flare at the flash of clarity. But he sought we he thought what he bought; what he thought but he bought what he sought. Then air was arrowed and there was a road.

Cal Nipper by Henderson Will

As if he had just spent weeks blundering among the rattlesnakes in the heat of Wenatchee, Cal Nipper arrived at the track in a visionary daze. He came by bicycle, via a rooftop party near Lake Washington, where a pal from The Prop lived. The occasion was a Blue Angels air show before a hydroplane race. Nipper had pumped up his tires, oiled his chain, and wheezed as far as a hundred yards up Beacon Hill between Georgetown and the lake before he had to get off and push. He expected to have to walk uphill, but not for as long as it took him to reach the party, and so he only stayed for one beer, leaving way before the chicken was off the grill, so he could get to

Emerald Downs while there were still a few races on the card.

As strange as he looked from his ordeal, we shouldn't have been surprised that he did something totally out-of-character. He aimed at a bigger payoff to win than he ever had before. In this cheap maiden claimer for two-year-old fillies, his 29–1 flyer ran well and finished fourth, just as he figured she might, off good works and a bit of bad luck in her last start. Finishing fourth on a longshot pleased him more than just missing and finishing second or third.

In the next race, Nipper reverted. His co-favorite speed horse went wire-to-wire, putting him only $6 below zero on the meet.

He might have gone back to his usual betting habits, but he still was under the influence of his extended time away from the track. Something had happened to him out there, and he still hadn't figured out what it was. Despite the greasy sheen of 48-weight sun block, his face, neck, and arms throbbed bright red against his blue-green Hawaiian shirt. Every few minutes he went to the water fountain or the bathroom, then came back jittery to loiter under the monitors in the ground level betting area.

Although we hadn't been there much longer than he had, we had each come our usual ways to the track, and so would have settled directly into the routine, if only Nipper hadn't still been so charged up by the adventure of his ride. He thought he was on the verge of a major breakthrough, and this vaguely spiritual sentiment kept him from paying much attention to our specific wagers while he focused on the complete wagering program as a manifestation of some all-encompassing quest.

We tried to ignore him, but there he was, demanding attention even as he kept still.

Cal Nipper was more receptive to procedures than either of us, and as he brightened to reflect upon his new routine, he would have to work through it before realizing that it, too, must culminate in delusion. He thought he was onto something big, though. For years he had planned to take the bicycle on a major excursion, and now he had done it. Accomplishment. For years he had thought of doing something about his approach to the races, and now he had done it. Accomplishment. For weeks he had done well at this approach, but then faltered. Adjustment. Now, in one day, he had made a serious adjustment in the way he went about doing what he had to do, and then he had done it. Accomplishment.

Cal Nipper nodded at the odds flickering overhead, and, as if by whim rather than need, submitted himself to the room with the mirrors.

Cal Nipper by Kelly Lane

He might have pretended to agree that Henderson Will held the key to what we were all about, but what Cal Nipper thought was that we were all about Cal Nipper. We were all essentially one person whose focal point was the identity Cal Nipper. You could say this about any of us, he conceded. The idea of anyone being the center of this silly little universe was a notion he mentioned as if to dismiss it while also asserting that such a hero-based regime was inevitable. Coming back to the track by bicycle after a two-week layoff, he had made a play to draw attention to himself. And by finessing his first race with a bold fling at a longshot before hitting his second with a classic return to Nipperian form—yes, he did fashion an adjective for himself—he had almost single-handedly changed the course of the course of The Course as it applied to what we would accomplish.

And so now it was up to hero Nipper to wield his Nipperian authority to get us back into the winner's circle, as long as he didn't drink too much water and piss himself away. What this assumption of authority did to his way of thinking was to redirect all of his efforts toward helping us. What he thought he did for me was put my third bet of the day on Premo Copy, a second choice in the wagering who had the pace figures to run down the solo speed, Exclusive Molly, even though Molly would blast off to a big lead on the backstretch. When Premo Copy ran her down and put me up $86 for the day, Nipper opened his arms and smiled.

Then he applied himself to the fortunes of Henderson Will, who, Nipper might have acknowledged, had some hand in guiding my pick to a second choice in the last race, because it was more like Will than Nipper to take on a solo speed favorite by picking a second-best horse. But hero Nipper had no time for such thoughts. He set to work on Will's game.

Just because Will played Miss Pixie, whose past boasted by far the most back class, in a typical bottom wheel, Nipper put his stamp of approval on the play, even when Miss Pixie faded after a bid to finish a respectable but worthless third. He didn't say it, but thought of it as a match for his loss on that longshot in the first. Never minding that Will's loss, after a scratch, was $60 for the day and $262 for the season, Nipper thought of this kind of result as a latent win, bound to pay dividends in the long run.

The latent win! Nipper had an inspiration. Some day he would become the author of a book on handicapping. From him, fledgling horseplayers and veteran railbirds would learn the one true way to visualize victory. He would call the book *Visualize Victory,* with chapters called "The Latent Win," "The Second Serve," and "Spank Me, Laddie," but first he'd need a subtitle. *Visualize Victory: Pump Up and Ride On.* It would deal with the mental aspects of the game, with the ways you handle pressure and the ways you trick yourself into losing because you just don't have what it takes to look in the mirror and say, but no, he would steer clear of that. No seminars in the office park for Nipper. Nipperian theory would be celebrated in book stores. Nipperian insights would cross over from tout territory to the land of letters. Beyond self-help to philosophy, the consolation of philosophy. "'All he ever lost, he lost in kindergarten: a modern Boethius'—R. Fulgum" on the back, an appearance at Town Hall as part of Seattle Arts and Lectures; and, no mere Pulitzer: a National Book Award, a special citation for the invention of a whole new literary category, Memoir Actualization. As he confided to George Plimpton for his long-awaited interview in *Paris Review* (unaware that Plimpton had to be channeled by spiritual medium to do the interview), "There I was, at the end of a losing streak on the first Saturday of August, and it came to me: spank me, laddie, but there is a certain power in the latent win, even if you must rely on your second serve. Pump up, ride on, and visualize victory."

Cal Nipper by Kelly Lane

Nipper was well into his third ale. The Braves had lost, an exhibition football game loomed from the TV nobody would turn off, and what had promised to be the culmination of his life's work now struck him as thoroughly pathetic, thanks to the encouragement of everyone around him. Nobody would have said anything about this, but when Nipper had wheezed up to The Prop, filthy and sweating on a bicycle, they wanted to know what got into him. He said nothing got into him—he just felt like going for a ride, and the party was halfway to the track, more or less.

He knew better than to take himself too seriously, especially when he was taking himself too seriously, so when he told them about going for a long ride to clear his head, which led him to dream up the book he should write to tell people how to win, he made fun of himself. That was the only way to act. They liked him. He liked them. They weren't close friends—none of them had ever been to his house—but they knew each other well enough to keep each other from getting away with pretensions.

His business at the track was well known and accepted here. It figured that Nipper would get mixed up in a scheme like that. Taking or getting taken by The Course was what he had been born to do. But teaching? Running his own self-help scheme spun out of a book he was going to write that would make his reputation? Nipper reminded them that he had been a teacher, was a teacher, and so could be a teacher, all the while realizing that he wasn't currently and therefore never had been cut out to be a teacher, let alone a writer/guru to lead a cult of fiends, who based their lives on the assumption that all could depend on how they won at the track, because they would win at the track.

Wobbling home on his bike, he supposed that all of his life depended on not just winning but making something of his success. If he won and didn't go on to write the book to start the cult, all would come to nothing. Even though it was absurd to get started on this obsession, because he never would have written a book like that, the thought of framing what he did in terms of potential acclaim depressed him and made him feel worthless and ridiculous and so made him want to laugh.

He knew none of this would bother him in the morning. In the morning he would make drip coffee from his five-pound stash of Starbucks/Costco beans and heat up the remains of some day-old Hostess factory outlet store pastries from a week ago. He would go for the paper. When he got back with the sports page, the buns would be warm, the coffee would be ready, and the Braves would still be in first place.

Kelly Lane by Henderson Will

Kelly Lane had a good feeling about this muggy Sunday, even when she had a blow-out on the way to pick up Nipper. In less than an hour, AAA came and got her rolling again. She knew her spare would be flat or her jack would be missing, and when it wasn't and it was, she felt smart about having kept her auto club membership, because having it and never using it would have been only as good as having a talisman to ward off bad luck. Kelly Lane did not need a good luck charm.

Nipper fidgeted. He must have been calculating how much time he had lost and how long he would have waited for her not to come before he took off on his bike. She had called to say she would be late, and that made him more nervous. Better nervous than cocky.

They made it in time to play a six-furlong $12,500 open claimer where each took safe exactas, only to lose to an 8–1 closer in the muck. They lost the next, a non-winners-of-two $8,000 claimer for three-year-olds, to another closer.

"You need a horse with stamina, but he can't come from too far back."

We knew what she meant, and Nipper ratified the idea when he zeroed in on the ninth, a stakes at a mile and a sixteenth. She keyed on Stratoplan, the second favorite in that race, who was fresh off a win against similar in Vancouver, boxing him in exactas with the likely lone pacesetter, Knightsbridge Lane, and putting him on top of the old warhorse Condotierri.

This was the inverse of my bet, when I keyed on Knightsbridge Lane to finish second to those contenders, and also covered the possibility that he might win. She liked that. It was consistent with how I normally played, and our bets were bound to reflect each other sometimes. We were both a bit surprised that Nipper should have skipped Condotierri this time around and taken Stratoplan to win.

Cal Nipper by Kelly Lane

"What did you expect me to do?"

He said it wasn't like Father's Day, where he and I got stuck on the same bet because of some perverted sense of guilt. There were races where our separate approaches could get a fix on the same outcome, as they should in a successful multiple betting strategy.

Sure enough, Knightsbridge got the lead, Stratoplan stalked, and Condotierri came up to take third as Knightsbridge held second after getting run down by Stratoplan in the stretch. Nipper's $98 profit for the day put him up $92 for the year, but he was really thrilled to see Henderson and me both hit the exacta, making this the first day all of us won the same race, and boosting us collectively into the black. My profit left me down $32 for the year. Henderson's payday put him up $18.

Nipper wasn't about to get into the pipedream of advising people how to run their lives, but this three-way payday did confirm something he confessed he had been thinking about, ever since our weekend away from the track: we were all parts of the same whole. He knew we weren't supposed to think that way. The Course said each of us had to think of the others as autonomous heteronymous beings, but maybe The Course was just testing us, deliberately misleading us to rave like entrepreneurs when the most productive way for us to act was to work together as a collective.

Nipper wanted to develop this theory, but there was a problem. We were walking out the door, and the time we were all together was quickly coming to an end. If he was going to keep on developing his theory for us, he was going to have to propose something for all of us to do. To do that, he realized, he would be putting himself in a position to buy a round of beers or even a round of beers and pizza. He was the one who was most ahead, even if only weeks ago he and we had been way behind. In one more week, we could be in the hole again, and he, of all people, had no right to play the big shot. We knew that. And so we, of all people, made up from aspects of cheapskate hysteria, didn't expect him to invite us out for squat.

While Nipper processed this rationalization, Henderson had time to hop on his scooter and scoot.

"First round's on me."

The voice of James Bond slipped his arm around my waist and kissed me on the neck.

Henderson Will by Kelly Lane

Systematic minds missed thematic signs, whereas air has ways haze weighs. Automatic notions taught a manic showman's brag of tics bag of tricks. While he knew better than to abdicate control, bile he knew wetter. And to tab trick aide on cold dunking cunning of lumbers unknown numbers alone was a blunder. Plus, a wonder tit hook it took to start a cult. The defying card at the stultifying sucker's jamming monte deck was a mucker's damning jaunty trek. That is at this, a certain enticement at this terse, thin at mice scent hoard of soap sort of hope you knew to do due to you: work the angles, irk the wangles.

For one or fun, he'd pre-depict your deed predictor pout tics tout picks. To meet the lasses and lead the masses, what better than a shuck? Shut wetter than a buck, Will's tip shop shills whip tops call the bay to the wank all of the way to the bank.

Latch key finds of catchy lines for each horse would whore each force:

> Can do a damn coup.
> The speed to catch the key dispatch.
> Will run down the speed till spun round the deed.
> Hucker source sucker horse.
> Few tack glories? Glue factories.

Kelly Lane by Henderson Will

She knew I wasn't about to start a tip sheet, and Nipper wasn't going to write a book, but there had to be some need to make her have us contemplate those possibilities, just as there had to have been some desire to make her make Nipper kiss her. Could she have made him kiss her—and, granted, it wasn't a sloppy plunge, but a friendly smack and a squeeze which, nonetheless, was hardly ambiguous—just because it was in his character? After so many weeks of riding together, playing together, drinking together, wasn't this something that she would have to have him do, whether she liked it or not, because he was bound to do it?

After she inspired Nipper and me to start cults, write books, devise systems, and formulate conclusions about the true nature of what we were supposed to be doing, Kelly Lane had to wonder if the whole scheme didn't come down to her own search for the fulfillment of desire. What did Kelly want? If she knew, would she have taken The Course? Was The Course to help her discover what she wanted by forcing her to ignore what she wanted or to reconfigure what she wanted by manipulating these heteronyms? Desire was hysteria, an aspect yet to be discovered.

What Kelly wanted: she had wanted to win the last race, and she did win; she had wanted all of us to cash in, and that also came to be; and now she wanted a beer, so she parked and went with Nipper into The Prop. So far so good. Kelly Lane was getting what she wanted. The Course was working. We were all getting what we wanted, and we knew what we wanted was what we were getting. Nipper and she had won and then stopped at a winner. They had a round of beers. They would have another. She guessed they would, but, as The Course instructed, take it point by point. Point by point, Kelly Lane was satisfied that she was getting what she wanted, but what did she want beyond that?

If she went home with Nipper, there would be consequences, and these consequences would be there to be dealt with by her and him and even me. If she didn't go home with Nipper, there would also be consequences, as one act must follow another, even if said act were essentially a failure to act.

She liked Nipper, but did she like him well enough to want to go home with him? She wasn't sure. She was sure he would kiss her again, and each time he touched her, he would be feeling her out—feeling her up, before long—and it was up to her to set limits, or not.

She could shy away. She could say something. She could go for it or just let it go on and on and on to wherever it went. After all, she was an attractive woman in her late thirties/early forties, living alone in a hip neighborhood of a "most livable" West Coast city, between jobs, beyond careers, away from all she had known and toward a future of days at cafes, nights at bars, plays, movies, restaurants, concerts, parties for a while until she moved on, loitering, to die. What the hell.

She sat opposite Nipper where they always sat, drinking the same pale ale.

"You said we could be parts of the same whole. If our bets compliment each other, how is that different from being one person?"

Cal Nipper by Henderson Will

"Maybe it's all attitude. If you think you're thinking as I would think when you think for me, then you think for me and not for yourself. When you thought I would play to win instead of playing exactas, you made me play to win. And I made you play exactas."

Nipper tried to sound sure of himself. What was he going to do with her? Shouldn't she have responded more? She had kissed back, hadn't she? Or nudged back, but not as much as he hoped she would. She might have done more if he hadn't jumped her in the parking lot while people poured out of the gates. She was classy. Making out in the parking lot of Emerald Downs after the feature race, to put on a show for the hordes of losers plodding to their cars? Not Kelly Lane.

What about him? Would he have pressed for more if she'd given more of a response? How much more? He knew he wasn't in her class. A starter allowance for nags who had been put up for a $3,200 tag, that's the company he might have kept, when he wasn't racing at the $6,250 to $8,000 level. She had to be a few notches higher. Not so high that she couldn't drop into a field of the likes of him for a quick score. She had responded, and they were enjoying each other, drinking beer, but then he had another thought.

"This business of hysteria. I wonder. We took The Course and things are fine. We went in thinking The Course was set up to make things better, but suppose it wasn't."

"Wasn't what?"

"Wasn't what we thought it was. I thought it was supposed to make us winners, so each of us could deal with life on better terms. What if it wasn't?"

"You're saying it was set up to make us lose? Henderson is just making you think that. Don't you see?"

"Maybe. But don't you think that's possible? The Course didn't care if we won or lost. It was there to take our money—not to make us feel more well-adjusted. More like it was set up to drive us crazy."

"Like you said, it's all attitude."

Nipper was crazy about her. He had the perfect moment to say so, but she got up to go to the can. Better, though, that he didn't say so now. Now he had to relax, to regroup, to think about Kelly in terms of what Kelly wanted, to think as she would think. Or feel or whatever.

Kelly Lane by Cal Nipper

It had been a while since she felt this way. How long? What way? How was she supposed to feel, as she caught sight of herself in the stainless steel towel dispenser of a mirror in the ladies room at The Prop at the end of a day in the middle of August? Like a winner. To the winner went the spoils. Second prize, two weeks in Philadelphia. Fine. In the disinfected sunset air as she washed her hands and watched herself, Kelly Lane felt relieved. Not so much to have won as not to have lost, she felt relieved, and as she realized this she realized that this wasn't what she should have felt. This was how I made her feel. It was more like me than her to feel relief at not losing rather than pure joy at winning.

Then she realized she had spent too much time in the ladies room at The Prop. Not that she was in the way.

The only other woman here was the bartender. If they thought about it, they would only think she was shooting up. No. She didn't think they would think that, but that's what they would say, to seem hip to the possibility that a person could do such a thing when a person spent too much time in the rest room of a bar. If they thought she was shooting up, they also would have thought they didn't want to have a junky shooting up while locked in the rest room until somebody broke the door down and called the paramedics before the overdose killed her.

But she didn't care what they thought; she cared what I might think. She knew I thought she had something of a past, a past she had put so far behind herself that it was not to be mentioned, except via rumor and innuendo that couldn't help but break out like a rash of a latent disease in too long of a stretch of time spent in the ladies room of a bar.

She opened the door and nobody noticed. She saw I was looking out the window and then wondered if subconsciously she hadn't devised this little rest room episode as a test. What would I say when she came back late? What I said might reveal what I thought, she felt, which she thought might reveal how I felt about her and all that.

Not how I felt about her, because it was obvious to her that I was crazy about her, but how I felt about her and this past she was supposed to have had. Having dwelt in the gate of The Prop ladies room, would she set off an inquiry?

When I said nothing about her being away so long, she wondered if I was being considerate or self-absorbed.

As for the rumor and innuendo of this something of a past she was supposed to have had, she supposed she would have to say something about all that to me some day, even if I said it was O.K. because it was none of my business. She knew, though, that I might have thought I knew her from somewhere, whether or not we had ever met. If this thing we were going through ever led to that thing we were aiming toward, it might have been better for her to say something about what she had been through rather than let me file it away forever in the imagination, even if what she said was a lie. Wasn't all memory a lie?

Kelly Lane by Cal Nipper

"What were we talking about? I forget."

"Memory is fiction."

"Something like that."

"Let's do something crazy. Let's get a pizza."

She laughed as she was supposed to laugh. She knew we weren't crazy any more than we were capable of being driven crazy by The Course. Some people had real problems, and the problems we had weren't even remotely real. We could drink and eat, go home with or without each other, show up for the next day at the live workout. At the end of the season, we could count ourselves out of the running, tally it up, and move on. She felt good about that because, hey, she had been through a thing or two, and so, sure, here she was now, over the memory of all that. She also was getting sick of throwing around this careless notion of "crazy" that trivialized and romanticized and therefore dismissed some very real personal problems each of us had more than a little share of and some of us had up the yin-yang.

Up the yin-yang?

We walked a few doors up the block to the pizza joint, with her taking my arm in a wrestling hold of an escort grip, like we were going to fight or dine. Trains softly smashed their way along beside us, freeway traffic hummed above. The sky rose whiter than stars inside the yellow glow of the warehouse security lights, and the breeze from the north of the chemical waste dump held the breeze from the south of the animal rendering plant to a standstill.

"If we're aspects of Henderson's mania, maybe he's our psychic toxic waste dump."

"But we made him what he is."

"We dumped the worst of us into him, so we wouldn't have to deal with it."

"Thought for food."

Kelly Lane by Cal Nipper

She wanted wine instead of beer, but they had better beer here than The Prop had and worse wine than she had seen in clubs that took pride in serving rotgut, so she had a gin and tonic because it was idiot-proof. She really wanted a margarita. I ordered one, and we shared.

We ordered one slice of each pie and shared them, too: gorgonzola and walnuts, pepperoni and onions, sausage and peppers, arugula and tomatoes. The music was what she would have expected: rockabilly and punk, lounge and western, soul and reggae, electronic and hip-hop. The windows were so wide open, we could sit inside and feel outside. We watched people play pool badly. It was like watching ourselves play, and so saved us the trouble of doing that, too. Did it matter how pairs formed, things coupled, or one went with another? What were the consequences of the sequences of finding herself subject to my account of what happened to be going through her mind as we sat at a table together in what was our first date?

She looked around at the others who shared slices, swapped drinks, and scratched shots. They looked happy, carefree. They looked like they were dating, even if they were in a lopsided group of five. The girls wore tank tops baring firm, tanned midriffs, and the boys flopped about in Hawaiian shirts open halfway down the chest. One girl's plaid pants could have been made from one of my sport coats, Kelly said, as she looked from it to me. Should it have made any difference to her that they were all younger than we were? We were older than everyone at The Prop, too. Where were the people our age? The people with something of a past. At home watching TV? Portland? Who cares, she thought, I'm on a date?

She didn't want to think about the idea of being on a date as funny, because the part of it being funny was the part of it that went with being with me. Even though she knew as she thought this that I knew what she was thinking, she didn't want to come out and say it was funny to be on a date with me. Being on a date with me wasn't funny; the idea of being on a date with me was, because, not to put too blunt a point on it, what the hell was I? I was an aspect who happened to be recording everything she thought. And then suddenly none of this was very funny at all, because, well, do we have a choice? Are we not all subject to the aspects within us, so that every single moment of our lives, like it or not, we are, in effect, going on dates with them?

Whoa. Kelly Lane got up to go to the rest room. This time she wouldn't dawdle.

Cal Nipper by Kelly Lane

Cal Nipper didn't want to think about frequency and order, not now, but what could he do? There were only so many opportunities each of us had to tell of one or the other of us, and it was on these occasions each of us not only developed who the others of us were, but also developed what happened between and among us. So although Nipper felt good for not getting ahead of himself, for not rushing the sequence of events when he had three whole occasions in a row to make what he would of me, he also wondered whether he hadn't blown his chance.

This was the second run through the sequence. Whether the sequence derived from post position surveys or some other pattern, he suspected that the frequency and order of each of our accounts in the second run was similar to if not identical to the frequency and order in the first run. It was rare, he knew, to have three occasions in a row to have his say with me. Was it also theoretically possible for him to check the sequence to see whose turn it was to say what came next? Sure, he could have relaxed and let things happen as they would, but he didn't want to have come this far with me only to have to wait while some other bit of business took place.

What he really wanted was for Henderson to take over. Henderson had been treating us fairly well, especially when you considered the mental obstacle course each of us put him through, and Nipper had been hoping for someone else to take us from here. Someone other than himself, but me? Shouldn't the gentleman lead? At least it wasn't time for him or me to deal with Henderson.

So here we were, at the end of our stay at the pizza joint, with me coming out of the restroom and him picking up the check. Picking up the check made Nipper feel like a real sport, but then he realized who gave him that idea. Rather than leave his usual fifteen percent, he rounded up to twenty.

"So, do you think we should see whose turn is next?"

"Even if we could, just because it happened one way once, doesn't mean it will happen the same way again."

"If it doesn't matter, what's the harm in looking?"

"Maybe none. Maybe the harm is in thinking that it might matter to know in advance, or that the pattern of the sequence makes any difference in the end."

In the meantime, we weren't walking to the car. We could have just been walking in the warm night across the tracks by the empty soccer field, but Nipper knew we were going to his house, and he felt that this was fine with me. Then he thought I might worry about the car.

"It's O.K. I left it unlocked with the window open. Nobody will break in."

He smiled like he finally got it, and kissed me like he meant it.

Kelly Lane

What do you want? A blow-by-blow account of the frequency and order? Kiss and tell? That's not Kelly Lane.

That I should be seen walking in Georgetown on my way back to the car on a Monday morning in the same clothes I had on yesterday—what of it? Anyway, the question wasn't what then, but what now?

What went on can't help but influence what comes next. Consider the scenarios: we become a couple, and this leads to some exclusion of Henderson, which knocks the betting scheme off-kilter; we had great fun but it was just one of those things, so we can still hang out together but we agree to stop at a winner; he loved it and I didn't, and he spends the next several days chasing me until I finally lay down the law; I loved it and he didn't, and I... not likely; we had a miserable time and we agree it was a mistake we won't repeat; we had a miserable time but he (or I? not likely) wants to try again and again and again until we get it right; we were (or one of us was) too drunk to make sense of any of what when on. Whatever odds you make for any of these outcomes, what we did will be reflected by how we do, on and off the track.

Then there's this: in nearly every remark here I have been, say, less than wildly enthusiastic in conveying the wonderfulness of one Cal Nipper. It's one thing to be friends with a guy you think of as I have thought of Nipper, one thing to hang out with him over beers, but quite another to start something with him. Except maybe we didn't start anything. Maybe we just got it over with, and now finally we can get on with whatever it is we're doing.

Some say that's how all dates should be, especially first dates: get it on and then get on with the rest of your life, so there's none of that tension hanging over you, as if anything's wrong with that tension. If I know my Nipper, though, he is far from over the tension or anxiety or mystery or whatever combination of feelings you get when you get laid. Are men more inclined to be romantic, or is romance a function of lack of experience?

Then, why Nipper and not Henderson? Or, if Nipper, then Henderson? Please. Kelly Lane's tips for girls: get out with a plan. I told Nipper I had business to take care of, that I'd call when I could.

Henderson Will by Cal Nipper

Rest the like of us, Henderson Will tracked the miss. The weekend next the *Form Racing* arrived to fail from the Coast East in the races for time. So us of none traveled to bother to the races of day, rather waiting to choose until the week following, when the race biggest of the season racing, the Mile Longacres, drew miles from around crowds.

In the time mean, did Will ordinary out of the nothing. To bar the hits, to pick a make-up there and here, to out hang with the vagrant rubbers in the lot parking next to the hospital veterans—else how one should time one's pass?

There then was bowling lawn, at the Park Jefferson Club Bowling Lawn. Membering as a pose prospective, went Will day every other to bowl rolls on the pitches green, where after hour after, worse seemed to get him better than rather. Less the none, it timed to help the pass and, hill on a high, the club bowling a view commanding had of around all.

Wards after, walked he Hill Beacon around, down maybe to the Valley Rainier for a wagon taco and up back the ravine through Boulevard Cheasty on, heading to before some dive neighborhood where might he night his spend board shuffle playing, on those games of one rules whose based were on the principle same as bowling lawn in rules, the game of the object being to turn takes to bowl or puck your put target to the closest, target the be a "jack" ball or the court of the end. At game this, too, Will wasn't player of a much.

All after, should he win to like when no line was on the money? Yet and, he only could long so go nothing for playing. He backed to get had at the track race, where all mattered to seem.

Cal Nipper by Henderson Will

Try as he did to come up with something else to do in the days before he saw her again, all Nipper could do was think of Kelly. She had called him a few days before this Sunday when she was to pick him up, and he asked if she wanted to get together. She said she couldn't. Couldn't or didn't, he wanted to know, but couldn't and didn't ask. He rode his bike, thinking up other hobbies he couldn't or didn't or wouldn't do, like lawn bowling, and foisted them on me. At least I got to eat at the taco wagons on Rainier.

When she pulled up, Nipper felt like a fashion model on the runway. Days he had been wondering what to wear, how to walk, what to say, and just how he would kiss her when she came for him, as it were. Sorry. I would really rather spare you, but the memory of all that, too, is what Nipper couldn't stop thinking of as he replayed the scenes of their big night, and so, although he had felt not especially confident in the days that followed, he had felt more or less good and, yes, I'm afraid the truth is, he had felt confident, until the days passed without a call, and he called her and left a message, and she finally called him back and said she couldn't see him until Sunday.

What to wear? To dress for success, Nipper thought he should go casual, nonchalant, breezy, but dark, mysterious, edgy. He would wear the black Hawaiian. Trouble in paradise? No, not the black one; the blue Hawaiian was better, except the flower parts were so blatant, even strangers had said it looked like a shirt full of penises. Madras? No, Mexican. He had a pure, white short-sleeve

Mexican dress shirt with ornate patterns in cotton. This would show that he thought to dress up for her.

The walk would be breezy, casual, calm. Unless she came to the door. What if, now finally, she wouldn't pull up and toot or pull up and wait, but pull up and jump out before he might even have the chance to emerge—pull up to rush the door and pound her way in to—he should pause. Casual, cool, collected, he would wait when she pulled up, to give her a chance to throw herself at him or, no, make the kind of gesture a woman makes when... then, when she didn't rush the house, he would come casually fumbling out, *Form* under the arm, keys dangling, maybe smile and hold the wave. And, after locking the door, he would stroll to the car, slide in, and, as he put one hand on her neck and one on her thigh, he would kiss her just like that.

There. That wasn't so difficult. And then they would talk about silly little things that occurred to them over the last few days, the things you do when you do the laundry or shopping, the people you might run into, the movies you might have seen. Maybe he'd even tell her about that awful game when every infielder made an error in one inning. Oh those Braves were a riot!

No, not the Braves. He would think about what she wanted to discuss and talk about that, but he wouldn't be obsequious. Casual, cool, collected—not overly solicitous, let alone uxorious, Cal Nipper would finally be here, at the track, dressed for success with Kelly Lane at his side, trying but somehow failing to look like a man who wasn't trying too hard.

Cal Nipper by Kelly Lane

Nipper tried hard to think of the races. He knew he had to relax. I had told him he looked nice, I had kissed him right back, I had looked at him as he looked at me (well, maybe not in the same way, but for the same amount of time), and now he had to get down to business. He knew that, but he kept pointing at my *Form*, leaning over so his head grazed my hair, as if it were no big deal to be this close to me here, under the monitors, closer than he used to get when we talked about the next race.

We had reminded each other that this was another one of those occasions where you had to watch for a coup. With a crowd full of tourists on Mile Day, some trainers were apt to sneak one in.

A big favorite won the first, but in the second, a cheap maiden mile, a longshot coming off a sprint wired the field. Neither of us had either race, although Nipper was wary of the jockey switch on the winner in the second, and of the weak field. You could do worse than take a flyer on that longshot, he'd said, but had played his usual sort of horse.

He had to loosen up, but kept thinking about what came later, in the Longacres Mile. He liked a scenario in the Mile and, ignoring The Course, said he wouldn't mind waiting to make a play on that race with his final maximum wager. I told him he should concentrate on the next race, but he kept dreaming up Mile upset scenarios. Did he really think Handy and Bold would steal the race at 14-to-1? Did he really think Alfurune would get up in time from as far back as he would be? There were some tantalizing exacta possibilities, I said, but how could he throw out Sky Jack?

"I know. I mean, I think I see a way."

Kelly Lane by Cal Nipper

She knew what she was doing. She had a clear idea of what she needed to do to get what she wanted, and the kinds of horses she needed to play. The speed of the speed. Even in the Mile, she shot down my scenario of Handy and Bold dueling Sky Jack out of the race so Alfurune could sneak in. Sky Jack was the speed of the speed, and Handy and Bold was old.

In the first, her Cigi got hooked on the lead. In the second, her Sleeve Target, out of the one-hole in a flat mile, backed out of a duel with Prince Stately, who took the gift of that lead to the wire. In the third, her North of Rio, clearly the speed of the speed, was going off at near 7–1 in a $10,000 nonwinners-of-two claimer for fillies going six furlongs.

"Am I missing something?"

"Maybe they think she'll fade at the half."

She didn't have to ask what I thought. She knew I'd take KD Implosion, off of the usual gamut of indicators. Nothing against KD: the filly had made money for her a while back. Still, I liked how she had asked what I thought.

Kelly Lane went to the window, got about 8–1 for her $60, and watched North of Rio stalk the cheap speed to the half and then run on with her to a $410 payday, putting her up $378 for the year.

"Thanks, boys. Nice boost."

She pecked me on the cheek.

Henderson Will by Cal Nipper

In that race same where Kelly pot jacked the hit, also might have Henderson Will timed the hit big, only if had he played his usual make. Stead in, he hit to try an entry coupled. The duo this one entry coupled was, was as the favorite off-going, so and Henderson played simply the nose on. $62 down he was, with the $80 of loss.

Worse even, one entry of his horse second finished duly, with horses of the neither taking what it had to top on finish in the pace of the heat Kelly's horse forced by. The loss that the fact inevitable made him to play to continue the Mile Longacres off him pissed, but better far was it that Kelly raced the take.

"Time any us of one score can that like, better the so much."

With Kelly together, the them of two down sat to see over my play getaway on the Mile Longacres. As a bonus added, this year of the race would be TV on broadcast, live either or in run-re, so us of all could bar it from a watch stool, hand in one beer, another in the shot.

"Case in any, potjack Kelly's is celebrate to reason."

Henderson tried to want a pub in City Columbia, Avenue Rainier down from the wagons taco.

"Place the know? There you race."

Legging one swing the over of his seat and helmeting his strap-on, went off Henderson Will before us of either had a reply to chance.

Cal Nipper by Kelly Lane

"I have a good feeling about this. Sky Jack can beat me. I'm O.K. with that. I'd rather lose that way than by counting on Sky Jack to win at 2–1. In that company, nearly half the field has a shot. Poker Brad or the invader from Canada. Handy and Bold."

"Sky Jack can go as fast as he has to."

"You'd have taken him on top? The exactas will pay nothing, unless a longshot gets second."

"You know what I'd have done as much as I do."

"Handy and Bold."

"Not this year. Without Sky Jack, maybe. A few years back, even with Sky Jack. Not now. And at this level? Never again."

We took the valley freeway to Renton and drove along the lake. Nipper said it would be fun to hang out at a different bar, and with Henderson, but the wrinkle in the routine bothered him. Getaway plays were for reading about in the paper the next day—not for watching on TV.

"I thought you had a good feeling about this."

"About the bet, sure. It's just the TV. Remember when the Longacres replay show was on? I usually missed it, but one night, it was the Fourth of July, at an apartment where you could go on the roof, and someone left the set on in the place, and when we came down after the fireworks, the replay show was just finishing, on the last race, a $4,000 claimer, full field of twelve—those were the days, huh?—and as they're coming down the stretch, there are just two horses in the picture, my horses, a 40–1 and a 30–1, neck and neck all the way to the wire. The exacta paid $800, but I only had it one way."

"Better not to have bet at all."

He didn't like what that made him think of, so I tried to explain.

"Do you think you'd be ahead overall if you boxed every throwaway exacta? What's $800? You go broke in no time if you try to cover every angle of every longshot you might like."

Henderson's scooter was in front when we arrived at the pub. Nipper took this for an omen. Given an easy lead on a 30-mile-per-hour pace, he was bound to beat us here, no matter how clear the freeway was. No algebra story problem in the world could change the reality of that, or give a closer like Alfurune any shot at beating Sky Jack in the Mile.

It only got worse from there. Nipper realized the beers came in extra-large, expensive imperial pints, and there was no happy hour. The walls had photos of other pubs, in Ireland, Scotland, and England. He dubbed it an Anywhere But Here theme park, to fit in a neighborhood whose older businesses were giving way to Sicilian trattorias and tequila bars.

The TV coverage added to Nipper's misery. The sportscasters acted like the Mile was the Derby, giving lavish profiles of the owners, trainers, and jocks of the contenders. They made it out to be Sky Jack's race to lose, and never once showed the odds.

Then it was over. The fractions told the story: 22.2, 44.4, 108.4, 133. Handy and Bold dropped out at the ¾ pole, Poker Brad picked up a distant second, and Alfurune managed to finish the race.

Nipper was down $108 for the year.

"Beers on me, fellows. It's the least I can do, after sending you out on a day like that."

Then Nipper decided this place wasn't so bad. It only bothered him that, misfit that he was, he belonged among the gentrifiers more than he did in the bar across the street, with the folks who had lived here forever. He could have been more at home among people who looked like they could have traveled to the pubs in the photos than back at The Prop, hanging out with a bunch of kids.

A guy his age, height, and weight walked in, wearing an Atlanta Braves cap. He took the remote with the assurance of a regular and switched the channel to the ballgame.

Kelly Lane by Henderson Will

She wondered what she was trying to do, dragging a Nipper doppelgänger into this pub and making him turn on the Braves game. She couldn't help thinking that this would spook Nipper, especially after her big win had carried the day for all of us. Was she trying to tell him something about what she thought of him and therefore, now, inevitably, of him and her? Take it easy, don't get serious, make a game of it.

Well into our second round of imperial pints, Kelly Lane knew the drill. She would be driving Nipper home. On the way, they would talk about where to go next. Maybe stop some place for dinner. And then?

She had no choice. She had to spend the night with him again. If she didn't, Nipper would get feelings of inadequacy that would infiltrate his consciousness as a horseplayer and undermine any confidence and usefulness he had, as an operative in her or my gambling mobs and as a deployer of each of us. She wanted him to succeed. She wanted him to win for her. She wanted to succeed and to win for him and herself. Did it follow that she wanted to go home with him? What Kelly wanted was more complicated. Perhaps she did, eventually, as in maybe not tonight but some time later, want to spend another night with Nipper, but she knew that she had to spend tonight with him, or risk sending him into a tailspin swoon. The fear of spooking him made this outing a fucking chore. But she couldn't admit it, not to him anyway.

I found myself in the position of having to play host. They had fallen quiet, with him taking more looks at the baseball game and her trying not to pay attention to this parallel universe Nipper she had conjured up.

In this real "pub" where we were surrounded by pictures of "real" pubs, I felt responsible because I had suggested this as a rendezvous. It was a place none of us knew from before. I apologized. She said no need to apologize. Where else could we have gone? This was a good place to go to get to where we would be going next.

She asked what I was up to tonight. I could have said that was up to her, but didn't want to embarrass her, because in the scheme of how we did what we did, it was up to her, and so it might occur to her that there were other places she could go that didn't necessarily stick her back in bed with Nipper, one of these places being, if she read me another way, in bed with me, which, at this point, she was sure she didn't want to do. Maybe later? She knew I could have said it was up to her what I did tonight, and she could have made me do damn near anything, and she was grateful that I hadn't blurted that out in front of Nipper. Addled or not in my scrambled way of processing the world, I wouldn't do that.

I said I didn't know what I would be doing, but for some reason I had been doing a lot of lawn bowling and tabletop shuffleboard playing lately, and, to tell her the truth, I was getting sick of those games because they were the kinds of pursuits that you learn just well enough to see that you would never be good enough to satisfy yourself with how you did. Like golf.

"Like handicapping, before we took The Course and became winners."

We toasted. She looked at Nipper and at the guy with the Braves cap. She looked at me and shrugged.

Henderson Will by Kelly Lane

He said, sea head, to take the ride to rake the tide of the waterfront. Fraught, our want of tough stew stuff to do, to beep us out of cars and keep us out of bars was wetting to kill was getting to Will.

Come sign the sad gent for some kind of adventure, a la French Foreign Legion wench lore and free gin. An hour before sunset fanned sour, a flame in a cash came in a flash in the mines of the lap lines of the map: to ride the border of the city. To abide this order of the writ, he at once set out.

At dunce sweat doubt, he took the lakely hook the take full of bard boulevard, zapped his din mark around Madison Park, through the Arboretum far roar bee thrum, over the broad ditch drawbridge to roar a lurch to Laurelhurst to the town berry boundary fake poor rest lark at Lake Forest Park. Then a toss crown runaround fat trick crosstown done around traffic rolling over potholed hills holing over hot poled rills juice suited pound to Puget Sound kiss bomb lob belated dim hit discombobulated him a bit, sighting all the ray into one riding all the way into the sun. Over the cliffs glow for the lifts descent to the sea then, he passed a marina in the gloaming masts up a glare arena in the moaning, took a shortcut, shook a court shut a loss the crocks across the locks, and landed land-ended in Discovery Park in pisscovering dark.

The night skyline of the city light high sign of the skit he starred in as he rode hard, and he stowed to coast the posts of the coast to post the coasts of the post by the sea-dirted deserted weird pun pimp warts Pier One Imports/Trader Vic's fate or tricks. The shoes dip crocks cavations of cruise ship docks swag vacations lit up like yuck food fuck you penitentiaries. The derelict abandoned customs gauntlets rarely decked the can gunned dust bums gauntlets, as he went by fishermen who were then always there on the bridge, sent by wish or when the brawl fazed wear on the midge.

Zesty waddled West Seattle loomed in the future. Fumed in the jewel lure, he was getting a bit bored betting bare it gored to seep keying keep seeing the lit sea hit up the city lit up. Yet pretty soon the city pruned itself from sight. Some fright, in the tape of a dive lake or a shed pale snipe shape of a live snake or dead tailpipe materialized at once. What leery dull eyes at months of riding at night taught him tiring at height gnawed him into making energy matter.

Aching men, orgy adder asp bitten Cleos, clasp spit in glee hosed rapture chapped your tined from mime to mime mind from time to time. Apt snout of it, he snapped out of it and motored on south and so toured on mouth, winging as he sent singing as he went songs of days gone by, gongs of bays gone dry. Back over the ridge, rack over the bridge, past the airfield, past the fair deal, slack bowler to the fake, back over to the lake, and then at last lend that as he went we sent him home to the been away go Winnebago, boot head to bed.

Henderson Will by Kelly Lane

But then what pends? If you're in a nut shell of a shut hell to start from, you fart, strum to a different drummer. True, a referent dumber than this could hardly be brought to bear here.

He bought brew. Tearing beer from the pick sack's sixpacks seephold of toys, he told the boys about the long night. And out the bong light turned boo curse all the tizzy burned to circle the city.

"Could the bounty we, would the county be...?"

"And the whole state stole, wait—the American frontier?"

"The carom undone freer."

"None can dent the continent."

"The earth's ethers? The soul stirs this hum, the solar system, the will key. May the Milky Way?"

"A few you nurse, the universe."

Gunning rout of ass running out of gas logistics toe gist licks that lickspittle spat thick.

An expedition on spec sedition sop rose to propose a more realistic ordeal mystic charlatans go for. Far shall lands goad dormouse men to flit duly to see them, then sit mootly to flee them. The rust of that ode dust of the road became gold in their eyes. The aim, bold in their guise, was to do a quorum all nest normal quest, something thumb sink easy and say, big. Seize the grand basic!

They'd go bar to bar like Bogart to guard the fleer rank of the rear flank of the hundred suckered drunkards of herd paratroopers, rare trap poopers sailing bout bailing out to the blue yonder you blonder, bluer eyed types, too, blur tide wipes on the hankies skank. He's no romantic of a road nomadic for the sake of the ride, but Will will go roar the fake of the side.

Better ends fed or fit veterans' benefits, but checks and all chuck beck and calls. These guys're hauling a higher calling.

Henderson Will by Cal Nipper

On the end of the brink of the season racing, opened Henderson Will the *Form Racing* for the weekend Day Labor of Saturday, also which was the Saturday last of August. A card Thursday resembled it.

Now why? Ever what next came, barring from hike to hike with the wounded walking Charlies timegood, or housing around the hang between the bowling lawn and the board shuffle games, anything was ready for him. For as the track at the business, he was he thought in position good—neither at the behind way nor the ahead way no return of point, but position in to all and for once top on finish.

So and, the card lousy didn't bother with him here. To Meadows Bay went he. There the race first was better here than, but horsed he a key that schemed into the figure of this race to the approach. For horses older sprint in a claimer open $6,250, he horsed a pick off coming race in the last trouble. The lightning that reasoning couldn't twice strike? Case in any, again once his horse key got up fucked by some race in the trouble, when the favorite big he out set to out throw tracked in its stops, up pulling front in of his key to exacta the hits. This chanced all ruins and, time one more, down he went, of the tune to $80 minus bat the off and $142 all over.

Deal big. He shouldered his shrugs. Lane and me he turned a take on.

Kelly Lane by Henderson Will

Did she think of us now more than she did of herself? Whether this was the herself we made from impressions cobbled together, or herself, the woman between two men, she couldn't deny that she stood apart from us while also hovering in the midst of us. More than Nipper and I, she should have wanted to downplay her role as the lone representative of her sex. Sex was beside the point, wasn't it?

She did not think it was necessarily a mistake to have started something with Nipper, but there was a pat quality about this arrangement that bored her. At first, this development in their relationship made it easier for her to deal with him. The stupid awkward tensions of what to say and when to move, and of what the slightest remark might mean, en route to some grope that could have been obviously ambiguous—all of that was over. They had moved on to what? Another way of dealing with each other?

He was losing. It was her job to get him to win. He (and I) took good care of Miss Kelly Lane. She had to reciprocate. In the oldest way imaginable, she had.

Was that all it was? Payback? Sure, she felt like going home with him some of the time. Some of the people, some of the time. It wasn't just for him—it was for her, too. And she liked having him over to her place every now and then. If every now and then wasn't as often as he would have liked, it wasn't an apology or an act of mercy. The moment she thought it was, it would be over.

It couldn't end now. Maybe later, after they were through the last few weeks of what felt, at this stage, like a very short run: twenty-some dates to establish the value of an idea. She knew she owed it to herself to do all she could for us while she could, but the closer she got to Nipper, she wondered whether she wasn't cheating him out of finding out for himself how to deal with this thing they had thrown themselves into. Before, it had taken too long; now, it was agonizingly easy. Agony? Kelly Lane did not do agony. It was not agony. Agony was just an expression, a bit of hyperbole. But then, ecstasy?

She didn't worry about me. For me, she figured, the odds were set up to let me win enough to keep from losing, in the few times we had remaining. Nipper was another thing.

She had put him on a schedule, like a trainer planning workouts: a pair of short gallops, a longer run breezing, a hard hand ride to a blow-out, then a few days off before the next race. He was no gelding. He was a man—or, not a man, exactly, but... an aspect of hysteria? Right. Fucking crazy it was.

But she felt good, she was winning. I was in position to win, and so was Nipper. So Nipper was her boyfriend. She'd had her share of them. Maybe none like him, but she knew how members of a couple had a way of sorting out what each wanted from the other, so any gap in experience usually eventually closed. And down the stretch they come.

Kelly Lane by Cal Nipper

She pulled up with her top down, feeling good, feeling ready, but feeling maybe a bit odd. Now that we were together more, she felt we had to be apart before we were together again on the day we went to the track. This made her wonder why we didn't just stay together the whole week, the way people do, but then it must have felt better not to do that. So fine, we would go about doing what we did apart, and it would feel better to be together when we were together.

What had made her feel odd was the way Labor Day set up the weekend's races. After a throwaway $20 bet on an unlikely double combo in a baby maiden claimer, she said we might have picked a better day than this for our day this week. We could have got together and decided to come out here Sunday, which seemed more like a Saturday, or Monday, which seemed like Sunday. Anything besides a Saturday version of Thursday. Since we had picked this day at the beginning of the weekend, it was understood she and I might go somewhere afterwards.

The coast? The mountains? Portland? Vancouver? Not that we had to drive. We could go by train. Now that I had been set up with a throwaway double of my own at Hastings, she remembered: it wasn't understood. If she and I won, we might take a break together. No pressure. It all came down to how we did. Simple as that.

Was that simple? Weren't we a couple? Maybe we couldn't be a regular couple, whatever that was. That would mess up the gambling mob scheme, even if The Course now suddenly seemed, more than anything, like a dating service. If each one made up two, there you were, the two of you at the mercy of one, even while each of you also had some influence on the other, in conjunction with what the odd man out might have you do.

She should have been paying more attention to the races. The first races had gone off up and down the coast, and within minutes we were all on to the next step.

Kelly Lane by Cal Nipper

Our losses didn't surprise her, and Henderson could have cashed in if his horse hadn't been mugged at the top of the stretch. So she only had me to advise. Advise, guide, influence, inspire, provoke. Whatever.

The second at Bay Meadows was a $40,000 allowance for three-year-olds going six furlongs, a far classier affair than any of the local heats today. We didn't have to cherry pick. This was just the next thing going.

She didn't want to rush me. We could have waited for the second or third at Emerald, or taken another look at Hastings. Was I sure I wanted to take this one? I said I was; I wasn't. I didn't know what I wanted from Bay Meadows.

She seemed to know that. She seemed to know exactly what I did want: to win and go home with her, pack our bags and head for the train station. She was wondering if you needed a passport to get into Canada, or if a birth certificate was still good enough when she should have kept her mind on the next race. Vancouver rather than Portland, but were the Beavers at home?

She didn't know where she was or where she was going. She had bets of her own to make, and here she was stranded between race simulcasts and weekend plans. At least she made her mind up not to drive. The coast was as unthinkable as coming back to the track. Why was that? Why did we limit ourselves to no more than one day at the races per week? We had skipped a week or two. We could make up dates by coming back this weekend.

Before she knew it, I was holding a $40 ticket for the second at Bay Meadows, on the usual solid contender at low odds. He ran well and lost, to a horse that went wire to wire. She might have touted me onto the speedster, but this was my kind of bet.

In the shuffle of bets and races, she realized she hadn't bet for herself. There was action all around the country she might have got in on. She could play and win and stop. The sooner we won, the sooner we left.

Did she not want to leave? Staying meant losing. And yet, she didn't feel pushed to get on with it. She liked Emerald Downs and the view of Mt. Rainier and the ambience of the track. She loved betting, but The Course had tapped a feeling she had been noticing in herself in recent seasons: this wasn't a place she wanted to be stuck at for more than a couple of hours. A full card of ten races took half a day. Even with other races beamed in from elsewhere, she would get bored. But for some reason, today she was in no hurry to get on with the day, the night, the weekend.

Was it something I said?

Kelly Lane by Henderson Will

It wasn't like Kelly to lose track of where she was, but there she was, looking at the fourth at Emerald and thinking that it was her third bet of the day, when she hadn't yet made her second.

Her problem was Nipper. She wanted him to win and be happy, for her own peace of mind as much as for anything she might have expected him to have expected of her. It was time to make her own bet, and while she and I slapped together a typical Nipper play, at least she could see for herself the kind of bet that was, for her, automatic. She didn't have to think about it. All she had to do was get Nipper to the window, but then it happened that she held not a $40 but a $60 bet on Hope You Dance, a likely pacesetter in a sprint for cheap fillies and mares.

She stood at the monitor under the grandstand where we usually watched the races, crossed her arms, and watched the odds fiddle around 4–1 until they closed at 3. Hope You Dance—hadn't she bet her before?—took the lead at once, settled down, and netted her $198 for the day, putting her up $576 for the season.

Nipper's horse also ran.

This put us in position to have Nipper either bet on the fly, so we could go and he could read the results tomorrow, or to sic him on the very next race. But Nipper couldn't wait. His weekend depended on it.

Kelly got to thinking about the awful significance of Nipper's final bet for all of us. If he won even a small exacta, it could put us up for such a lead, we might lose the rest of our bets through the remainder of the season, and still we could finish ahead. But here she realized she was thinking like a Nipper.

Kelly Lane by Henderson Will

She didn't want to go anywhere for the rest of the weekend, so leaving without knowing how Nipper's last play turned out became the perfect strategy. He would either have to call the results line or wait for the morning paper to see if they were both winners. They couldn't leave town without knowing.

She thought he seemed content not to take a trip, but now that they were a couple, courtship was over. He had no need to play the big spender, the international traveler, the professional dog handicapper. They might as well have been outfitted for matching shirts and neckerchiefs and signed up for square dance lessons, like many another middle-aged pair. Maybe they would do something wild tonight. Rent an R-rated video and grab take-out sushi, hang out by the tube, knocking back martinis for a bit of light head on the couch before slopping it off in the sack.

As she drove Nipper to the point of deciding on Georgetown or Capitol Hill, she dreaded the Sunday paper. She didn't want to be there when Nipper read the results. She didn't even like getting the Sunday paper: the news was written way in advance, the arts coverage wasn't worth the trouble of throwing away the ads, and the sports she didn't follow were reported upon as the major events of the day. Nipper had told her he didn't get the Sunday paper, that he just read the sports page at The Prop, but if they spent the night together, he would go out for the paper, and there it would be for them at breakfast. Couldn't they just go out for breakfast and look at someone else's paper? Stranded among the fresh-made couples in a world of Formica, drip coffee, corn syrup, and eggs. Christ.

That would be Georgetown Sunday. If she took him home with her, maybe they'd go continental—double latte and croissant. Then what? A stroll to nowhere that would end up at Bumbershoot, for which they might have sprung $40 for tickets at the gate to justify having not taken the train anywhere. But to endure the extravagance of having to wait in line, first just to get into the festival grounds and second just to be able to see any of the shows? No, they would not go to Bumbershoot.

She drove to her place, dangling the promise of a pub crawl. She'd said it without thinking, but it made methodical sense. They could eat along the way, and she could get rid of him easier.

Could she? Wouldn't it have been easier for her just to go home when she was ready than to throw him out when she wanted him to go? Now she had him for the night. In Georgetown, she might have finished him off on the couch and gone home. Who was she kidding?

Cal Nipper by Kelly Lane

Nipper stood in front of my mirror.

"Now, let's see if you're a winner."

He couldn't fool himself any more than he already had. He preened to be in my apartment on a Sunday morning, before we went to breakfast to a cafe, a hip cafe, a cafe so hip, they might not even have a Sunday paper. He would either have to buy one or poke around the tables of other places where we might have to go for more coffee, just so he could sneak a look at the results.

Meanwhile back in the mirror, Cal Nipper thought of himself as the kind of winner he had dreamed to be. Having spent the night in my apartment, he wore yesterday's clothes—a rumpled Mexican dress shirt that looked absolutely filthy, khaki chinos, sandals. He thought he looked rugged. He liked looking as old as he was, looking the part of a guy who had been around, going with a gal who had been around (but who didn't show it as much as he did). He was a guy who knew what to do. Spend a night bar hopping in the hip neighborhood of a West Coast city with me, go home with me, wake up with me, and now take me to breakfast. What a sport. What a life. It just doesn't get any better than this. Who says you can't have it all?

Then he remembered where those lines came from, from commercials for beers that were plain rotten or for beers that pandered to some mass-market estimation of an upscale niche. As he turned from the mirror, he saw that he was trapped in an adolescent fantasy of not just acquisition but conquest. He never had quite gotten over the self-aggrandizing sense of accomplishment at having become the boyfriend of a woman like me, whoever I was, since I was, after all, no more and no less than an aspect of his.

We went out into the cool heat of the morning. The humidity stirred the smells out of his shirt from the night before, of sweat and booze and smoke. Would it rain? What did he care? He wondered if the Braves were on today. He hadn't checked, because of the certainty of doing something with me, but now that we had had our night on the town, he knew he couldn't stay. We would have breakfast and walk around. He wouldn't expect me to drive him home, but I would, because I had to go somewhere—somewhere I wanted to go alone and so wouldn't say it was the West Seattle Farmers' Market, or he'd want to go, too. Shit, that did it. Now he knew. Now he would want to go, too. In order to go without him, I would have to drop him at his place and then rush up the hill to West Seattle and get done with my shopping before he made it up the hill on his bike. He wouldn't ask me to go with him, but if we were to meet at the market by chance after we had spent the night together...

We came to an internet cafe on Broadway that would definitely have a paper. Soon we would know.

We got our drinks and pastries and took a table by the window. It was early. No matter how late he went to bed, Nipper was an early riser. Not just with me, he claimed, proud of that, too, like every other man who ever poked you awake at dawn.

Here was breakfast and there, on a nearby table, was the paper, barely undone by the last person who went through it for who knows what piece of useless news. The sports page was intact. Nipper took it and looked at the stories about the Mariners and Seahawks. His getaway race had been the eighth, not the feature, so no headlines let him see how he did.

We sipped and nibbled. I couldn't rush what had to be a ritual. If he came to the results first, he would go through them methodically until the race he bet on appeared. Otherwise, he would go through all of the baseball box scores or anything else that he wanted to read, if it happened to be laid out before the racing page. I waited, he went on, page after page, and then I read it in his face.

Cal Nipper

It's all in the charts. Tavy's Plan shot out to set the fastest fractions of the meet, from 21 flat to 43 and change, led deep into the stretch only to get passed by two horses. I'm looking at another $200 drop, to put me at $308 under. I pass the paper to Kelly and say it's just as well we weren't there.

At least she's riding high, and Henderson is fine. I should feel better about us at this stage of the season, even if I'm one more bad day away from having to take a plunge to get my head above water. That's the point here, to get them to win, not to win yourself. If you don't win, it's their fault. Why do I feel like a loser?

Maybe the problem is, no matter how well they do, we still haven't settled much of anything. After wagering thousands, what good is it to be a few hundred to the good? It's only a trial run, sure. It's all anyone could expect from some self-help pitch in the form of a handicapping seminar. I figured it might work. It was worth a try. What was there to lose? And so here I am, almost a winner near the end.

Near the end. One step at a time. Maybe that's the problem. When it ends, it's over. Better to have bet and lost than never to have loved at all. Love? Her. It has to be her. Did she really pick a horse named Hope You Dance without flashing on the name? All in the Game, Billy White Shoes, Dance on a Table, and Hope You Dance: stablemates, all.

I don't want to lose her. I don't want to lose Henderson, either. We're a team. We're doing fine, even if I'm a weak link in the betting chain. Don't they see what the deal is? Each of us makes these bets as if our lives depend on it.

As if? Because!

You bet, you live; you pass, you die. Either that or what? Replay the season over and over in an endless cycle? So what if we're duplicating the frequency and order of the first half in the second? Is that all there is? The 2003 racing season at Emerald Downs, Auburn, Washington.

I want to tell her what she means to me. How can I do that without sounding like a loser? Is it selfish to want to live through another person? To want to win and to make a winner of her or winners of them? To keep doing what we have been doing? But I know, I made her out of my own insecurities, anxieties, whatnot. I know she knows what she means to me, and she means to put up with this for only so long. She has a life, she thinks. She thinks she has a life that means more than just holding hands, more than just one of those things, more than all or nothing at all, more than the memory of all that, more than just a season of playing the ponies at the local track, because she has interests! Because she goes to plays and movies, reads books and discusses them at cafes in a hip neighborhood of a most livable West Coast city. Because there's more to life than gambling.

Because? As if.

Kelly Lane by Henderson Will

All she wanted was to drop him off and go to the West Seattle Farmers' Market, but other feelings were getting the better of her. She thought she had been looking forward to the end of summer, the end of racing season, the end of our time together, so she might move on to, what, another course? Go back to school and learn how to get by in Spanish and then move to Baja and write creative nonfiction? She wanted to work, to contribute, to create, to get into another set of interests besides going to the track and the theater, cafes, and bars. She didn't worry about her age the way most people did. She looked younger than she was supposed to be. She felt younger, too, but as Nipper resigned himself to the ride home, she wondered where she was going and why she was going there.

When she dropped him, she didn't ask what he was doing. She headed for the First Avenue South Bridge and zoomed up the hill, speeding light to light to keep from being caught up in the untold story problem of Nipper's retired algebra teacher brain. Within ten minutes she would reach the market, and then she would have a leisurely twenty to thirty minutes to go through the basil, tomatoes, and frozen organic meats before Nipper, at his Lance Armstrong best, might come wheezing into view. She had all the time in the world, she thought, but then a sudden chill came over her: in this world of my devising, she had no time at all.

It so happened that a number of mishaps delayed her, such as the circumstance of not knowing where her destination was. Signs said where it was, but Kelly Lane didn't know West Seattle. Where was she? Delridge? Delridge went back to the West Seattle Bridge. She had to go up the hill to the left, maybe take, what, Henderson Street? They named a street after me, or was it the other way around? Never mind. She remembered Nipper telling her how some streets of West Seattle had been platted but never built, how he would spend days riding to where the map said these streets were, up the cliffs by traversing through ravines until he ran out of trail. Nipper knew West Seattle. He had been riding his bike up steeper and steeper hills, in quest of nonexistent roads, courtesy of quixotic cartographers and unhinged engineers.

She was lost. In a maze of cul-de-sacs, walled in by overgrowth a bicycle couldn't blast through, Kelly Lane took forever to find her way back to the main route along the top of the ridge. She should have just followed the signs back to downtown. She should have blown off the market and gotten on with her life, but there it was, brandishing its harvest in the sun.

She had to stop, whether she wanted to or not.

Cal Nipper by Henderson Will

Cal Nipper didn't know he was in a race that he couldn't help but lose for winning. He pumped his tires hard and oiled his chain with some discount hardware store goo that would make the drive train go smoothly today and destroy it within a few weeks. He wasn't going to change clothes, then thought of socks and underwear, and so he got together a load before he remembered the laundromat was closed. What laundromat? Wasn't it time he broke down and bought a washer? Dryers burned down houses, but a washer was just... not Nipper. Nipper would not buy anything new he could get a deal on used and would not buy anything secondhand that would just break, so he threw his socks and underwear in the bathtub with some soap and filled it with water, like he was living in a foreign country where the laundry service cost more than a week at a hotel.

Washing his clothes by hand and riding his bike to market, he might as well have been living in a foreign country.

He thought of taking the First South Bridge bike lane to loop around to the Duwammish trail, but he was curious to see how fast he could get to the top of West Seattle by the direct route. Within minutes, he was on Spokane Street headed for the bridge under the freeway. He cut back to reach the road that went up the hill past the steel mill to Avalon and then chugged the rest of the way to the market, in practically no time at all.

What was he doing here? He would never splurge for organic meat and flash-frozen seafood, he had enough Costco vegetables to keep him for months, and he didn't eat fruit. He had to buy something, though, or the trip would be a waste. Pickled peppers? Wild mushrooms? Nipper moved among the tables, discerning as any connoisseur. Kelly Lane should see him now.

Then he saw her. She was poking around the fringes of the makeshift arrangement of tables and pick-up truck tailgates, waylaid by berries and jams. She seemed in a hurry, but determined to find something in particular. He started to enjoy watching her like this, like watching the girl next door go about the ordinary business of living, but she wasn't the girl next door. She was his girlfriend. And the place she had been going to all along was where he had got it into his head to go, but for some reason, they hadn't come together. Was that the problem? Coming together. Not that. It was the part about not telling that bothered him, but why should they tell each other? Why shouldn't they each choose to do something on their own? Their own. Whose own was that?

He had two choices: stay hidden and slip away, or go right up to her and say hi. But there was a third choice: ignore her so she could decide what to do. She could see him, and take it from there. It had been her idea to come here in the first place, hadn't it? They were a long way from the track. Maybe they didn't belong here. Maybe it was better to pretend they weren't here, but then if he didn't say anything and went about what he was doing here, and she didn't say anything and went about what she came to do here, even though she would have to have seen him (unless he disappeared immediately, which he still could do), how would he feel to be seen and not greeted? What would that say about their relationship? Maybe she just wanted to be alone for the rest of the weekend, like he did, but he didn't want to be alone for the rest of the weekend. He wanted to go home with her tonight. Then why not go up to her? No. No way could he do that.

Be a man. Don't run. Just go through the bins of food. Let her see you and say hello. Or not. Go about your business as anyone would. If you meet, say hi, hug her. Let her decide. Don't run and hide. Stand tall. Shop like a man.

Kelly Lane by Henderson Will

If it wasn't Nipper in the zucchini! What a dope. Nobody had to buy zucchini this time of year. People threw it away. There he was, though. He probably even beat her out here. Probably even saw her. Poor boy, he must have had a Hollywood inspiration: meet cute in the cukes. How do you meet someone you already know? How well did she know him—better than she knew herself?

He had to have seen her. Why didn't he say something? He was waiting for her to say something. She could do that. It was only a funny coincidence. It didn't have to be an episode. Episode, as in vignette or breakdown? Now she had to say something, or Nipper would pitch a fit. Why did she have to be the one to talk? He could act like a fucking adult, come up to her and hug her hello. And then? No, she did not want to spend the rest of the day with him. It might be easier not to say hello, easier for both or each of them.

If they didn't say hello, neither had to mention it when they met next Sunday. For now, they could go on with the charade of picking fruit and greens. Eye contact, and it was over: you had to greet. After a decent interval of doing what each was supposed to be doing, they could go back to where each wanted to go, without saying anything, and next week they could be content to continue to say nothing about this day.

What if he came up to her and wanted to spend the rest of the weekend together? She liked to think that wasn't her problem. Nice try. Let's see: an aspect of the hysteria within her, who also happened to be the guy she was sleeping with, has decided not to talk to her when they cross paths by accident at a farmers' market right after they have parted for the weekend, because he wanted her to take the initiative to speak up if she wanted to spend more time with him, which is what he, the figment of her craziness, really wanted to do. Whose problem was it if it wasn't hers? Don't look at me!

Problems are solutions, she remembered from somewhere. Since she didn't want to spend the rest of Labor Day weekend with Cal Nipper, Kelly reckoned the best way to handle the situation was not to say anything. This would send a message to Cal that if each of them wanted different things from each other in this relationship, that they weren't entirely made for each other. Partly, of course; entirely, no. Maybe it was better he find out this way. If he could parse the contenders in a starter allowance for nonwinners-of-more-than-$3,200-since-June, he could figure this out. He would see that she simply wanted to do something else for now. It could mean just that. It could mean a lot more than that, which was to say, it could be the beginning of the end, so when the end did come, as it had to come, because the end always came, he and she would be ready.

So then, on the Sunday of Labor Day weekend, Kelly Lane and Cal Nipper each went through the motions of whatever it was they were supposed to be doing, among dozens of hundreds of real people who, for all they knew, were doing just the same.

Cal Nipper

The question should be, where are we going? Not, what are we going to do about each other? All of these worries about meeting and greeting are beside the point.

Granted, to flesh out these operatives, you need to give them things to do, send them to farmers' markets. You need to get involved with them outside of the confines of the track. But love?

Love is a mistake. Falling in love with an aspect of the hysteria within you is not a good idea, no matter what she looks like or how well you get along. Well? We don't get along very well, do we? If we did, she might have said something last Sunday. But that's not the question. The question is, where are we going? In the short run, the answer is the track. We are going to the track to do what we do with each other. Afterwards, we'll see. In the long run, though, the run that might go past the final day at the races this season, it's a question of a different color. Where are we going? To be or not to be?

When this is over, and it is going to be over soon, what are we going to do? They know as well as I do. I don't have to explain. I don't have to say that, by not saying a simple hello when you happen to see someone you know, you are choosing to be not to be, especially if you happen to be seeing that someone. So I don't have to explain. I can take it like a man. Death.

All I am saying is, we do have a choice. It doesn't have to just stop at the end of a season. We could go on to the next thing. Or consider: there is no choice. We are stuck with each other, no matter what. Go ahead and ignore me, but I am not going away. At the end of the season, whatever the next scheme turns out to be or not to be, there I'll be and we'll be there, forever together, making something of each other, whether we want to be alone for the rest of a weekend or not, messing each other up or helping each other out.

Kelly Lane

Is it selfish of me to feel good about winning while my guys are in the red? At the end of the run, my wins might offset their losses, so the only success we claim from this workout will be measured by the profits I made, thanks to them.

And yet, I am who I am: call me an aspect, but I do have ways of making choices that, like it or not, are paying off. One of these ways—and I can't believe Nipper hasn't mastered it yet—is I take things step by step. You're dealt the cards, you play them. You find yourself in this situation or that, you act. Maybe what you do has certain consequences you would rather not have to live with? You live with no regrets. The race is over. The race is on.

Ha! Now there's a tune I ought to plant in Nipper's brain. So what if I didn't fawn over him the morning after at the market? The race is on, and it looks like heartache, and the winner loses all.

No, don't drag him into that. What does it have to say about yourself when the guys you pick all turn out to be losers? It says a lot worse if you then dump on them for being losers. Don't dump on them. Pick them up. There was something about Nipper that made him who he is, something I liked and still like. I can work with that. He can come to the track and go through the *Form* and make a pick that'll make him a winner, no matter what song has him by the balls.

As for Henderson, maybe what makes me more confident about him is his playfulness. Losing doesn't bother him, either in the long run or in the thousands of tiny setbacks someone suffers in a month, week, or even a day. Intention is meaningless. You want to win. Who doesn't? You want to stare into the mirror and say, "You are a winner." Bully for you. For Henderson, wanting to win has nothing to do with winning. You win or you don't. You chant like a zombie, or you think like a player. He plays like nothing matters, but it does. If he wins, he plays again.

Henderson Will

What, me worry? I'm having the time of my life, the life of my time, the lime of time I've—well, all right. Consider what they have said about me: The Course took me the year before, so this season I set out to do everything wrong. Then why have I made up two perfectly legitimate players who follow the rules, while each of them has me thinking backwards?

When it comes to making up your heteronyms and setting them loose, I ask you, who has done the best job of fleshing out his players? Nipper, with his beer babe poster fantasies sprung to life, and his nature-of-freak executive from a fugitive gig? Lane, with her baseball fan retired math teacher, and her misted twine twisted mind notion shone in all its roar glee glory? Or I, who managed to make up not only a pair of quirky, even somewhat likeable characters, but a love story! Think of it as a made-for-TV movie trailer. Complicated lives get a little more complicated when Cal and Kelly spot each other cruising for meat at the market the morning after she dumped him at his place, and hilarity ensues.

Back to the game at hand, it's the first Sunday of September, the seventh. It's a little cooler, with wind out of the southwest and some pinpricks of rain, a slight turn in the weather that makes people wail about winter, even though there will no doubt be several weeks of hot, sunny afternoons well into October.

We have maybe two more times to come to the races this year. One more win, and Kelly will be ahead, no matter what she does later. I'm in good shape, and so is Nipper, whether he knows it or not.

Now, because of me, all he can think of is last Sunday, as Kelly pulls up and toots the horn. What does this have to say about their relationship? I'd get into that, but fortunately it's not my turn.

Cal Nipper by Kelly Lane

Nipper took his time to come to the door, to lock it and double-check it, and then to walk to the car. He let the drizzle pock-mark his *Form* as he pretended to study what could wait. A squeeze of the knee and a peck of the cheek, and we were off. Don't mention the market unless she does, he kept telling himself. Don't be upset if she doesn't. Keep your mind on the game.

He said he had an idea about the double, where the betting in each race stood to be dominated by an odds-on favorite. One had to lose and other had to win. Odds-on favorites won more than other favorites, but not enough to cover losses. His strategy would be to pick one to win and one to lose. Then it was simply a matter of pairing the one who would win with a likely winner of the other race in the double. I had him finagle the scenarios and pick a contender to knock off one or the other favorite, but this was really more of Henderson's line of work, finding the second-best horse and playing for miracles.

Sure enough, in the first race, Dawg Fan tanked at 3–5, and Nipper held a live $20 ticket to Persian Harmony, who opened at 4–5 and dropped from there. My flyer in the first got hooked and died, while Henderson held back for one of the later races. In the second, I took a pair of unlikely exactas by putting Persian Harmony on top of two longshots who might have picked up the pieces of what figured to be a blazing pace in a bottom level restricted claimer. Persian Harmony didn't belong there, if you looked at back class, and would probably leave the field behind at the half mile and walk to the wire, but if you considered the two-year lay-off and the front leg bandages, 3–5 was the price of dog food.

"Nothing like being alive in the double, hooked to a live one."

I was glad he no longer smoked cigars. I was also glad I hadn't bet against him, not because I thought the favorite would park, but because $40 seemed like a cheap investment in solidarity that would give him a boost.

His hope to close the deal on the double tore away from the gate and made the half in 44 and change, and Nipper was about to let himself try to remember what the payoff would be, when the bandaged animal broke stride, lugged out, and wobbled the rest of the way home.

He tried not to let it get to him. He skipped the third. A race popped up for me from Bay Meadows, a mile on the turf, where a solid contender breaking from the one-hole was going off at 4–1. Hazen was a horse Nipper should have played, but Nipper was too busy working on bets for Henderson and me to notice.

"There's one aspect of the hysteria of simulcast betting."

My $60 win ticket rode not at 4–1, but at half that price, with a late rush to the tote board as the smart money from casinos, tracks, and OTB joints all over America suddenly awoke to his massive underlay in San Mateo and surged to make it right. Hazen netted me $100 on the day, putting me up $676 for the year.

Nipper was proud of me, Henderson, too. But now the pressure was on to do something for Nipper, who seemed determined to ignore his own advice, as another even-money favorite threatened to run away in the fourth at Emerald. Rather than realize that sooner or later one of those chalk monsters was bound to win, he tried to beat it and lost.

It was obvious he had his sights set on the fifth, where a perfect set up for Henderson also offered a tidy Nipper play. The horse he had in mind was Aquaduck, who had just lost a race to the favorite, Superior Kris. Aquaduck had similar figures and a running style that fit the race well, but Nipper liked was the tandem factor, the tendency horses have to take turns beating each other in back-to-back races. Did the fact that this was an open claiming sprint for fillies and mares make him even more confident on the tandem play? He didn't have to say so. Last time it was Superior Kris; today it would be Aquaduck.

For Henderson, Aquaduck was a key horse to back-wheel in exactas, a solid runner who figured to finish no worse than second and, like most horses, usually lost. So Henderson played Aquaduck under the contenders, Nipper put $60 on the nose, and Aquaduck lost by a neck, to Superior Kris. The exacta paid Henderson $342 over expenses and put him up again for the year, at $220.

Nipper should have been happier at Henderson's win than frustrated by his own loss. It paid more than he would have won, and it gave both of his players a winning day. But he couldn't get over his losses. He should have made more bets, for himself, for Henderson.

No. Nipper had had enough. Down $120 the day, he stopped. He didn't want to fall lower than $428 under for the year.

Henderson Will by Kelly Lane

A pursed thirst in a first-person take-in made Will awaken as he weighed: We marry, "What, me worry?"

Mad's icon sensation adds to my concentration a look of bewilderment.

We built or bent a fop-writ profit from the grand seine of a sand grain in a ludic haul to lick all of the pomp canned shit in competition. Like a lipper's naps, Nipper's lapse of corps vetting forgetting to bet after failing fed after bailing. End in sight? Send in night. The buckled coupled pair of them there puff ahem, hedging and shedding.

For example or fix ample, they stopped me at a winner, staid opting at a thinner, count'em, outcome. Up $220 with two more days due, Torme's Mel-fit velvet melodies low medleys accompany me to bump any keen fear re: losing. By this leer refusing to have me lay a bet, they bay a let, as sinister pleas rate your tennis serve replays. There was no time remaining where thus though I'm, me, reigning. To coast, I'll enthuse. The most I can lose is $160, then finishing me at $60 up, diminishing the fat dixie cup that hunts swelled my drake of a stink that once held my stake of a drink.

Whoa Kelly, and ice her!

So Kelly and I were, as said for the ease in, ahead for the season. Now on to wake, whip, or render to make

Nipper a winner. No sinecure that, though insecure gnats fight the ban that heeds them to bite the hand that feeds them.

The again, can a then last-minute mass limit cake up moll of a make-up call close to pass all who pose to class? Bled from wrack, from red to black, could he tag us drowned, daft, or dim to drag us down with him?

Henderson Will by Kelly Lane

Looking ahead, hooking a lead pipe cinch of a wager wiped pinch of a sager way to deal. The day to wheel exotic bets hot tickets redeeming pawned hopes. He, deeming pond ropes a better metaphor to fetter a bet her fore Nipper's blast lunge last plunge into the deep side of the swimming hole, heaps wide of the dimming soul a lifeguard stand in a kife starred land.

Stinking like a sewn wound or sinking like a stone soon, oozing lends a losing end's self-fulfilling prophesy to a fell, lull-selling sophistry. Conservative fun tours a gift given with interest on a shone lark by a loanshark, but Will has come to figure what bill has come to give your principle stake, as in pistol brake, a brisk pull take. A quick hitter of a hick quitter bam kit gambit he sees for Nipper.

See, he's for Nipper.

As for me, he has more elliptical tip lick cull key show fake hints evocations of what to bet. But too wet a downpour of recommendations would pound or deck immense rations of tryst-mussed distrust.

What butter be walking a tout, but what are we talking about? Bliss hands his plans to the weighed often fate of wind. Not lucking fuck or fucking luck or any chortle dance sort of chance, but something predictable to predict trouble, like a core fast forecast of a fine tuned typhoon.

West of the reek of the rendering plant the rest of the week of the then-blurring rant of luck versus design, a duck serves us a line, zigzagging one way and quacking the other.

Henderson Will by Kelly Lane

How the year reduced to the roost of a vast culture cast vulture whose fur pew purview sun kissed dead consisted of some horse races! A rum source stasis made him philosophical. Kill a fossil full of a dinosaur night of sore REM, or ease memories by turning them inside out, earning them in snide tout rear spit spirit beamed to see seemed to be on tap for the night. A nap for the tight? Um, smother time some other time.

Nearing the last portion of summer searing the past lore shun of number hazy days in a lazy haze, Will read the maps southward and said the raps mouthward, on a low song lease addled a so long Seattle to toke a coda. Will would take his chances to shake his dances. A thick heist of brass could pay the price of gas. Fish for food, beg or buy beer, his traded hitchhiked rides for rated rich striked hides would speed down the Pacific coast.

A good deed wound the specific post around a finger and found a king for a load that read a way on a road that led away. After the races, raft, or the aces, after we stop following The Course staffed or we cop wallowing the force, after all fizz oh were daft or all is over, woo till wit ill, to Will it will be over, moan or low next, no more no less, under the dimply sun, done are the simply done.

Cal Nipper by Henderson Will

Without having to show his work in this little blue book of the personal math finals, Cal Nipper knew where he was and where we were, with respect to the opportunities remaining. Kelly and I had all we could do to save him.

Save him? He knew we were in this together, but part of him also knew there was an element of competition in the by-play, an element that could make one of us not only gloat over the misfortunes of the others, but also arrange it so that he, Nipper, suffered more than his share of setbacks, leaving him no choice but to project his response to defeat on his prospects for success when he tried to make something more of himself, especially as this projection drove him to make more of something happen between Kelly and him.

Thanks to them, I had no hope. My circumstances were hermetic, confined to this makeshift ring where a tag-team of verbal grapplers took turns slapping holds on me to put me through ludicrous contortions, but my hold on them told a different story. Lane could exist as if there were no past and future, but she also had to deal with Nipper, who was in thrall with the hope for what came next, and each of them knew that more might come of this scheme, this life, this ink land.

And Nipper, of all people (people!), was the worst one of us to be under by more than $400 with the end of the meet bearing down. He knew he had to play differently now. He had to play even more conservatively, to keep from ruining it for us, but he also had to play more recklessly, to go for the big win. He could win and come out a winner. He knew he could. He had done it before, he could do it again. He was—had been—a winner. But now he understood how everything he did mattered, and it was this awareness that made him more awkward than ever. Some might say he couldn't "be himself" because he couldn't "act naturally" or such nonsense. Nipper knew he couldn't help but be himself, no matter how he acted, and the truth was, he never had acted naturally in his life.

Take this thing with Kelly Lane. She had whipped through the day at the track like a pro, summing up the races, giving the results, sorting out the winners and losers, and setting us on the way to the next week, but here he was, along for the ride and still thinking of last week at the farmers' market. He couldn't say anything about that. Would she? She could have said something, about anything.

He pulled out early. He lost track of his bets and my bets and left without making a getaway play. She was the reason it had to go this way, but he was the numbers man. Could he blame her for sending them home early? The least he could do was not lose count of the bets. Had she forced him to stop so he wouldn't blow what they had won? It was her car and she was driving, they were going where she took them, and he could suggest, but she would decide. If she couldn't trust him to make a simple getaway play, if she was already so far into her endgame strategy that he wouldn't be allowed to play to win, let alone to play to keep from losing, maybe, in her mind, it was over.

Over. This thing between them, this live workout of a handicapping theory, this reverie of a life: over? Nipper didn't want it to end. Nipper had to do all he could to keep it from ending, to make it go on, somehow, anyhow. He could live in the moment, but he wanted to go on to the next moment and the one after that, even if it meant going back, moment-by-moment, through every single time they had ever spent together, living these lives over again: not over but over and over and over again.

Yes, Nipper wanted her and he wanted to go on, to live, to keep it going through her, through me, through it all, no matter how it ended, because it couldn't end, not like this, with the three of us just dissolving into nothing. The record was here, the results were official: the way we made our bets, the way we worked the scheme, the memory of all that, no, no, you can't take that away...

Henderson Will by Kelly Lane

From me? Mum free. Wary velvet, very well fit.

Gabbing the constrained patters, I'm bagging the pun-strained tatters. No more moan or mooner's piss hum Spoonerism booze kick of the Meerschaum sigh music of the years gone by for this grub for pay rent rubber vagrant. No pipe dream tripe beam of a won array of runaway tick foray victory for me.

As parasites pass air as sight-set goals and get souls pacified, facts descend as if by accident. Who could win or wink? Coo hood winner/wink whispers deny winning by skill.

Dispersed, we tie loose ends, skinning by will.

Why bill? Bye, Will.

Whose lens ever saw beating the races as the way to succeed? We sever awe weeding the basis. As they who tuck greed into their pants thin to pair rancid dares for stares with stares for dares, such codpiece pod geese were no less disingenuous. Low gests list in tenuous torpor, over a porter torpor a port or muscatel custom hell shares re: rare she sherry reshared, Dover end over.

Out of control trout of uncold miasmatic sulfur sprang spry asthmatic wooer sewer crooners, who soothe nerves in this swan song's on swung onslaught no salon ought to fete lest defy or let testify.

But was it fun? Fuzz but it won. Well, so far, fell woes are laid to rest. It's all show, but for the outing's all over but the shouting, or singing sore ringing, Henderson surrenders inner renders on the internalized in urinal dives the pole court or dance stirs Cole Porter standards, the teen marred din Dean Martin loon mitts our rye like a pig beats a high moon hits your eye like a big pizza pie where hazed doe fed in the stairways to heaven of middle-aged rock anthems, idyll raged mock anthems, and the sundry gongs of country songs no more well known nor well moaned than what looks behind what hooks bee-lined to the inner woozes' loll to the winner loses all.

Cal Nipper

There's that song again. The George Jones song, with the race call refrain. I'm going down fast, at the races and in my personal life, and all I think of is that song.

Personal life?

O.K. I'm doing O.K. My two operatives are there. Even Henderson. We'll get him back on his winner-at-a-stop plan next week. Kelly and I will start as usual.

We will win and we will stop. And then? We are in the moment. When the moment comes, we are there, and when it ends, we are in the next moment. It does no good to think of what I might do then, because I'm here now. This is all I know. I am in the car with Kelly, riding home. what happens next week follows what happens now—just follows, not depends on or stems from, just follows.

It does no good to replay the past. The past is printed in the result charts. Who won, who lost, what happened: it's all there.

As we near the end of this second run-through of the order and frequency, it must be there that I am here now alone, looking back at the project for what may be the last time, the last time for me or for either of them to deal not with each other, but with me and my take on what is going down. Going down with the ship in a captain's log to the bottom or in a black box of a jet to crash in flames, here it is.

Shouldn't we speed this up a bit? What's the hurry? You can't go back, you have no choice but to go on. Step by step, I can beat this game if they let me. I am a winner, I made them winners. They can't lose, and I must win. Two more days, a winning day in each, and it's winners all around.

Cal Can-do Nipper, winner at large. Cal Earlybird Nipper, daily double specialist. Cal Getaway Nipper, master of the last ditch.

I must do what I know and know what I do. I must apply myself to do what I can do.

Cal Can-do Nipper, at your service.

Kelly Lane by Henderson Will

Kelly was more concerned about what to do with Nipper than she was about how to handle her own affairs. But he was, apart from an aspect, one of her very own affairs.

We all went into this season with expectations, but mostly we went into it with a healthy new sense of curiosity. We wanted to see how it worked, and we discovered it could work. It might end up losing overall, depending on how Nipper composed himself, as it were, from here on, but that would have to do.

She should have said something to Nipper. She drove along the lake, taking it easy. She didn't want to go to that pub with the pictures of pubs on the walls, but they might eat at the Sicilian place in Columbia City, or at a taco wagon on the way back from there. She did not want to take him home with her. A drink and a meal, no more. She was not in love with this character, and that was good, but what bothered her was the feeling that he seemed to have developed intense feelings for her, so she had to deal with them: with them, the feelings, and with him, the aspect. Specter? Symptom?

Kelly Lane took one step at a time, but she had to plot how to avoid going home with Nipper, and how she might make it seem more natural not to go home with him. Here on Rainier Avenue, she thought of telling him what she wanted, to begin by telling him what she wanted to eat. She set Jackson Street as the limit. There were plenty of good, cheap Vietnamese spots on Jackson. Noodles. She said she had a yen for them. Noodles sounded fine to him, noodles and Chinese beer.

She felt his hand on her thigh, an affectionate, passionate, but weary hand, or a last ditch hope for what came next.

Cal Nipper by Kelly Lane

Cal Nipper couldn't help thinking that he missed his chance when he opened up the morning paper to find the track had been washed away the night before. Two weeks into September, with one week to go, and already the weather was shot. Trainers would be scratching their entries and hauling them south, and in the few races remaining, with fields even smaller than usual, anyone trying for a score to win back all that he had lost wasn't going to be looking at good odds on any proposition with a shot to win.

Rain was still in the air when I picked him up, but he wanted me to put the top down, promising to put it back up when we parked. He said the wind was good for his head. He looked like he needed it. He looked like he was coming down from a bender that began when I dropped him at his place the week before, after noodles and beer. He hadn't invited me in or called in the meantime. He wanted me to make a move, but I was losing him and he was losing me, as if he was out to prove that even a cheapskate of an early retirement algebra teacher, whose life beyond the track hangs on little more than the ups and downs of the Atlanta Braves, has his dignity, and you can't take that away from him.

Nipper sat rumpled and damp in the wind, in a seersucker sports jacket that hadn't seen the cleaners since it left the Goodwill store years ago. He claimed it was his lucky coat, sneering at the word lucky, with a double-edged sneer to knock luck while also knocking The Course for saying luck didn't matter. He was ready to take a chance on luck, although he knew this was the worst possible time to take chances.

He said it was like baseball, when you came to bat in a situation where your job was just to move the guy over from first to second, to give yourself up with a bunt, but instead, the manager gave you one swing. Just one. One chance for a hit, to fool the defense, to give you a break, especially if you were in a slump. Fool the defense, drive in a run, don't waste an out, get on base: win, win, win, win. But if you missed your chance, you were one strike down, behind in the count, closer to failure. Today, he said, he was going to swing. We were in scoring position. We were ready to come home. He knew what to do. Nipper was a team player.

The first step of his last swing was a five furlong maiden race at $8,000, won by an odds-on geezer whose record was littered with seconds and thirds—just the kind of maiden that needed a depleted field. He thought of taking the 3–5 shot in the double, but saw no value in the payoffs any contender in the second offered, and so went down swinging on a 5–1 also-ran.

Henderson Will by Cal Nipper

Toting the notice on the pool place for the race first, spotted Henderson Will a system in the crack. The favorite on-odds more paid to second finish than to race the win. Unheard of this wasn't, but unusual it was. Gamblers most in zeroed on the double dailies and exotic others, aside setting the bets straight, in especially the pools show and place. When the large were pools enough, no plunging minute last could out of the water bet the blows, so and, board the hit your horse providing, you gained to stand a payoff modest on a layunder.

So and in case this, Will flawed the spot in the line betting, and placed the pool hit tune the to of $60 on the on-odds horse sucker in the race first, to only see the wall on the writing in the tote last of the tick, as air into vanish thinned, him making a winner of nothing practically.

$10 up, Will flew a taker of an away throw on a Frisco race maiden, $40 burning, end to $30 day for the down, up leaving him $190 for the year whole.

Landing the survey of what to him was available, Will passed to decide the races of the day's rest. He wanted he said to bet on our works, though even our settled seemed to be minds, that so nothing could shape the change of come to things.

Were we who we were, did we what did we, and the action of pattern set was as it set. Patterning the follow, us of each would lose or win, and in the losses and wins of the amount it was that the result end would itself resolve.

Kelly Lane by Henderson Will

She had to admit it felt good not to think about losing, and that, no, she did not feel all that responsible for Nipper. She would play out the day, and then, who knows? Maybe she'd stop for the season.

She enjoyed being here, among the stragglers looking to change their luck while the horses of better trainers deserted their barns, and clusters of old maidens and nonwinners-of-two got slammed into the gate for however many races we'd be able to see before the next deluge washed the track away again.

She had thought of taking the bus, of calling Nipper to say the car broke down, and we'd meet here, but that would have left her no way to go home except by bus, and the ride back to town offered the gruesome possibility that Nipper would ride her all the way home in order to walk her to her door.

She couldn't beat the favorites in the double races, and so resigned herself to picking one more winner at odds high enough to recover her stake for the day. She didn't blame me for playing out my string from last week and stopping at a loser, but she did wonder why she, too, now thought of the season in the shape of a whole process, an arc or plot or sequence that leant itself to some meaning or theme rather than as an artificial construct of actual opportunities to win money, wherein the opportunities themselves constituted all that should have mattered to her or to any of us. Was it realistic or fatalistic rather than existential of her to be so aware of the end?

In the third, a cheap sprint won by a co-favorite, Kelly Lane returned to form. She went down on the speed of the speed, who got hooked on the front end by the eventual winner. So many of these races went this way or that. Win the duel, win the race; burn out early or come on late. Nipper was right there with her, picking the wrong contenders or the right contenders in the wrong exacta combos. He was doing what he did best, and it wasn't good enough. She couldn't hold his hand forever. She had her own race to win.

I told her not to worry about Nipper, that I would see that he got to the window, but no. She put off making her own last play for one more race, while she and I turned our attention to him. Pathetic. With our expert advice, she coaxed him to key on a running style play, choosing a closer to finish second to the speed (my money management plus her handicapping), and just missed. Then, rather than leave well enough alone and let Nipper be Nipper, she sent him plunging with his last $80 on the longshot in a field of five, a stalker who should have handled the pace, and who, like so many of his horses, showed enough promise in various attributes to be competitive, but who threatened to affirm a season-in-microcosm view of Nipper's fate. Bid and hung, the chart would say.

Catpasser finished last, putting Nipper $628 under for the year, which made her see she couldn't afford to go home without a win.

Kelly Lane by Cal Nipper

She claimed she would do it her way, but in the sixth the pick was so obvious, even Henderson would have had a hard time playing it to finish second. Firefall had speed on the rail in a mile, with steady improvement and sharp form. It was a walkover. Her $80 profit for the day put her up $756 for the year.

She wondered if she should sit out the final day, to make sure we didn't fall under for the season. How could I argue? Part of me wanted her to stop, and no part of me wanted to lose. But if the point was to play out the season to see how the scheme operated, she owed it to ourselves to play through to the end. To ourselves? She had the will to go on, the devil's advocate spirit of what-the-hell to see what she could see. She also had the urge to cut herself off from the rest of it. What does anyone owe to the aspects within her? Certainly she owed no explanations. Even if she had a feeling that by continuing to ignore how we felt about each other and acted toward each other, she was undoing all we had ever hoped to do. What did we ever hope to do? Lose ourselves and beat the races, to see if we could. Very well, she could. She decided to take us out for pizza.

Kelly Lane wanted to celebrate like a winner. She wanted all of us to celebrate because, here we were, coming to the wire. We were on the brink of a discovery. Next week, a victory lap, tonight a party. We would toast our success, her success as a player, mine as a mob boss, Henderson's as both.

The sky opened and dumped, flooding the surface to make them cancel the rest of the races again. Maybe next week there would be no track at all, but a lake over quicksand. She was thinking of the future. She had no choice but to wonder what she would do next, at the party, at the last day of the season, when it came time to decide what we really meant to each other and what to do with each other for good.

Did the big winner have the right to decide? Maybe it was her responsibility. Maybe it was her role to be the one to say hello and good-bye. Winner take all.

Cal Nipper by Kelly Lane

What more did they want? Pizza and beer on me. It had seemed like a good idea, but now, into our second pitcher, Nipper moped and Will dawdled through a celebration that felt like an obligation.

Nipper thought we shouldn't have ruled out discussing the races, but feared we might have been better off ending it like this. We could split with no illusions about what each of us would do with the others once we were done here. A trio of misfits we were, parading our collective pointlessness with all of the casual precision that tedium could muster. This had to occur to Nipper as it did to Will, but Nipper knew he wasn't Will, any more than he was me, and the part of me that was Nipper, like the part of Will that was Nipper and the part of any of us that made up the others, was a part sprung from hysteria. And so, no, he would not go gently into the good night. He was waiting, for a thank-you, an apology, a kiss. Cal Nipper would mope and fume and rale and hack, all pent up inside himself. We couldn't help but notice, because he didn't stop until we did notice.

He knew it was better not to cling to each other, but he didn't want it to end this way, any more than he wanted the Braves to crap out one more time in the postseason after they won yet another National League East "pennant." Give him some credit. He did know that what he wanted and what he could have were worlds apart from each other. That he had successfully managed a mob of two gamblers of disparate approaches to the game through an entire racing season, that he had once in his life managed to have a relationship with a woman? Some would take these feats as signs of life. He could live as a man through that. He had seen the future take shape in an outcome he had predicted. Sometimes, he got to win.

But he knew better than to hold out for a miracle to turn his life around. Wasn't it kinder to have him realize the fix he was in rather than to dangle some unrealistic expectation? Beat the races, yeah right. But doctor, doctor, but will I ever play the violin? That's funny, I never could before.

I might have tried harder. I might have done better for him, given him a bit more to hang onto, a quick, shy, morning-after hello at the farmers' market. What's the use! So we go back to that scene and what? Take the plunge of a roll in the hay of arugula, pawing each other all the way to my car to his house to our weekend of nonstop double-header action beneath the blue glow of the Braves? Better to have bet and lost, his motto for the season, was tattooed to his brow, as his balding noggin turned red and sweaty. Nothing could have been crueler than to give him hope, but I couldn't deny him hope, either. He did see me as more than what he might have seen me as, and it was as stupidly romantic to say he was beyond hope as it was to hoist him on a dream. He was no less human than the rest of us. He hoped, he loved, he needed, and he lost.

I ordered another pitcher. Will smiled. Nipper laughed. We had been hungry, and we ate too fast, and so we started to burp. Oh the good life, full of fun, seems to be the ideal. What more could he ask for?

Cal Nipper by Henderson Will

Cal Nipper was doomed to hear "The Race Is On" not only as a catchy melody with a clever lyric that underscored every move he made with what he could only hope was ironic counterpoint, but also as the dirge that came closer and closer to summing up his life as a player, and therefore as a man.

The other groups of drinkers and eaters and pool shooters were beginning to sneer at Nipper, with his pathological trips to the jukebox, his fitful fistfuls of quarters repeatedly investing heart and soul into D-8. We should have been well within our rights to stage an intervention. This character was, after all, sprung from within each of us. But this was a pizza joint, therefore there was a jukebox. Given a jukebox, there was that George Jones song, ready for the punching by any palooka drunk enough to take it for a personal anthem, celebrating himself and singing himself, and what he assumed, you shall assume.

Fortified by the hops-fueled logic of a peculiar determinism, Nipper felt free to think of himself as the equivalent of an odds-on favorite at a minor track, with all of the relative advantages of speed, stamina, and back class, who would take command at the top of the stretch as if nothing might have (yet something must have) stood between him and the winner's circle. Kelly and I had to get him out of there before somebody threw him out. If only we could pass him off as drunk. He wasn't drunk, he was way under the Nipper limit, but the combination of beer, pizza, Jones, jealousy, and losing swirled him into a draining vortex, so that what he had only thought of as a longshot now loomed as the dominant scenario before him, and whatever inside track advantage he ever might have had in this matter of a relationship between Kelly and him had been neutralized if not reversed by something as real as the line of a song, where someone else came up to win her, and he wound up in second place.

Maybe it was a virus, a bug, not the flu but some stomach ailment from the tension, like an ulcer. He would have to survive whatever it was on his own, as he had no job with health insurance. Nipper wondered if he could be the opposite of psychosomatic, i.e., he was prone to think the worst and most flagrant symptoms of some perfectly likely disorders were imaginary, but he knew he didn't have an ulcer. How could he know? I didn't know, and I'm the one who put that notion in his head. He only knew the pain in his gut couldn't be serious.

There, he felt better. He felt better to realize he didn't know anything. Whether he won or lost next week, what would become of each of us afterwards, how any of this would change the way he was in the world, he didn't know. He knew the math, he knew the odds, he knew how to play, but he didn't know the future, other than what the chances were.

We got him to her car, and he rode in the middle, calm, secure in the assumption that he would be O.K., that we were taking him home to bed, that I would hold him up by one arm and Kelly would hold him up by the other, and that—why was this necessary, since he wasn't sick or drunk, other than as a chintzy plot device to get him out of the way so Kelly could spend time with me?—we would dump him in bed, and then bolt the door after us, locking him in as we left together.

Henderson Will by Cal Nipper

A quandary was in Henderson Will. He didn't do what to know. To pass a make at Kelly too easy seemed and, frankly quite, the it of inevitability sported him as unstriking. A gentleman was he, all above. If needed Kelly a feel for him to bone her jumps, then well, was it her to up to move the make. Lowing me lay with sickness some vague so just could be alone get her? That do never would he.

Here was he, end the toward of the meet entire, with a spread maximum between us of each whose fortune of turns he saw over. Though even the madness of our methods lapped over, $1,000 than more us separated. Down deep, wasn't he concerned too. All after, a winner was he.

Admit I had to, drunk had Will share of his more of those ale of pitchers, and car in the here Kelly with, as him she drove bar to the back where could he scooter on his hop for a hill up the ride, his actions for him weren't responsible entirely. The do me made it devil? Quite not, yet and, the responsibility of lack us of each had this scheme in an alibi did offer. Pass a make or make a pass was same the all, fact the after in the day of light.

Might even be it not of him rude to car out of the get out with some gesture that was just than more handing holds. A knee of the squeeze or a cheek on the kiss, not if a blown-full throat down the tongue good kiss night and a grope body full crotching into the plunge? No but.

All after, him she knew well as did I.

Cal Nipper by Kelly Lane

Cal Nipper sat on his porch drinking coffee at the end of summer, wondering why he never sat on his porch in the morning on a Saturday, as the sun slashed colors from the weeds across the street in the yard of a house like his. When was the last time he mowed, and why hadn't he? He was running out of excuses.

This was our last day at the track. We could go on Sunday and Monday, but that would break the rhythm. Still, Nipper counted on the sequence of turns of the frequency and order to keep us going. If the second half matched the first, there were more slots left.

He ate a fried pie from the stash of day-old pastry he had replenished weeks ago. He tried to concentrate on breakfast and on the weeds across the street, the feel of the air, and the records of the *Daily Racing Form* that had nothing to do with today's card at Emerald Downs, but here it was again, the same notion that had been pounding him ever since he woke in the middle of the night in bed with his clothes on, alone. Either something happened to change everything, or nothing happened and everything would, what? Stay the same? Matter?

It had to matter. It was all that could possibly matter to him, as things were or weren't between us. So he thought he might just ask, but knew he never could. Why was I putting him through all this? What sort of hysteria was making this aspect twist and turn and torture himself to begin to think and therefore never stop thinking that I had to have gone home with Henderson Will?

There. He said it. To himself he said it, and what of it? He never had to ask me, and I never had to tell, because, really, would it do any good to deny it? Maybe it would have been better to say I did, whether I did or not, just to let him get used to the idea. Used to the idea! That was the only idea Nipper had, as they say, entertained for six days. If I told him what he dreaded, just to get him over it, regardless of the truth, maybe it would be better for everyone.

He had to get back to the races at hand. Here it was in the past performances, squirming in his lap, the race that would make him a winner today, and maybe even hook him up to a miracle finish. If we weren't going to bet on this last day, wasn't it patronizing of Henderson and me to put him up to this? Henderson and me! He couldn't help but imagine.

He looked at the *Form*. He couldn't look at the *Form*. He had to follow the rules by looking but not paying attention. An easy chore: no matter what he began to think about the day at the races, he kept slipping back to wonder about that night a week ago.

He thought he should have called me. He could have called me. He usually did, on one pretense or another. After he thought he might have made one too many calls in the middle of the week for apparently no reason other than to talk to me, he had ventured to say so, and he distinctly remembered that I said I thought it was sweet. That did it. He knew that I knew he would be calling about getting together. He should have come out and said it. I could have helped him say it, one way or another. If I wanted to see him in the middle of the week, I could have said I did. I could have said anything. Anything but that I thought it was sweet.

Never would I have said it was sweet, but that didn't matter. Nipper thought what he thought, and these thoughts were in part partly and at most mostly my fault. It would be in part partly and at most mostly my fault if this guy didn't buck up and bear down and fucking deal with the next few hours. He knew he had to deal with it, whatever it was. He couldn't be thinking about what might have gone on after Henderson dumped him in his clothes in bed. He had to be here.

Kelly Lane by Cal Nipper

Why did she even bother to buy the *Form*? The races on this last weekend seemed to have drawn entries at random: fillies with geldings, maidens with multiple winners, $3,200 nonwinners-of-two in $20,000 open claimers. The fields filled to the point where they would allow show wagering, but not trifectas. Although it would take a lottery play for a trifecta to drag me to the good, she knew she couldn't do that to me.

She didn't feel like betting; I told her not to bother. She wanted to do her part, but felt she could do her part by helping us. She didn't want us to think about betting for her. Was she relieved? Could she feel guilty? Not on her life.

Kelly Lane had earned her way to the top by not letting herself think of what came next, by not plunging at hopes or falling into regrets. Still, she wondered why we had chosen today instead of Sunday's card of stakes races, or even Closing Day's assortment of occasionally blatant set-ups for a feedbill exacta keyed by the most obscure longshot.

She wasn't doing this just for me. Or maybe she was. She had to get me to the window. She couldn't think of Henderson. Henderson would be fine, but I had become a project. After a promising start, I had blown it all, leaving me one last bad day away from failure. Had she let me stray from my methods, or were my methods the problem? She wasn't one to go back and check to see how, where, and when I failed. She thought she had a clear idea of who I was and what I should do, that she had deployed me faithfully.

She wanted me to play within myself—to do what I would do. She knew that it was because the total of all of us was on the line that she had me here today and not Monday, here where I could be counted on to win just as I would have won if I played as I always did. No plunges for longshots. That's not Cal Nipper.

She cared. She was concerned, considerate, but love? Had she ever really been in love? Forget the aspects, maybe that was the root of all her problems. What a joke. She must have been in love. Maybe not to that Oakland thug or that San Mateo impresario, but there had to have been some time way back where or when to form a basis to know what it was to be in love. And so, if she had fallen in love with me, if she had come up to me on that Sunday and just said hello… No. Such a love could only lead to madness. Kelly Lane did not do madness. Idiosyncrasy, sure; hysteria, of course; lunacy, no.

She looked over my shoulder, her hair dangling to graze my cheek as she read the past performances in the first and second races. Henderson had his own *Form* and might have made suggestions, but she knew what I would do.

"It's O.K. You can bet $40 on your first play, to cover two doubles. Why not?"

Couldn't we deviate? Each of us had lost track of bets, gone out of order. She wanted to say we were only human, then didn't, then laughed. She didn't want to distract me, but did.

She wandered down the rail not far away—where was that from?—and watched the post parade up close for the first time all season, recognizing the jockeys from TV replays, watching the muscles of the horses ripple, and looking for that bent neck in the shape of a question mark she liked to see in the horses she thought about betting on, the flexed neck, the prancing toe-dance gait, the lack of bandages or nervous sweat. Who was she kidding? Body language? Count the legs, and play one with four was about all any of us did when we paid attention to the appearance of these animals.

If she had ever had a special thing for horses, as some girls did, would she have been better at the game? Maybe in another lifetime. And yet, what if she played on paper today, using the stop-at-a-winner money management plan but picking the winner by body language? On paper, as in, without money? Kelly Lane did not play on paper.

Cal Nipper by Henderson Will

The first race was a six-furlong nonwinners-of-two $5,000 claimer with no contender Nipper could find to beat the favorite, True Bucks, whose running style, speed figures, and current form drew such a heavy tote, even the double payoffs shouldn't have been worth chasing. There were a couple of favorites in the second that paid better than 5–1 when paired with the odds-on choice in the first, so he figured we wouldn't mind if we covered them.

This was how he did so well at the beginning: play the exotics keyed by chalk. A 5–1 payday wasn't going to get him out of the red, but winning a double was better than winning a straight chalk bet. By going back to basics, Nipper aimed to start over, so if he won he could look at this outcome not as the end of all we had done, but as one more step in a cycle that was bound to continue.

There were no surprises. Suspect speed took them out of the gate to the turn. True Bucks stalked, pounced, won. This left Nipper in his favorite place to be, a leg up on the double, with two contenders to close the deal. Even better, he had a half hour to wait for the next set of results, to watch the double payoffs blink on the screen, along with win and exacta odds, odds that again confirmed he was alive. Even if he didn't win, the action told him he was right.

How? Only the results were right. He had won the first, but for him to think that the betting alone justified what he had done was, Nipper saw, the key to nothing more significant than a character flaw. What kind of man needed the approval of a pari-mutuel wagering pool? Better he should have picked winners that the vast majority of bettors shunned than shoot for minuscule underlays on co-favorites. To think that he had practically cashed in at this stage was to surrender.

Kelly Lane wouldn't ever have counted herself in before the race was run. She had even had a 10–1 winner disqualified. Week after week, she had seen her picks knocked off the board by the stewards or knocked out of the running by horses the stewards didn't take down, but here she was, in command.

He might have figured my style of play was a preemptive surrender, but he knew better. He knew that once I dug in to key on the horse to finish second in exactas, I worked it, win or lose. If he thought that losing didn't bother me, that was his business, and none of his thoughts on what I wanted made any difference now.

So here he was, within minutes of post time to the second race on our last day here. If he not only practically but actually won the double, he could not be happier than he was now.

Kelly Lane by Henderson Will

She was relieved of having to express her anxieties through a character like Nipper, even though those episodes must have been easier for her to imagine than whatever she had in mind for me. I welcomed her retirement and could only wish her the best of fortune in what she chose to do from now on, regardless of how it might have involved either him or me. And she welcomed my release of her from any obligation to bet or to do anything for or through either of us, regardless of whatever I might have had to do to relate her involvement with one Cal Nipper.

She turned to me. She knew me, she knew what I would do. The third at Bay Meadows was going off just before the second at Emerald, and so she was certain that I didn't want to jump into Nipper's double. Nipper had made the play he had to make, and whatever exacta wheels I might have spun wouldn't spoil his thrill. I shuffled entries to come up with Glo Pirate to finish second in a $12,500 turf route claimer.

She said I barely seemed to watch the race, that it seemed strange to make my last play of the season on a simulcast, but every race we played we watched on TV. She didn't think it was a bad bet, but it felt wrong to her for me to go out like that. What could I know about a cheap turf route? The strategy of playing tactical speed breaking from the rail to finish second might have worked at Emerald on dirt in a mile, but turf was another game. This wasn't a graded stakes turf race, but the first of its kind I played all year. She said she was sorry. She could have done more to make that last bet something other than an $80 loss, to leave me up only by $111 after, what, how many months of weeks of days?

"Twenty-one days to make five dollars a day. Divide and conquer. Here's to the winners."

She handed me a beer, and we bumped cups in a toast.

Nipper roamed from monitor to monitor before the second at Emerald decided his fate in the double. She said he was trying to see more of a future he liked in one screen after another. She added that he probably wouldn't think it was enough for a valid sample.

She gazed at me, curious, not about valid samples or what I thought of Nipper, but about how I might respond to what her look conveyed, a look that didn't have to be explained, because words themselves might be no more than a string of sounds and tones in lyric incantation.

"A salad vamp'll eat a valid sample for lunch. What do you think about dinner?"

Cal Nipper by Kelly Lane

Nipper was in shark mode: on the prowl and out for blood. Numbers kept him occupied, so he didn't think about how restless he was. He only thought of the next few minutes.

The race was a six-and-a-half-furlong maiden claimer at a $12,500 tag. All that bothered him was the heavy betting on the one-horse, whose record showed nothing. Heavy tote on a horse like that in a race like this at this time of the season was a definite threat. But the double payoffs and exacta prices on the one-horse hadn't been bet down to match the play in the win pool. Anyone aiming to score big would have been all over the one in the exotics. Besides, Nipper knew the one-hole at six and a half was the worst place for a debutante to break from, out of the chute before the backstretch. A slight bump or funny step, and he'd get squeezed by the rail. One check of the reins or even a slight steady was all it would take to take him out of the running. The rest of the betting seemed normal, with his horses going off at 2–1 and 3–1. The second choice would be on the front, the favorite would run late. How could he lose?

Out of the gate, his speedster gave the lead to the four-horse. He hadn't figured the four would do anything, but there he was, out by a couple of lengths. His early runner, though, kept pace, stalking along the rail, well ahead of the one, who maybe did get squeezed, but Nipper wasn't watching the one. The other, the closer favorite, started his move, but was too far back unless something went wrong. At the turn, the leader bore out and quit, and at the top of the stretch, it was over.

His speed horse, Victory Venture, netted him $124 for the day, leaving him $304 down for the meet. Henderson and I combined for $866, putting us $562 up for the season.

Nipper wasn't satisfied. Nipper wanted more. On our last trip on the last day of summer, he saw no more chances for me to have my say, and he wanted us to go on, with me making him into more than just this guy I helped dream up for a while, more than all that music of the years gone by, but what was left? The Braves would win the National League East and lose in the playoffs. It was better to have bet and lost than never to have bet at all. These schemes and sayings and songs we lived by were but the configuration of a single moment, and we lived in the moment of the moment we lived.

Ladies and gentlemen, Cal Nipper.

Cal Nipper by Henderson Will

Were eternal cycles eternal only within themselves, and therefore nonexistent elsewhere? Nipper lost himself in questions of hermetic systems and eternity, questions to provoke anxieties that threw him off the exercise of tracking the frequency and order that ruled the aspects within each of us, and so he wasn't sure where he stood in the scheme of who had what to say about anyone. For all he knew, this was it for him or me and so for all of us, one way or another.

While I took off for The Prop on my scooter and they walked to Kelly's car, Nipper had an idea of a way to bridge the time from the here to the there: from here at the track now to there at The Prop an hour from now; from here, at the end of the betting season, to there, in the afterwards of an indefinite future; from here, with Kelly and me today, to there, with others at The Prop, weeks later. By picturing himself there in the future, Nipper thought he might create a link between the here and the there, the now and the then, a link that might connect this cycle to whatever must follow. Wasn't that the trick of getting into heaven? In the moment of death, think about going to heaven. Then, shazaaam.

So here he was in the car with Kelly at the end of summer, thinking of sitting at The Prop in the dark of an autumn happy hour on a Sunday, long after the Braves had made the final out. A football game would be silently beaming from the TV to light the room as the music from CDs played on, mercifully free of any associations he would make to what anyone said, as he and the folks he usually saw at happy hour teased and argued, joked and remembered and forgot about all they ever did. This was a place where nothing really ever could have been declared or concealed, believed or denied.

When the ad came on for the Breeders Cup, someone would ask if he was going to the track to bet on the simulcast. Someone new might ask why he would be doing that, leading another to try to explain what it was he was supposed to have done.

"So, how did that turn out, anyway?"

"It worked."

"What do you mean, it worked."

"I took a handicapping course that told you to make up these characters and have them bet for you according to a plan where you quit when you were ahead, and they won."

"You won."

"You could say that."

"But why did they do that?"

"They?"

"The people you made do that."

"They took the same course. That was the deal. We made each other up. Same as anyone makes up anyone, in a way. I mean, what you know about anyone is what you think about anyone, right?"

"You couldn't have made them up. I saw them. Her, anyway. Her I remember."

"Her who?"

"Don't you remember? She used to come in here after the races."

"Who was that lady I saw you with?"

An aspect of the hysteria within me, someone I figured out as a woman I once thought I saw and then later got to know, he thought as they rode to watch the land speed by, imagining a conversation that would take place in the future in the bar he was going to now, where once and for all it would be established what he did and who he was. That was no lady; that was my life.

Henderson Will by Cal Nipper

After one week the track of the closing, Henderson Will was handing shakes with the lot around the parking guys by the hospital veterans. Them of some hadn't as long waiting as others been, so and those of a few wondered well what wrong was with him.

Then so would Will them tell, into going this malady of his odd, part the omitting about having served never in the forces armed. If shove came to push, tell would he them of parting take in marches peace and demonstrations war-anti, which, not as like, them of many now would join also, to account their leaders cowardly to call. The truth but it was that little knew Will of the years of memories by gone, and, as by went time, it remembered him less.

Yet and, he'd lived to learn it with, and, the confines in with the memory term short out turned to be rewarding in a way peculiar. Instance for, remembered he to seem a lady with a night week last. Her he knew and loved even in a way exceptional, and versa-vice, so the them of two time some spent that now to him sublime seemed so, for the him of life said he could not, for to tell and kiss wouldn't close come to saying it was what. As such, she was what or who? Say he couldn't.

Though even a job and a wife and a mother once had him, that life of his part put him aside. For there, the memory of confines out turned to be a freedom of source. Less the never, difficult was it to sure for say what were the results.

Ruling the follows or ruling the breaks, won he had. The scheme the stranger, the success the more? As was it, the sensible most action of course out crapped like a holiday on binging sailor, and by losing to try, a success of measure had him.

Now but it was leave to time. The California of tracks well might score the settle with The Course to respect. So if, well would do him to take with him Kelly. What but of me? He didn't need me like someone to configure help him and her? Rate any at, that night last together at The

Prop were we, each other phones and addresses we gave, leaving him up to it if us he called to want.

Him up to it? Life to sprung as a thought after was he, and we minded his twist to do him make the things craziest and himself express this like a savant idiot, or a proof that ruled the exception.

Gentlemen and ladies, Henderson Will.

Kelly Lane by Henderson Will

California was no more than the moving pictures on TV screens of the races at Golden Gate Fields, Bay Meadows, Santa Anita, Hollywood Park, Fairplex, and Del Mar, and she could go there from anywhere, and so didn't really have to go there again. She had thought of traveling with me as far as Astoria, where she'd once seen a saloon by the Columbia that boasted off-track betting, but it was too soon to take up the action again, least of all in some smoky dive. And, she had thought about dinner, without Nipper and with me, to think of the possibility of what it might lead to, but such a scenario only made her remember how it was in her twenties, when she might not have thought twice about that. Regardless of how it could have been, it had to exist outside of the scope of our time together here.

She needed a break, now that the summer was over: the summer, the live workout, the expression of her fears and anxieties, and all of what made her who she was through Nipper and me—whatever it was and whatever it would become when she thought of us. Had she really lost herself and beat the races or simply given herself away? We used her, sure, and she used us, exploited us, manipulated us, and in the end, we came through for her. Sitting pretty she was, on a tidy bankroll.

How did she feel, though, to be here, at the end, with nothing to show but a pile of measly hundred-dollar bills? What was all this supposed to come to—a cure, a resolution, a statement, a discovery? A relationship! She was the woman, so she had to pick a man? This wasn't the Dating Game. This was simply a game.

It was what it was, no more and no less than a game, and she, ladies and gentlemen, was a winner.

Now that's Kelly Lane.

Kelly Lane by Cal Nipper

Long after it was over, Kelly Lane tried to buy *Divide and Conquer: Lose Yourself and Beat the Races.* The Course had only handed out copies of the introduction, printed on an ancient mimeograph machine. She was curious to see the rest of the book. Her internet searches found no such title, so she tried the name of the guy behind The Course. No luck.

The publisher, Off-track Books, Reno, Nevada, was listed on a website of a Phoenix bookstore that specialized in gambling titles. Her e-mail to the store bounced, so she was surprised when someone answered the phone at the number posted on the site.

The guy on the line had nothing to do with the store, but he knew all about it. People were always calling him, in quest of some book that would make them rich, even though the store had been closed for two years. At first it had been annoying, he said, but the conversations with crapshooters, card counters, and horseplayers were livelier than his dealings with family and friends. He became interested in gambling. He tried his hand at the ponies and the dogs. He even went so far as to buy some of the books the store used to carry. He had heard of Off-track—it went bust long ago—but not of *Divide and Conquer.* After his own search, he assured her that no such book had ever existed, except in the mind of this grifter who had sold her on that cockamamie system. Book titles, phony degrees, wild claims of success were all tools of the trade, he said. Nobody made money gambling. They made money telling you how to gamble.

"Come on, if I could beat the races, I wouldn't be writing about it. I'd be at the track. Winning at the track! Imagine."

She liked the guy. She might have talked more or called him again, to tell him something about herself and the season she had spent going to a track near Seattle, in a gambling mob, spun out of the work of a Portuguese poet, where each made up the others and played according to a plan described by a Scottish novelist. But he would never believe her. The more she thought of what to say, the crazier it seemed.

Only the results were official.

Acknowledgments

The preface to *By Kelman Out of Pessoa* first ran as an eponymous story in *Fence*. One report on the project that the novel sprang from, "Methodical Mad Science," appears in *TrenchArt: Recon Aesthetics,* and another report, "Experimental Novel Experiment," lurks behind a door of *Trickhouse* at www.trickhouse.org, thanks to Rebecca Wolff and Lynne Tillman; Les Figues; Selah Saterstrom and Noah Saterstrom.

I'm especially grateful to Teresa Carmody and Vanessa Place, Amina Cain, Janice Lee, the rest of the Les Figues crew, and to Louis Bury.

Thanks also to the people and horses of Emerald Downs.

And many thanks to Vincent W.J. van Gerven Oei, Eileen A. Fradenburg Joy, and the crew at punctum books for making this new edition happen.

Made in the USA
Middletown, DE
05 April 2023